Blood Red Vines

Blood Red Vines

A Novel

Best wishes to Kathleen —
Dick Wheat

RICHARD WHEAT

ISBN: 1515049477
ISBN 13: 9781515049470
Library of Congress Control Number: 2015911373
CreateSpace Independent Publishing Platform
North Charleston, South Carolina

Part One

Helmand Province
Afghanistan

2007

1

"**M**ORPHINE!" YELLED THE camouflage-clad doctor bent over the struggling Marine with his torn and mangled leg. "Goddamit, more morphine!"

Even as he spoke, the blast from an incoming mortar round exploding just outside the makeshift aid station almost knocked the surgeon onto his patient. Before the dust and smoke had settled, the Marine's body armor, bloody sweater and shirt were yanked off. In moments, a young corpsman jabbed his second morphine loaded syringe into the now exposed shoulder. Throwing aside the empty auto-injector, he searched for a vein to start an I.V. The exposed, needle scared, vein plugged arms were those of a full-blown addict. "Look at those fuckin' tracks!" The corpsman cried out in frustration. "No wonder that first dose didn't touch him. Where'n hell are they getting this stuff?"

The doctor looked briefly at the rows of needle marks on the Marine's forearms. "Whatta damn waste!" He exclaimed as he quickly inserted a central line in the man's neck and started Hexamine running fast. "Thank God for that stuff when there's no plasma around," he muttered as they covered the Marine's pale, now limp body with a heavy blanket. The two men, clad alike in camouflaged Marine utilities, heavy winter jackets, body armor and combat helmets were now splotched with blood. They looked more like victims than a medical team. "Jesus," muttered the corpsman as he peered down at the bone fragments and torn muscle of what was once a leg. "Whatta ya think Doc, any chance?"

"Don't know, Mark, but it's sure as hell worth a try. Let's see what we can do before the choppers arrive."

Lieutenant Senior Grade Jeff Thomas, United States Navy Medical Officer and Hospital Corpsman 2nd Class, Mark Taylor, had helicoptered into this rocky, inhospitable hilltop just the day before. With its few scraggly, ancient apricot trees, low stone walls and long abandoned mud-brick houses, Firebase Chagai was the home of Company Bravo, 3rd Battalion of the large Marine expeditionary force based at Camp Leatherneck many miles to the north.

Stretched out before this small band of young Americans were the dark, forbidding. Chagai Hills which form a natural border between Pakistan and southern Afghanistan. Here ancient trade routes, threading through parched canyons and over barren ridges, have for centuries given access to the empty deserts of Helmand Province. The Marine company, positioned strategically on this ragged hilltop, was all that stood in the way of Taliban fighters headed north.

For Jeff and his corpsman, their assignment had been simple. Spend two days to review the firebase medical readiness and investigate the extent of drug use among the men at this remote outpost. The growing epidemic of heroin spreading through the Province was as dangerous to these young Marines as the Taliban.

That first afternoon and evening had been spent reviewing Bravo Company's medical status. After a long day, the two men were still sound asleep in their sleeping bags when the first mortar round landed not far from the aid station. It took only moments to strap on armor, helmets and grab the M-16's loaned them the night before. "You never know," the Marine Captain had said as he handed the surprised doctor the two rifles and a pouch of ammunition clips.

As mortar shells, RPG's and rifle fire tore into the Marine positions, the wounded began to arrive. Jeff, a Trauma Surgeon by training, was in his element. The furious firefight lasted all day. One of the two corpsmen attached to the rifle company was among the first casualties. By nightfall two Marines and the corpsman were dead and there were a number severely wounded.

In spite of brilliant sunshine, the hilltop was bitter cold. Wind whistled through the flapping camouflage tarp covering the absent roof of this makeshift aid station. Jeff, Mark and the surviving corpsman worked steadily through the long day and into the night. When the sun at last rose next morning, it was to a mercifully quieter scene. Most of the surviving Taliban fighters had melted back into the surrounding hills as silently as they had arrived. As two Medevac helicopters arrived, Jeff and his small team had stabilized the surviving wounded sufficient for the long flight. Their destination, the Helmand Province Forward Operating Base Shukvani with its Role II trauma facility.

As the wounded were being evacuated, a fresh platoon of Marines and two replacement corpsman were flown in to replenish the remnants of Company Bravo. Together, the Marines cleaned out the last remaining pockets of bearded Taliban fighters. As the day wore on, some semblance of order returned. Ammunition was resupplied and distributed, food served and the men took turns trying to catch some sleep.

The Rifle Company Commanding Officer, a dirt encrusted, bone tired, young Marine Captain, came into the aid station to check on his wounded. Leaning his M16 against the mud brick wall, he hauled out a crumpled pack of cigarettes.

"Sorry 'bout your reception, Doc," the Captain chuckled, "But you guys sure arrived at a lucky time for Company Bravo. Damn lucky!" Cupping his hands around his lighter's flame, he lit up and took a slow, deep, satisfying drag. "I know, bad for the health, but so's this fuckin' war."

Eyes bloodshot and sleep deprived, he looked at the three body bags resting against the wall, at the confusion of tossed aside body armor, torn bloodied utilities, used battle dressings and empty I.V. bags. With a sigh of anger and fatigue, he took another long drag and slowly exhaled a grey haze of smoke into the frigid air. Looking at the equally exhausted medical team, he leaned his shoulder against the wall. "Just wanted to thank you-all an' tell ya we've got things pretty much under control out there." He pointed his cigarette out the broken down door speaking in a broad Texas drawl. "You better get the hell outta here while the gettin's good ... the last choppers are about to leave." As he turned to go, he paused and walked back. Looking directly at Jeff, the young Captain's stubble covered face turned grim. "Doc, you gotta find how our boys are gettin' their heroin. That stuff's killin' my Marines!"

Jeff's eyes took in the scene outside. There, the three body bags were being loaded gently into the cabin of the last Medevac helicopter.

"Captain," Jeff looked back into the tired eyes of the Marine officer. "Why the hell do you think I was sent to this God forsaken lump of rocks?" He nodded towards the chopper and gestured. "Every last one of your men, including those three poor bastards out there are as much my Marines as they're yours. We're all doin' every thing we can to shut down this miserable plague!"

2

BACK AT THE base, Jeff peeled off the layers of armor, jacket, sweater and blood stained utilities. Standing in that wonder of modern civilization, a scalding hot shower, his sun darkened face, neck and arms were in stark contrast to the pallor of the rest of his tall, muscular, frame. If dressed in a dusty robe, turban and sporting a beard, he could easily pass for one of their Afghan neighbors.

"Hey Jeff," Called a barely visible figure through clouds of steam. "How was your jaunt down south in the hills – heard you got into a real meat grinder"

Jeff peered through the vapor at one of the helicopter pilots who shared the male half of the Bachelor Officers Quarters with the doctors. The nurses and female pilots had the opposite end of the building. "Yeh, Tom, it was pretty bad. Peace and quiet when we arrived but all hell broke loose the next morning … lost three good men and had a bunch of badly wounded guys. I was glad I was there and damn happy I got out in one piece."

"I know what you mean. You shoulda seen my chopper when I got back from my last run … looked like Swiss cheese it was so full of holes."

Jeff toweled his lean, muscular body dry, pulled on clean utilities, the standard desert tan Marine combat uniform, and waved goodbye to his friend. Time now to relax!

The small trauma hospital was just a short walk from the B.O.Q. These wind blown, sun bleached, plywood structures were home and workplace for the doctors, nurses and corpsmen of this forward operating base. The building euphemistically named "Doctors Lounge" was a bare, plywood walled room with a vaguely functioning propane stove, a dozen folding chairs, a table piled with ancient magazines and a large Navy issue coffee pot. A decrepit lamp of ancient vintage, "acquired" from who knows where, dimly illuminated a small circle. Above, two bare bulbs hung from the rafters casting shadows around the room. Jeff claimed a seat by the stove and was soon telling the story of the firefight. Listening quietly, a half dozen doctors were sitting around the sputtering stove drinking coffee and trying to stay warm.

Jeff's voice was animated. "How the hell are these jarheads gettin' their heroin? Two of those wounded Marines had been hitting it up big time. One guy told me it was all over the place, easy to get."

"Yeh, it's a big problem and it's getting worse." replied a short, fast talking New Englander with a barely disguised Beacon Hill accent. "The corpsmen say it's good stuff, too."

From the far corner, a dimly visible, bearded, sweater and watch cap clad figure spoke up. "I heard they get it from one of our contractors – makin' a mint on the side. Miserable bastard, he's robbin' the government and killin' our guys."

Unnoticed, a lanky, older but similarly attired figure came quietly in, closing the door against the freezing wind. Taking a quickly proffered seat, he pulled off his scarf and looked around at the men now gathered close. "Heard what you said, George, and I sure agree. I've been talking to the M.P's about this situation," came the quiet reply. Aside from his apparent age, crease-lined face and graying hair, what set him apart were silver patches sewn on his utility collars denoting a Commander's rank. "They tell me the same story but apparently this guy is a civilian and out of their jurisdiction or some asinine excuse like that." Carefully extracting a cigar from his jacket pocket, Commander David Williams, the Senior Medical Officer of this Forward Operating Base, bit off the end of his cheroot and scratched a match on the stove. Clamping the cigar between his teeth and cupping the flickering flame carefully with his hands, he sucked several times and smiled with satisfaction as the tip began to glow. With his erect posture and bright penetrating eyes, Dave Williams looked every bit the leader he was.

Holding his cigar with care, he spoke quietly to the men gathered around. "I've been talking to our boss, Captain Ross, down at Leatherneck. The brass are all aware of our problem … and madder'n hell. Gentleman, do you realize that half the world's heroin originates right here in Helmand

and Kandahar Provinces? "He paused looking thoughtfully at the young doctors seated around him before continuing. "There's a lot being done as you all know. Eradication of poppy fields, try'n to pay farmers to plant other crops, but so far it's not doin' much for our Marines." He paused to take a few puffs on his cigar and look around the room. "The latest idea is this: the M.P.'s and the Navy brass know we have a special relationship with our Marines. They think we might be able dig out information they don't seem able to reach." He paused with a slight smile. "They've decided to use us as a test to see what we can do to help."

"Just hold it right there, Commander," piped up a short, cigar-smoking doctor wearing a very thick, very non-regulation, red knit sweater. "Our guys are doin' urine testing as often as they can, but son of a bitch, we're supposed to be doctors, not damn cops. We got way too much to do already." There was a rumble of assent from around the room.

"Hell, I know that!" said the Commander as he sucked on his cigar and moved his boot-clad feet closer to the stove. Everybody liked Dave. He was a first class trauma surgeon and a good administrator. Like all the men in this small group of Navy doctors, he loved his Marines. He was dead serious when he continued to speak.

"Captain Ross and I agree we can't wait any longer. What I'm getting at is we're gonna try an experiment. We've decided to appoint one of you guys to do some extra-curricular snooping around and try to pin this contractor down. We think he's here in the province, probably working with the Taliban. The M.P.'s think he's an American. Not only are these people hurting our Marines but they're flooding the streets back home with heroin. It seems to go from here to Pakistan, then Mexico and up into California and Texas. Gentlemen, we've got a problem that's got to be fixed!"

The room erupted with angry questions but the Commander raised his hands to quiet them all down. "Hell, I know you're not detectives, but you're smart and we think one of you docs can get more information out of these Marines than all the M.P.'s in Helmand Province. They trust you docs and we're hoping they'll talk. We've got to bust this bastard's ass … and soon!"

There was a creaking and rattling of the beat-up old chairs as the small group of unhappy doctors pulled in closer. No question about it, somebody was about to get stuck with a miserable, dangerous job!

"I know this kind of work isn't in your job description but somebody's gotta do it." Dave stopped and looked around at his young medical officers, all now paying close attention.

"Most of you boys went to places like Harvard and Yale. You grew up on the other side of the track from these kids. Half of 'em are Latino, grew up on a ranch in Texas or California. Spanish is their first language – most of you guys speak a little French or German if you've got a foreign language at all." The Commander stopped, taped the ashes off his cigar and looked around with amusement at this unlikely appearing team of Navy doctors. "Well, it just so happens that there's one of you gentleman that grew up on a ranch and worked his way through school grubbin' it out in the vineyards back in California - speaks ranch hand Spanish like a Mexican *bracero*."

Jeff, who was sitting in the back, suddenly realized that everyone was looking his way, many with a big grin. "Now wait a God damn minute!" he exclaimed. "That's not fair! I'm no Sherlock Holmes! Furthermore, you know I'm due for rotation home next week … I'm outta here! Hell, you guys can draw straws or somethin'"

"Don't you think I know that?" quietly replied the Commander. "None of us are M.P.'s. We're not policemen, we're doctors. But Jeff, you're the best qualified man on our team. These Marines like you, trust you, know you're one of them. I think you feel the same way about them." The Commander stopped briefly and looked directly into Jeff's angry face. "You know and I know, many of these boys of ours are in deep trouble with drugs. You understand how our Marines tick better than all the rest of us combined. Captain Ross and I know it's not fair to put the finger on you like this, but we need you … need you right now. I'm sorry Jeff, but as of today your date for rotation has been indefinitely extended." He paused momentarily to let that news sink in. "And Jeff, this is no suggestion, it's an order!"

———

The next morning an unhappy Jeff sat perched on a chair in the SMO's small, cramped office nursing a cup of luke-warm coffee. Dave Williams sat behind a once green metal desk, feet propped up on an overturned wastebasket, chair tipped back, an amused smile on his face.

"Come on, Jeff, this isn't so bad. Give you something to tell your grandchildren. Just think, you won't have to shave, the bigger the beard the better. You'll get to see all the off limits parts of this lovely garden spot. Think of the poppy fields, marijuana crops, the bazaar in town – hell, you might even come out of it alive!" The Commander chuckled, brought his chair upright and declared with a slight grin, "And here's the best part. You're gonna have a partner."

Jeff slammed down his coffee. "What do you mean a 'partner'? Come off it, Dave, I need a partner like a hole in the head! Hell, I wanta find this guy as much as you and Captain Ross - maybe more - but it's bad enough I've gotta risk my own neck. Havin' somebody else tagging along is just going to make this whole crazy job more dangerous!"

The Commander grew serious as he leaned across his desk. "Alright Jeff. Let's agree on a couple of things. First, you may want to help our guys but you don't know your ass from a hole in the ground about drug trafficking. Second, you may speak Spanish but how'll you do tryin' to have a conversation in Pashto? Not so hot, right? Jeff, the only reason we're asking you to do this, dammit, ordering you to do it, is because you're our best chance of dragging information outta some of our Marine junkies. You're also tough and know how to handle a gun. But, Jeff, you're gonna need help with the rest. A lotta of help."

Opening a drawer, he pulled a sheet of fax paper from a folder. "Let me tell you a bit about this 'partner' we found. It's kind of interesting."   Putting on his reading glasses, he scanned the page and began. "Agent Smith is attached to the Navy from the Alcohol, Drug, Firearms and Explosives Agency … Agent Smith Is an acknowledged expert on drug interdiction …   Smith volunteered specifically for duty in Afghanistan through the Navy Judge Advocates Corps … plus Smith's been here almost three years… knows the language and knows the territory."

"It seems," he said, looking over the top of his glasses, "Our Agent Smith lost a brother, a Marine officer, right here in Helmand Province. That brother was shot by a junkie high on drugs … let fire with his M16 … killed his captain and three of his platoon members."

Jake leaned across his desk and handed the page and a photograph to Jeff with a wry smile. "I think your gonna like workin' with Agent *Caroline Smith*."

Jeff stared at the blurred photo in shock. "Caroline …" He whispered. Jerking his head up, he spoke incredulously as he held up the photograph. "This is Caroline Pierce and that Marine Captain had to have been her twin brother Todd."

It was the Commander's turn to be surprised. "Do you mean to tell me you know this woman? How …..?" His voice trailed off, concern on his face.

"Yeh," said Jeff in a low voice, "I know her. I know her very well. Caroline Pierce was her name back then."

"I'll be damned! Where the hell did you know her?" asked the astonished Commander.

Looking up, Jeff's eyes seemed in another place and another time. "We were at Sonoma State together." He spoke slowly. "Caroline was in Criminal Justice and I was a pre-med. Her brother Todd was a good friend of mine. Caroline and I thought we were in love ….. " His voice trailed off. Staring at the picture, he spoke quietly. "Dave, I just can't do this!"

"Son of bitch!" The Commander exclaimed under his breath. Swiveling his chair, he looked silently through the dusty window into the brilliant sunshine illuminating the drab buildings with their backdrop of the distant, snow capped, Hindu Kush. After a moment or two he turned back to Jeff. Sitting straight, his voice was hard.

"Doctor, this may complicate things for you, but our heroin problem still exists. It's getting worse by the day. We're going ahead with this operation whether you like it or not. You two are going to work together, whatever your past history. I hope that doesn't translate into more risk for either of you but we're committed, your orders still stand!"

That night, Jeff lay wide-awake, unable to sleep. Caroline was coming … Caroline of all the women in the world would be his partner. Jeff had never forgotten this woman who had been so much a part of his life, even though seven long years had passed since they had bid a tearful farewell. He'd gone out with other women of course, slept with some, but it was never the same. With the passage of time he thought he had finally put her out of his mind. Now Caroline would be here, beautiful and bright as ever. He could see the cheerful twinkle in her eyes, smell the faint fragrance he remembered so well. What would she feel seeing him after all these years … would she even care?   Lying there sleepless, Jeff felt a hollow ache deep in his chest and was conscious of his pounding heart. "Damn! Why Caroline … why now?"

3

PROMPTLY AT 1500 hours, Jeff and the flight controller heard the heavy, thump, thump, thump, of a large Navy Sea Stallion circling in for a landing. There had been no radio transmission that might alert the Taliban to an arriving aircraft. Rocket Propelled Grenades, well aimed, could bring down a low-flying chopper. Even though broad daylight, the lights on the helipad had been turned on to aid in the approach. The helicopter was coming down fast.

"O.K., Jeff," mumbled the unhappy young doctor under his breath. "Smile and be real nice to the lady like the Commander said."

Half-blinded by the dust and sand swirling up from the ground, Jeff ran toward the now settling aircraft. Instinctively crouching under the still churning blades, he positioned himself to watch the new arrivals emerge. As the tailgate of the big, multi-bladed craft lowered, he watched 24 Marines, obviously male, jump out with full packs, M-16's and gear. Pallets loaded with supplies were manhandled out to the waiting ground crew while a dozen stretchers were carefully carried up for the flight to Camp Leatherneck, the Marine headquarters at Lashkar Gah, the provincial capital. He had almost given up when a crew member appeared in the open hatch accompanied by a much slighter figure. Although bundled in helmet, body armor, heavy jacket and wool gloves there was no question this was a woman. Stepping down to the tarmac, the new arrival looked quickly around. Her duffle was unceremoniously dumped on the ground and without further pause, the tailgate began to close even as the ungainly aircraft began its slow ascent. Agent Caroline Smith had arrived.

"Caroline!" Jeff yelled over the noise and flying debris. Grabbing the duffle in one hand, he took her free arm firmly and pushed the woman toward the dust obscured flight shack. "Jeff, Jeff Thomas." Realizing his voice was all but drowned out by the helicopter engines, he put his mouth next to her ear and yelled, "Head for that door, It's quieter inside."

As the door slammed closed behind them, the sudden drop in decibels was almost a shock. Jeff put down the duffle and with clearing vision took a good look at this woman whom he once knew so well. As he watched, she put her brief case on a chair and quickly pulled off gloves and helmet. No question, this was the same Caroline and as beautiful as ever. Turning back, she shook out her short blond hair and with obvious astonishment, looked intently at the man standing before her.

"Jeffrey Thomas!" she laughed with the same cheerful lilt he remembered so well. "So you're the Spanish-speaking doctor I'm going to be working with? God help us all!" She laughed again, then glanced quickly around the bare room. "Lovely terminal you've got here."

"Yeh, regular JFK," he responded. "We're a little short of the usual amenities." He was still anxious at having a drug-sniffing female agent on his turf. Not just any woman, but this particular smart, strikingly attractive woman he once knew so well.

Caroline paid no attention to his snide remark as she looked hopefully around the drafty room for an appropriately labeled door. "Jeff, right now what I need is a bathroom! It was a long bumpy flight from Bagram. They kept feeding me coffee and that final leg from Lashkar Gah aboard the helicopter … "

Picking up the duffle, Jeff pointed towards the door. "The closest head is inside the B.O.Q. Come on, we'll walk fast."

As they walked the few hundred feet, Jeff filled her in on her accommodations. "They're bunkin' you with our nurses, the female chopper pilots and few other women officers. You ladies have the north end of the B.O.Q. 'The Shukvani Hilton' is what we call our home sweet home."

"That," he pointed to his right as they moved rapidly along. "Is the Trauma Center where I work." He pointed again. "And over there's the B.O.Q." Arriving in a few moments at the door, he yelled in a loud voice, "Visitors! Anybody home?" At the same time he pointed to a door not far from the entrance. "That's what goes for a Powder Room around here. While you're busy, I'll see who I can dig up to show you around."

No sooner had the door to the small toilet room closed than a short, older woman dressed in a faded blue bathrobe stepped out from a nearby doorway, furiously brushing still damp hair. "Hey, Jeff, over here," she called. "The lady's gonna be bunkin' next to me."

When a much-relieved Caroline came out of the head, the two walked down the short hall. "Boy, did I ever need that stop!" She exclaimed as she shook the smaller woman's hand, "I'm Caroline Smith".

"Welcome to Forward Operating Base Shukvani, Caroline, I'm Madge Walker" came the reply, followed by an angry retort. "Damn men," she growled, indicating Jeff, "They've got a head to use every couple of yards plus they can pee in any ditch or behind any wall — but not us. Hell, women in this part of the world get stoned if they so much as tug at their skirts!" With a wry smile, the short, gray-haired woman attired in her vintage Navy bathrobe, slippers and wearing wire-rim glasses with no make-up, quickly pulled back her hair and looked up at Caroline. "Sorry about that. Sometimes I get a little worked up about what women have to go through in this God forsaken armpit of the world."

"A little worked up?" exclaimed Jeff in mock surprise. But Jeff, like all the personnel on the base, male or female, knew that Lt. Cdr. Margaret Walker was a very special person, a true diamond in the rough. Without exception, they loved this smart, tough, hard working, long time chief nurse. They knew they were lucky to have her.

"Saw your orders so knew you were comin'. Glad to have you aboard, Caroline, you'll be bunkin' over here." The bathrobe-clad figure turned, pointing to the small room adjacent to her own. "The showers and head are down the hall." Then turning abruptly, she glared up into Jeff's face and in a voice of unquestioned authority, loudly proclaimed: "Now Doctor Thomas, you big juvenile delinquent, get the hell outta here, You're off limits in my hen house". Madge never pulled rank but nobody talked back when this woman gave an order. She might be a small package but Madge Walker out-ranked everyone except Commander Williams.

"When you get rid of that old battle axe," Jeff called to Caroline as he hastily retreated, "Meet me at the bar about five. Madge'll give you directions."

"OUT!" yelled the Generalissimo of the women's B.O.Q.

"You need a drink, I need a drink, and we both need to talk." Jeff called, then laughing, he turned and ran for his life.

―◦◦◦―

No sooner had Jeff collected two beers and rounded up a couple of chairs, Caroline arrived. Even in her Marine utilities she was beautiful. Watching the men turn to admire this new arrival didn't do much to allay his concerns. It was bad enough having a female along, but this woman, in this ultra-conservative Muslim country?

Spotting Jeff, Caroline walked over and looked quizzically into his serious face. She seemed to read his mind.

"O.K., Jeff," she said without any pretext at small talk, "I know having me here is making you nervous," she smiled faintly. "But don't forget, I've been working this country longer than you. You know medicine and your Marines, but I know these Afghans and I know drugs." She paused and looked towards the dark windows. "Plus I've got a personal interest, a very personal interest in Helmand Province."

"I just heard about Todd ..." His voice trailed away.

"You knew him, Jeff," There was a catch in her voice as she looked up into his face. "He was my other half, my closest friend."

Jeff could hear the sadness in her voice. He saw the hands held rigidly in her lap, the moisture well up in her eyes. He could feel the sorrow and pain so evident in her face.

"I'm so sorry, Caroline," he said, reaching out to touch her arm. Trite and hollow as these words might sound, he didn't know what else to say. Both sat in silence for a few moments, then Caroline wiped her eyes and picked up her beer.

"O.K., Jeff, let's talk."

For the next hour the doctor and agent sat huddled in concentration. Jeff carefully laid out what little information he'd gleaned from the local M.P.'s and what he had found talking to the wounded Marines identified as users. Caroline could feel the anger in his speech as he outlined the epidemic of drugs in the area. As she watched this intense young doctor, she remembered college days at Sonoma State and the young pre-med she had known so well. She was not surprised at how seriously Jeff took the plague of drugs that infected Helmand Province. These were his Marines. She was used to jaded, overworked officers who just turned their backs on addicts. This man had always been different ... he always cared. Perhaps that was why she had once loved him so much.

"There seems to be a pattern.," he continued. "They learn by word of mouth where to find the stuff at any given time. The sellers are constantly moving. Sometimes in the bazaar, sometimes a street corner, sometimes just a motorcycle on the edge of town. Never the same place, seldom the same person. No names and they all look alike."

"Typical," she interjected, looking up from her notes. "It's the same around Kabul. As far as we can tell there are half a dozen drug lords covering the country, each with his own territory – not too different from the way it's done back home. We don't know that much about Helmand Province. They seem to follow a slightly different routine here. We need a lot more information. We need to identify an upper-level middle man, grab him and squeeze."

"I've got a Marine here, just a kid, a corporal." Jeff said in a low voice, pulling his chair closer. "He owes me his life. He knows it's dangerous but he wants to go clean and he's ready to help."

"That's as good a place to start as any. By the way," she looked directly at her companion. "If you have no major objections, I'm going to bring in a man I've worked with in army intelligence up in Kabul. He may be Afghan National Army, but he's a very tough, unbendable soldier who knows drugs. He's smart, speaks English near-perfectly, and like me, has a personal grudge against these miserable bastards. They murdered his wife and two little girls."

"Why not use the ANP? The local National Police know the territory around here."

"Because those poor guys are badly trained, low paid, and most are corrupt as hell. They can't be trusted, Jeff, a lot of them are part of the drug trade. They've got to be just to survive."

Jeff looked at her for a moment and then shrugged. "O.K., your call. You're the expert, but I want to meet this Afghan buddy of yours before we get too involved. I've got a bad feeling about this whole affair. The fewer people the better. it's just too damn dangerous."

"I know that, Jeff, probably a lot better than you, but we're going to need his help. Captain Ali Mohammad is the perfect man for us. He saved my ass at least twice in situations much like this. If you agree, I'll get on your satellite phone right after supper. The beauty of Ali is he looks, talks and thinks like the Taliban. He knows how to deal with local leaders and can talk with the mullahs we could never approach. He's good, Jeff. I'd trust him with my life."

True to her word, Caroline was on the phone as soon as they finished supper. Speaking in rapid fire Pashto, the conversation didn't take long. It was clear the Captain was not only free but more than ready to come immediately.

After hanging up, Caroline, tried to stifle a yawn. "Sorry, Jeff, I'm bushed ... it's been a long day. I really need my beauty sleep and ...." Yawning again, she mumbled, "Tomorrow I suppose I'll have to make a courtesy call on your commanding officer." With that thought in mind, Caroline stretched, struggled to her feet and headed for the door.

In the morning the two had a quick breakfast then walked over to Commander Williams' office. Introductions made, the S.M.O. outlined what he hoped they could accomplish. "Ms. Smith..."

"Caroline, please, Commander." corrected the agent with a smile.

"Right." Grinned back the man behind the desk. "Caroline, I'm sure you've heard from Dr. Thomas what we have in mind. I hope you understand how seriously we take this problem. It's become almost a personal crusade for all of us." He turned, including Jeff as he spoke. "The Medical Command at Camp Leatherneck and Bagram are well aware of the risks involved in sending you two out into this dirty business. We want results but we don't want either of you getting killed!" He looked at Caroline. "Agent ..." He quickly corrected himself, "Caroline, in spite of Jeff's jaundiced view of women in action, he's tough and he knows his Marines." Looking at the two sitting before him, he spoke deliberately. "The success of this venture depends on your being a good

team. You damn well better be!" Then his face relaxed
he smiled. "I've got a feelin' deep down in my bones you two
just might bring it off."

"I don't think you have to worry about our working together, Commander," replied Caroline. "Jeff and I may have
a past history, but we're both adults. "She looked over at the
man beside her. "You agree, don't you, Jeff?"

Jeff didn't speak for a moment, then with a slight frown,
he looked up at his commanding officer. "Yeh, Dave, we'll
do the job."

There was another half hour of discussion and planning
before the two took their leave. As the door closed, the anxious figure sitting mutely behind his cluttered desk stared silently at the now closed door. "Dear God, I pray those two
come back alive!"

⸻∞⸻

After their interview with the Commander, Jeff and Caroline
walked over to the small trauma hospital. Most of the injured
were only briefly treated here where they were triaged, trans-
fused, and urgent stabilizing surgery was performed. As soon
as possible they were flown for more definitive care at the
hospital attached to Camp Leatherneck or straight to Bagram
air base outside of Kabul and from there on to Germany.
Those few less severe injuries were treated at Shukvani, held
briefly, then sent back to their units. Such was the case with
Lance Corporal José Lopez. Arm in a sling, he stood in his

bathrobe and slippers as he nervously greeted the doctor who he hoped would save his Marine career.

"Buenos Dias, José," said Jeff to the Marine who was staring in disbelief at Caroline. "Si," he laughed, "This is the Agent I told you about." He quickly reminded the young man why this woman was here and what they needed to learn.

"O.K.," said Jeff, "He's ready, you can go ahead with your questions. José's got pretty good English but I want this to be accurate so I'll translate."

To Jeff's chagrin, Caroline turned to the wounded man and without further comment, launched into a rapid-fire interrogation in flawless Spanish.

Jeff laughed out loud. "Damn! It's been so long I'd completely forgotten - you speak Spanish as well as I do, maybe better!"

She smiled and winked at the Marine. "You, Dr. Thomas, are not the only one around here that speaks a little field-hand Spanish."

4

That afternoon Jeff and Caroline continued their interviews. Word had quickly spread through the unit that their Spanish speaking doctor and a woman were questioning men about narcotic use. All were well aware of the Marine Corp crack down on drugs and the dire consequences to their career if addiction was discovered. Even so, a few were ready to talk. Their stories were all the same: word of mouth, quick encounters, rarely the same place or person. Then just before lunch their luck changed. Held back from the morning flight to Leatherneck at his own request, one evacuee had told a corpsmen he desperately needed to talk to "that Mexican doctor" before he was shipped out.

Sergeant Jenkins, although badly wounded in the recent suicide bombing at the base was a realist. His left arm, shredded from the elbow down, had been amputated to save his life. His next stop would be Bagram, then Germany, and home. In spite of three deployments and a spotless 20 year career, Jenkins also knew his now discovered heroin addiction would mean the end of everything. Maybe being helpful, plus the loss of an arm in action, would let him keep his stripes and be discharged honorably.

The sergeant's gurney was moved into a small drafty cubicle just outside the flight shack. In spite of the cool temperature, the pale, anxious, Marine was sweating. The distinctive smell of disinfectant, anxiety and fear common to all wounded men permeated the room. As Jeff and Carolyn pulled up chairs, Jenkins was given a morphine boost to control both pain and his drug withdrawal. Dismissing the corpsmen, Jeff placed his hand gently on the Marine's shoulder.

"Sergeant, I'm Dr. Thomas and this is Agent Smith, We hear you may be able to help us. You know what we're here for, what can you tell us?

The wounded man surveyed the two with amusement. "Doc, you don't' look like no Mexican I ever seen, and she," he pointed with his remaining arm, "Don't look like no cop— but what the hell, ya never know what you'll find in this crazy part of the world." He chuckled quietly at his little joke before looking directly at Jeff. "You know all about my heroin problems, Doc, but the scuttlebutt is you ain't gettin' very far findin' who's selling the stuff."

"We've just started, Sergeant, but you're right." He sighed. "If we're going to shut down this miserable business, we need a lot more information."

"Well, Doc, I can help ya all right, but first I need to do a little horse tradin'." The pale man spoke slowly. "You know I'm gonna get dumped by the Corps 'cause of this arm but I gotta keep my pension." There was desperation in his voice. "My old lady is raising our two kids, trying to work an' she's not too well. She needs every penny I send home … and with me a cripple, it's gonna be mighty tough." He paused then looked directly at Jeff. "Will you write me a real official letter telling how I helped your investigation?" His face, showed both hope and desperation. "I gotta have that, Doc!"

"Sarge, I'm not going to bargain with you, but if you've got some good information I'll do whatever I can … and that's a promise!"

Caroline pulled her chair closer. "Sergeant, tell us where you get it and who you get it from. We understand you pushed some yourself. What do you know?"

The Marine sighed and lay back on his pillows with closed eyes. "They set me up for the first meeting in town. It was in the bazaar at a stand not far from the big Mosque, sells fruit. What's different is the guy who runs it. He's built like a truck, about 6 foot four an' his beard is flamin' red. Speaks pretty good English when he gets you alone."

"Does he sell it or is he just a messenger?" interjected Caroline.

"He's no messenger or regular pusher. I think he's important. This Red Beard's different." The sergeant paused and looked up hopefully. "Any chance either of you got a cigarette?" Although Jeff was not a smoker, he was prepared. Pulling a fresh pack out of his pocket, he lit one up. After a couple of puffs to be sure it was going, he placed it carefully in the Marine's mouth. "Go on, Sergeant."

After a long drag, the wounded man began to speak. "Red Beard's smart, he checked me out real careful. He wanted to know about the battalion, what my job was, who were the brass and a lotta stuff like that. I didn't like the way this was goin' and decided I better get outta there before things got out of control. I told you he was a big bastard. When I started to leave, he just shoved me back into the stall, put one big hand on my chest pinnin' me to the wall an' then pulled out his cellphone. He talked for a few minutes then said he wanted me to meet a man. There was an AK-47 just inside the door which he picked up an' stuck in my face." The sergeant looked up at Jeff and shook his head. "I was scared as hell. Shit, I was just tryin' to make a buy and it sounded like this guy's tryin' to set me up for a lot more than just bein' a junkie tryin' to push a little on the side". He paused, inhaled a deep, satisfying lung full of smoke, then slowly exhaled.

"Next thing I knew Red Beard walked me over to a tea-shop just outside the bazaar. We just sat there, didn't say a word. About ten minutes later, a big dusty Toyota Land Cruiser pulled up. First out were two bearded bodyguards, looked like Taliban. Then out steps a white guy dressed in a tan outfit a lot like our utilities but no camouflage. The two beards took up station at the door and this white guy come in and greeted me in real good American English. Funny, he talked like he came from California but somewhere in there I could hear a little accent. Then he …"

Jeff raised his hand. "Hold it a minute, Sarge, lets talk a bit more about this American. I need to know what he looked like. Height, weight, things like that."

"O.K., lemme think a minute." He paused. "He looked younger than you; he couldn't a been more than 28, right around there. About your height … " The sergeant tilted his head slightly as he looked Jeff carefully up and down. "Yea, Doc, he was just about your size. He had black hair an' his face was clean shaved – real neat. His eyes, they looked right through you - sharp, dangerous. He was what ya might call a good lookin' fucker." He winced. "Excuse me, ma'am."

Caroline looked up from her notes and smiled. "Anything on the Land Cruiser to tell where it came from?"

"Yeh, there was some worn out printing on the door. Somethin' looked like 'Afghan–American' was all I could make out. Strange, if it's the outfit I think it was, 'Afghan-American Construction', they was supposed to be kicked out of the country a couple a years ago. Heard a lot about 'em at headquarters on my last deployment."

"Afghan-American Construction?" Caroline looked thoughtful. "You're right. They were tossed out of the country three years ago. Graft, tax evasion, failure of completion and also involvement in drugs. That was just before I arrived. If I remember correctly they were thought to be deep into the poppy trade but nothing ever proved. Their C.E.O. was only here part time, and he skipped out before the axe fell. "

After a moment or two, the sergeant picked up his story. "He asked a lot of questions about the base and our guys. Where'd they come from, how many were Spanish, things like that. I think they thought my workin' at headquarters might be useful. Maybe give 'em a heads up if any investigations were comin' up. Soon as he found out my deployment was almost up he lost interest real quick. He gave old Red Beard hell for wastin' his time and took off in a hurry. Never saw him again. Red Beard was really pissed at me. We walked back to the fruit stand; he sold me my stuff and I got the hell outta there." Mouth dry and parched from the drugs and talking he stopped, looking around for something to wet his throat. Jeff quickly unscrewed the top of a plastic water bottle and handed it to the sergeant. "Thanks" mouthed the pale, drawn, man as he took a long swallow before continuing his story. "Those guys made me real nervous so from then on I only made my buys from small time pushers I'd heard about from my buddies. Once in awhile I saw Red Beard in town - I kept my distance."

It was almost time for the corpsmen to collect the sergeant for his flight to Leatherneck. Jeff and Caroline spent those last few minutes picking the Marine's brain for everything he could remember about the strange American. Sergeant Jenkins was clearly exhausted. It was time to stop.

"Good luck, Sergeant." Jeff said taking the man's one good hand as the gurney was wheeled out to the tarmac. "Those are the first good leads we've had. Agent Smith and I promise to get you one hell of a thank you letter from the Brigade Commander if this pans out and we get these bastards."

"Be real careful, Doc … an' keep the lady out of it. These mother-fuckers are too damn dangerous … they're killers, don't make no difference if she's a woman!"

5

T RUE TO HIS promise, Captain Ali Mohammad flew in a day
later. He arrived in his A.N.A. uniform, an AK-47 slung
over his shoulder and a pack on his back. Absent his uniform, he could well have been a Taliban commander. With
him were two beaded, uniformed men, both with Sergeant
stripes, dressed and armed like their leader. One hand up
to shield his eyes from the bright morning sun, the officer
spotted Caroline, waved, and jogged quickly across the tarmac. "*Namaste*," he spoke softly, pressing his hands together
and bringing them to his face with a slight nod of the head.
"Sorry we're late," he explained with a slight British accent.
Ali, last names being seldom used in this society, had been
held up selecting his two companions and going through the
red tape common to all armies. Caroline responded in like
manner as she slightly bowed her head and raised her hands
to her face. With that lovely, ancient, Eastern greeting complete, she proceeded to the mandatory Afghan small talk,
asking about his extended family, his work, and his health.

Not until this traditional acknowledgement was complete did she introduce Jeff.

Looking at each other, the two men assessed one another with unfeigned interest. Standing straight and alert, the tall, wiry, Afghan looked very tough indeed. Over his dark weather worn face, a grizzled beard left space for two piercing gray-blue eyes. A typical Semitic hooked nose jutted out over thin dark lips and his teeth when he spoke were stained yellow. A faint smile was fixed on his face. Maybe fifty, his age was indeterminate. Jeff was impressed. He found himself instinctively liking this Afghan soldier. Also apparently satisfied with what he saw, the Afghan turned back to Caroline. "Where do we bunk and when do we start?"

The rest of that first day was spent reviewing what they had learned, looking at maps and making plans for the next few days. All agreed they had to move fast as word was bound to leak soon that a team was investigating. Ali's first request was for 24 hours to reconnoiter the bazaar, check out Red Beard and get the lay of the land. "I've got some cousins that live here; they'll help me keep you two under cover." It was decided that with Ali busy in town, Jeff and Caroline would spend the time collecting what they needed to live undercover in the community for a number of days.

A day later when the sun was just rising over the distant mountains, two Afghans, a man, his wife following dutifully behind, passed through the checkpoints headed towards town. Both were dressed in traditional Pashtun attire, the only exception being a Marine issue Berretta hidden, but easily accessible under their loose clothing. Jeff's disguise had been no problem, but Caroline had angrily refused to wear Ali's suggested all-encompassing conservative Muslim burka. Caroline's eventual choices were shapeless gray pants, a dark-green long sleeved tunic that hung to mid-thigh and a large patterned head shawl. With help from Madge and a couple of nurses, her hair was now dyed jet black.

It was cold and crisp in the early morning sunlight as they slipped into a small tea shop not far past the razor wire surrounding the base. True to his word, Ali was already present sipping a cup of *Chai*, the sweet, milky green tea, which is the Afghan answer to a Starbucks latte. Sitting at a nondescript table, he was bent over his cup talking in a low voice to a small, gray-bearded man. On Ali's left was an unknown younger male. On his right were the two sergeants. The shop owner stood closer to the door. He seemed to be the lookout. In a corner, packs and weapons were stacked and covered with a large tarp.

The teashop consisted of just one modest sized room with two dusty windows and a door facing the street. A few tables and several mismatched, rickety, chairs were randomly placed around the room. At the back, the proprietor had returned to blow on glowing coals under a large, much dented, aluminum teakettle. Also perched on the waist high brick partition was an ancient samovar-like vessel – hot coals in the inner chamber and tea simmering in the outer. Close by stood a row of short, thick glass tumblers. A pitcher of long-simmered milk and a bowl of sugar were ready to add to the scalding brew. The entire room was cloaked in the pleasant fragrance of brewing tea and the aromatic scent of cardamom.

Ali looked up as Jeff and Caroline entered. As the door was pulled closed, another table was moved closer and room found for the newcomers. Bent over his steaming cup, Ali spoke to the three local Afghans. Tipping his head towards Caroline, in a muted voice, he explained why this American woman was present and dressed as she was. The older man frowned with concern but listened to Ali's explanation without further objection. Like Jeff, the men were attired in the traditional *Khet partug*: loose, baggy, pants and a long tunic-like jacket hanging to mid-thigh. Of neutral gray color, all showed signs of long usage. Each of the men wore a *Pakul,* the soft round wool cap so common with Pashtun men. The older man was distinguished by a black vest.

Ali, speaking English quietly and fast, introduced the men sitting around the table. His older companion was not only a close cousin, but a respected *Malek*, or elder, with a seat at the town council. Ali explained that this man and his wife had both been sent to Kabul for schooling when young children. That was in the last days of the monarchy before the communist coup and the Russian invasion. Ali went on to note that western education was very, very, rare in this small dusty city. He next pointed to the tall younger Afghan, who it seems, was the old man's son. The proprietor of the teahouse, now sipping *Chai* with the group, was a friend of a friend. He had lost his only son to the foreign drug lord's gunman. Sitting silently across the table, the two Afghan sergeants were dressed much as the others, a far cry from the uniformed soldiers Caroline and Jeff met at the airstrip.

The conversation was mostly about Red Beard. Efforts to locate the whereabouts of the American had so far been fruitless. It seemed that after the expulsion and dismantling of the Afghan-American Construction Company, two Caucasian men had been left behind to manage the very profitable Provincial poppy and drug trade in concert with an Afghan drug lord. Also an equal partner was the shadowy Taliban that had successfully infiltrated the local police and kept the growers and distributors in line. The poppy fields with their opium byproduct were an important part of the local economy and a vital source of revenue for the Taliban. The end product, heroin, was manufactured in several small laboratories scattered around the Province and across the border in Pakistan.

After an hour of animated discussion, most of which could not be understood by Jeff, a decision seemed to be reached. Caroline briefly summarized for Jeff. Ali and the two Americans would all stay with the cousin … crowded but workable for a few nights. The two sergeants and the tea shop proprietor would stay at the cousin's small farm a few miles out of town. Housekeeping having been settled, the talk moved on to the local drug leadership. There was immediate agreement: they would begin with the capture and interrogation of the red-bearded Afghan dealer. Ali grimly assured them all that he could and would quickly extract creditable information on the American's whereabouts. As they were talking, the morning sun had risen in the sky, and on the road outside the traffic and noise had steadily increased. The small, worn and battered pickup Ali had requisitioned at the base was parked behind the teashop. One by one the eight slipped through a hidden back door carrying their packs and weapons and crammed themselves into the overloaded truck.

Avoiding attention they passed quickly through town, taking a circuitous route well away from the bazaar, and soon arrived at their host's home. The ancient, once fortified, compound was enclosed behind a high ten foot tall, mud-brick wall topped with jagged glass shards embedded in the rounded mud top. Before them was a heavy iron-studded wooden gate now standing open. As they drove in they passed fruit trees in early spring bloom, chickens pecking at the hard dirt and close by a neatly arranged vegetable garden. Ahead stood two dwellings, one of two stories. Imposing by local standards, this appeared to be the main home. Another smaller home stood across an open cleared area. Behind the garden and fruit trees stood two sheds and a small raised wood framed structure.

Coming to a halt in front of the primary dwelling, all seven occupants climbed out, stretched and shook off the dust. Before the white bearded family patriarch could reach the door, it was thrown open and two young woman dressed much as Caroline stepped over the threshold. Shawls carefully covering hair and much of their face, they greeted the men with respect before stepping back to let the group enter.

Several windows, shutters spread wide, brought sunlight into the room. A large Persian rug covered much of the floor and a few chairs and cabinets were carefully arranged against the white washed walls. Standing alone not far from the door was a small, perhaps older woman covered head to foot by a long, all concealing, dark blue Burka. Her eyes, barely visible through the mesh-covered opening, shrewdly observed her husband's guests. The two younger women greeted Caroline with much interest and in rapid, low voices, ushered her to a corner of the room. That she could speak not only their language but also their dialect brought obvious pleasure

Shushing the women in irritation, the family patriarch turned back to his guests and invited them to sit on the pillows scattered about. Speaking as head of the household, a flowery welcome was extended. The speech was no sooner completed than one of the women entered with a large, ornately designed copper tray. Each visitor was offered a cup which was quickly filled with steaming hot tea poured with polite ceremony by the Burka clad matriarch. Ali, with a slight bow to their host, extensively thanked the family for their hospitality. It was then time to get down to business.

"My cousin and I have been discussing housing arrangements." He spoke in English to the two Americans. "It is going to be a bit tight and he is not sure of the proper protocol for you Americans." Ali smiled and continued. "He has decided that you two foreign guests, being of course married," the Afghan's eyes twinkled as he looked from one to the other, "shall be given the guest house."

"Wait a minute," whispered Jeff, "Who says we're married?"

"It must be so if you two are together in this country," replied Ali, his grin widening. "In fact," he spoke in a low voice, "Even though this family are all educated and quite modern in thinking, it would be inconceivable for you to be seated together in this home if you were not married. You must never forget that!"

"He's right," replied Caroline "Besides," she smiled sweetly, "I promise to be a dutiful wife."

Jeff scowled. He knew they were making fun of him. "O.K." He finally replied "What about the rest of you?" Ali went on to explain how everyone would be accommodated.

"Your sergeants and our teashop friend?"

"As I said before, they go out to the small farm of my cousin where there is a summer house. They will be needed there."

After tea was finished, and without further discussion, the family patriarch escorted Jeff and Caroline across the courtyard, Ali carrying a heavy quilt. The building was small by any standard. There was a tiny living room and one small bedroom complete with a sagging metal bed and thin mattress covered by another heavy, multi-hued quilt. The room was cold and the musty scent of long usage hung in the air. On one side stood a chair, an armoire-type cabinet and a small chest of drawers. As in most Afghan homes, there was no sign of bathroom facilities. Like the main house, a Persian rug covered the small living room floor.

Walking into the bedroom, Jeff sat gingerly on the aged bed and springs. "Alright, Caroline, you get the bed and I get the floor out there in front." Bouncing on the noisy, sagging affair, he chuckled aloud. "Lucky you!"

Caroline sat down next to Jeff and the bed sank still lower with much creaking of the old metal springs. "No way, mister!" She muttered. "I think our best bet is to move this mattress onto the floor in the other room. I get the mattress and you can wrap up in your quilt and sleep on the floor." She stopped suddenly and looking around the room saw no evidence of any toilet facilities. "I hope you brought a flashlight in case I need a midnight run... I have a bad feeling about this ... where do I run?""

Jeff nodded, amused. "My experience says you're right to be nervous, but I think I noticed a possibility back behind the fruit trees when we drove in. If not," he smiled smugly, "I'm glad I'm a boy!"

With that parting remark, Jeff left to collect their small packs and investigate the "bathroom" situation. Sure enough, there up against the back compound wall, not far behind the garden stood the family privy in all its glory. What Jeff found was a slightly modernized version of the dry, two vault system developed centuries ago in the parched and arid lands of Central Asia. Perched four feet off the ground and supported by concrete walls was a wood sided, corrugated iron roofed, fully enclosed structure. The interior consisted of a concrete floor with two squat holes, one now covered with a wooden plug. An adjacent trough by each hole diverted urine, thus separating fluid from the solid waste. After each use, a scoop of dirt and ashes from a nearby bucket is dropped down the hole. As a modern touch, a homemade tin urinal was attached to one wall with a tube that led through an opening in the floor. Below, Jeff knew there were two vaults; one under each squat-hole for the solids. Liquids passed through a tube to a large plastic container in the empty vault. The solids collect in one vault until full, then the squat-hole above is plugged airtight and they unplug the other. "Aged" for a year in its enclosed, dark vault, the resulting compost is a cheap, completely safe, ready-made fertilizer for use in field or garden. Simple, little odor, no need for water, no moving parts, these ancient marvels of ecological sanitation work to perfection.

"How lucky can we get? " thought Jeff as he stood admiring his discovery. "I bet there are not a dozen of these in this end of the province." Jeff knew from past medical inspections that these simple, ancient, solutions to mankind's basic needs are rare everywhere in Afghanistan even though mortality rates from drinking water polluted by human waste are so tragically high.

Carrying the packs into their quarters, Jeff couldn't wait to tell of his happy discovery. "Caroline, we lucked out again! There is a genuine, first-class, Afghanistan outhouse in back of the garden. No trips behind the wall. No lurking lions or tigers awaiting you in the dark. All it requires is a little gymnastic squatting. Considering the alternatives, you're gonna love it!"

He was pulling the mattress into the room when Ali came over to see how they were doing. "Ah, very cozy" He smiled, looking around, amusement in his eyes. "Good thing you two are such old friends." Turning to Jeff he continued. "I noticed you inspecting the sanitary facilities." He laughed aloud. "Pretty nice, yes? Must be the only one for miles around."

By the time they were settled it was almost noon. Breakfast and dinner being the primary meals, lunch in Afghanistan is always a simple affair. A bowl of fresh and dried fruit, a dish of nuts plus a slice or two of *Naan*, the delicious and ubiquitous Afghan bread. Just as they were finishing their small meal, they were interrupted by the sound of a pickup driving into the compound and coming to a quick stop. As they looked up to see what was going on, one of the sergeants jumped from the driver's seat and ran to Ali. After a rapid conversation accompanied by much gesticulation, Ali returned to the group, concern on his face. After speaking rapidly to the family he turned to the two Americans.

"We may have a problem. There is talk in the bazaar of two foreigners in disguise. Someone must have spotted you two leaving the base. It does not change our plans but we will have to be very careful. We will take this old pickup. There is nothing to identify it and it looks much like all the others on the street. Caroline, I will have the women of the house check you very carefully. You must look inconspicuous and wear your scarf around your head and face at all times. Jeff, your beard is still very short. We will have to put some coloring on your face. Always wear your cap. I have also instructed the family to keep the gates barred at all times.

6

I N THE EARLY afternoon the Bazaar was still teeming with
burka clad women, their younger counterparts more often
dressed less conservatively in long skirts or shapeless pants,
blouses and head scarfs. No matter their attire, all were noisily
bargaining with the many shop owners. Dust flying, children
happily raced in and out adding to the din. Boys in dirty
Mickey Mouse shirts, hand-me-down sweaters and patched,
worn pants kicked misshapen soccer balls toward imaginary
goals. Girls in a colorful assortment of pull-overs and bright
little dresses tugged at their mothers' skirts. Here and there
scrawny, dirt smeared, semi-starved, dogs snarled and fought
over the fly covered offal of just butchered goats and chickens.
The smell of rotting fruit, exotic spices and the excreta of dogs,
horses and humans perfumed the air.

Carefully navigating the narrow, crooked streets, the
pickup was soon parked in a narrow passage just outside the
bazaar. Here the cousins with their tea shop friend would
await a signal from Jeff. Spread out and walking with no apparent purpose, the team kept to the periphery of the bazaar

until they were near their target, close by the mosque. The fruit stall was a simple enclosed structure made of old boards and flattened 5 gallon kerosene cans. A multi-colored awning projected over the fruit giving protection from the sun. They found Red Beard arguing in a loud voice with a wrinkled, indignant, old woman. Tattered shawl carelessly slung over unkempt gray hair, eye flashing, the old crone was howling full blast. A large ripe melon, the apparent subject of the brawl, was clutched firmly in both her arms as she stomped off. Under cover of this loud but bloodless altercation, Jeff took up position behind the small shack ready to block any attempt at escape. Caroline stood shielded behind an empty adjacent stall.

As though on cue, Ali and his two compatriots approached from the front. Wasting no time, Ali, a good half-foot shorter and 50 pounds lighter, strode purposely forward. Reaching up suddenly, he grabbed a handful of the astonished man's luxuriant beard and gave a mighty yank. Taken unaware, the startled and unsuspecting shopkeeper was next the recipient of a well-aimed knee slamming hard into his unprotected groin. With a scream of pain, the drug dealer collapsed on the ground, clutching his crotch and retching uncontrollably. Protected from view by the tables of fruit, Ali and his companions immediately dragged the miserable man into the stall's small, enclosed area and as quickly, pulled closed a beaded curtain. Handcuffs on wrists and a gag stuffed in mouth, subdued the moaning man. Moments later, the pickup was backed up to the stall and Red Beard hoisted over the tailgate and covered with a tarp. When all were precariously loaded aboard, the truck edged away. The young cousin, crouched over the wheel, drove with caution out of the Bazaar. Now hidden in a maze of nearby alleys, the truck skirted a couple of checkpoints and was out of town in minutes.

Bouncing along a pot holed, rutted, gravel road for several miles, they abruptly swerved off to the right, winding carefully along a narrow track dividing small plots of cultivated land. Well out of sight of the main road, the dust encrusted vehicle slowed and came to a halt in a cleared area before a modest stone house. On the far side of the open area was a much smaller, windowless, square brick building as well as two sheds housing farm equipment.

Ali was first out of the truck. "Welcome to my cousin's small farm and summer house." Eyes twinkling in obvious pleasure, Ali continued. "Here we shall enjoy privacy to discuss life with this red bearded devil." With just four days stubble and his short military haircut, Jeff felt dangerously conspicuous among these tough, bearded men, AK-47's slung carelessly over shoulders. Had Ali not been present, he'd have been certain he was trapped by a Taliban patrol.

Unlocking the front door of the house, the proud owner walked to the shuttered windows, throwing them wide as he invited Caroline and Jeff to enter. After a welcoming *Namaste*, the old man proudly gave a brief tour of the simple dwelling. Just one story tall, the main room, with a hard packed dirt floor, was covered with a near room-sized rug.

Two adjoining smaller areas appeared to be sleeping quarters. Out a back door was a semi-attached but open sided shed that served as a kitchen. On the roof, surrounded by a low wall, a just visible shelter had at some time been erected, three sides open to catch any wayward breeze. Fixed wooden steps attached to the back of the house gave access to this shaded refuge from the coming, searing, 110° summer days.

The tour completed, the men unceremoniously hauled their captive out of the truck and variously pushed, dragged and kicked the struggling man over to the small structure across the cleared area. Gag removed and howling obscenities, he was shoved into the dark interior, a plastic container of water and several chunks of bread were dumped on the floor, and the door slammed shut and locked. Two small, heavily barred openings close to the roof provided the only air and light.

After Ali had carefully inspected this makeshift jail, the two sergeants along with the teahouse proprietor were delegated for guard duty through the night. It was getting late in the afternoon by the time all was satisfactorily arranged. It was time for the remainder of the team to head back to town.

———

The sun had already dipped over the horizon and twilight was fast approaching as the small group arrived back at the family compound. Caroline, acquiring a large aluminum basin and a pitcher of warm water from the two young women of the household, retired to the small house to clean up for dinner. Jeff, stopping at the old-fashioned hand operated water pump, a rare reminder of the Soviet's attempt at modernization during their short reign, washed hands and face then picked up Caroline before crossing over to the main home. This Afghan equivalent of a living room had been cleaned up and transformed. Two shaded electric bulbs hung from the ceiling. Electricity, always uncertain, was functioning fitfully, bringing light to the fast approaching darkness of this star studded, moonlit, spring evening. Below, a bright floral tablecloth was spread over the center of the handsome rug. The exotic scent of herbs and spices filled the air. As they watched, plates of food and two steaming copper teapots were placed in the middle of the area. The men, squatting comfortably on their haunches, seemed perfectly at ease. Knowing the difficulty of westerners holding this alien position, Ali had requested pillows for his two American charges. As food was being placed on the table, one of the daughters held a basin for the guests while the other poured water over extended hands. A towel was passed, used, and passed on. This ancient ritual complete, it was time to begin the feast. Tradition holds that three cups of hospitality tea should be drunk first at such an occasion. The first for thirst, the second for friendship and the third for tradition. Each person picked up a cup, already one third full of sugar, and waited expectantly for the scalding green tea to be carefully poured. The scent of cardamom wafted through the air and voices were hushed.

As honored guests, the two Americans were seated farthest from the door. Jeff, sensing all eyes on him, prepared to take the first taste. Looking at the array setout before him, he slowly leaned forward, extending his left arm. There was a sharp intake of breath from Ali on his left and at the same moment he felt a quick dig in his ribs from Caroline. "Right hand!" whispered Caroline hardly moving her lips. Without missing a beat Jeff corrected his near classic Western faux pas. Dropping his left arm as though to support his body, he carefully extended his right hand to take the first expected small taste. "Thanks," he murmured in reply.

The centerpiece of the meal was a large and colorful platter of *Qabuli pilau*. This traditional dish, a thick layer of rice held together with a saffron and cumin laced sauce, rested beneath a mound of boiled lamb, onions and raisins. Above, a second layer of rice sprinkled with slivered carrots, peppers and almonds, made up the whole. Colorful as it was with the yellow saffron rice, red peppers, bright orange carrots and oval shards of white almonds, it was the transcendent aroma hovering above that had mouths watering in anticipation. As is the custom, it was not until each man had taken a portion that Caroline took her turn. Carefully, using the second and third fingers of her right hand, she thrust deep into the *pilau*, rolling the retrieved mixture between thumb and fingers to create a small ball. Bringing this morsel to her nose, inhaling with appreciation, she slowly chewed and savored this special treat. It was delicious. Nearby was a bowl of *burnai*, cold sour cream and eggplant, a perfect foil for the lamb and rice.

Although still early spring, a few fresh root vegetables had been found in the bazaar. These also were dutifully served. Baskets of quartered hot *Naan*, the classic tandoori baked flat bread of Central Asia, circulated around the room. At last, appetites flagging, a final platter of dried fruit with slices of cool fresh melon concluded the repast. Predictably, the power had failed mid-way through dinner, replaced by the soft light of kerosene lamps. A very romantic touch, thought Caroline. After many an appreciative belch, a sure sign of the kitchen's success, it was unanimously declared a memorable evening. Ali and Caroline each effusively thanked the family in Pashto. Jeff did his best to follow suit bringing many smiles and some open laughter. Caroline again thanked everyone and apologized for the risk and danger their presence had brought to their lives. Ali completed the evening by giving thanks to Allah for their preservation from their enemies.

—◦◦◦—

Back in their assigned domicile. Jeff and Caroline again inspected their quarters.

"O.K. Caroline," said Jeff, inspecting the arrangements and picking up his quilt. "You take the mattress — I'll do fine on the floor."

"Ah, an officer and a gentleman! Nope, Jeff, there's plenty of room for both of us on this old mattress. I can just roll up in my quilt – I'm sure my virtue will be quite safe." Taking on a stern expression, she pointed at the door.

"Now vamoose. I have to dig my way out of this collection of clothes you found and I don't need an audience."

As Jeff stepped out into the moonlight, his thoughts were in turmoil. "This whole business gets crazier by the minute." Jeff looked up at the quarter moon rising high in the night sky. "How the hell am I supposed to act with this woman? It's been seven years; she's married," his voice tapered off as he looked hopefully into the star studded sky for an answer. The moon, looking down from above, regretfully gave no response to his unhappy query.

It was dark and silent when he returned to the room. Caroline seemed to be asleep. As he stood motionless looking at her mute form, there was a faint hint of the perfume he remembered so well. He'd smelled that sensuous, faintly earthy, jasmine laced scent when he'd first met Caroline. "Damn," he whispered to himself. "How could she do this to me." Turning away in despair, he stripped down to his skivvies. Carefully wrapping himself in his quilt, he hoped against hope not to awaken the sleeping woman beside him. It was not to be.

"Jeff," Caroline whispered, opening her eyes and turning to face him. "We need to talk."

"Not now, Caroline, it's been a long day — we've got to sleep."

"Yes, now!"

The faint light of that unhelpful moon was all the illumination present … it was all that was needed. During the next hour Jeff learned that Mr. Smith was long gone. A great lover and a philanderer par excellence. They had parted after two miserable years. There had been no children to her great regret. Other men had come and gone, but nothing lasted. She often wondered if it had been her time with Jeff that had jinxed any meaningful relationship. When she'd arrived at Shukvani and found that Jeffrey Thomas was to be her partner, she had almost turned back.

As she related her life over these past years her voice faltered and at last trailed away. "Jeff, I think I still love you … I think I never stopped."

Jeff said nothing for a few moments, then his own story poured out in the night. Of the hurt and heartbreak he'd suffered when they parted. Of the anguish he'd felt on hearing rumors of her marriage. Even the years in medical school and residency, though by no means celibate, had not dimmed the memories of their once bright love. Reaching out, his fingers tenderly traced across her soft lips. "Caroline, I know I have always loved you."

The silence of the soundless night was finally broken by the faint sound of touching lips. At first hesitant and tender, their kisses grew fierce and desperate as the two lovers, once so close, joined together in ever increasing waves of overflowing passion. Breathless, bodies still entwined in the embrace of love they rested but it was not long before a renewed urgency brought them together once again in a slower, gentler ascent to the crest of love. It was not until the early morning hours that the two lovers finally lay back happily exhausted.

Cradled in each other's arms, eyes closed in contentment; they soon drifted into a deep and peaceful sleep.

—∽∞∾—

Roused by activity in the courtyard, Jeff and Caroline quickly pulled on their Afghan clothes and met the family for breakfast. *Chai,* thick yogurt, assorted dried and fresh fruit, chunks of *Roht*, a round sweet flatbread plus the always-present *Naan*, made for a filling meal to last through the morning.

Ahmed Kahn and Ali, their heads together while drinking their *chai*, talked quietly about security. The two young women had gone to the Bazaar early to see what they could learn. They had returned full of rumors about Red Beard's disappearance. Rough, angry men suspected of being Taliban were already questioning women and shopkeepers. Although no suspicion seemed directed to the family, all knew there was growing risk. Before leaving for the country house, the men carefully checked the gates and instructed the women to stay secluded and within the high walls. Satisfied they had done what they could for the compound's safety, Caroline, Jeff, Captain Ali and the two men of the family climbed into Ahmed's truck and headed out to the country. Ahmed was driving with Ali, Caroline and Jeff jammed together in the front seat.

"My biggest concern," said Ali, turning to speak to Jeff. "Is that you two, having never been seen in the bazaar before and despite your disguises, might be suspected as being for-eigners. We'll just have to hope no one spotted Ahmed or his son-in-law with the truck as you climbed aboard."

"I'll feel a lot better when we're back at the house." said Caroline, obviously concerned about the women. "Saire and the girls aren't safe there alone."

"Don't worry, we'll get back by noon," assured Jeff. "No one will be looking this early."

The morning went fast. Pulling information out of Red Beard was slow but bit-by-bit they were making progress. Caroline sat quietly taking notes, occasionally interrupting to clarify a statement. Jeff, unable to follow the rapid fire Pashto, stayed well in the background. It was abundantly clear that Afghan-American Construction was primarily im-plicated in the drug trafficking of Helmand Province and for the heroin plague infiltrating the Marine troops. There were two Caucasians, both from San Francisco who were left behind when the company was ejected, one, the man Sgt. Jenkins had met at the bazaar, the other unknown.

For two and a half hours they kept up the questioning until all were exhausted. Putting Red Beard back in his makeshift cell, they broke for lunch. The Afghan Sergeants and the teashop proprietor would remain while the oth-ers would return to Ahmed's compound to check on the women.

It was shortly past noon when Ali and the Americans ar-rived back at the family compound. Dust flying, the truck skidded to a halt as they all stared at the frightening scene.

The massive gates were closed, the planks pockmarked with bullet holes. Just before the gate stood a nondescript pickup, windows shattered and a man hanging lifeless from the driver's door.

"My family!" rasped the older man, rushing toward the gate followed by Ali, his AK-47 at the ready. Not far behind ran Caroline and Jeff, pistols in hand. The two men banged on the heavy timbers and almost immediately a small grill covered window was cautiously opened. Staring out, the frightened face of a young woman appeared for a moment followed by the scrapping noise of the heavy bar blocking the gate being pulled aside. At last the big doors swung open. The burka clad older woman stood rigidly before them, an AK-47 hanging loose in her arms. The two younger women stood slightly apart sobbing in fear. Just to the left of the gate lay the bodies of two bearded men, a dark pool of blood slowly spreading around them.

"Allah be praised!" cried out the older man as he rushed forward to clasp the three in his arms. A torrent of Pashto flew back and forth between Ali, the cousin and the women as Caroline tried to translate. There had been an attack by three Taliban gunmen looking for two foreigners. They had searched everything fast and found nothing. Furious at coming up empty handed, they shot up the house in warning. Their mistake was trying to take the two daughters hostage. The mother had put up no resistance during the search but when the men grabbed the two young women, maternal outrage exploded. Pulling her hidden weapon from under her voluminous gown she had let fire. The result of her fury lay dead before them.

Ali quickly drove the truck in and the others swung the gates closed. Jeff and Caroline raced to their quarters and flung open the door. The small building was a shambles. The contents of the armoire were scattered on the floor, the dresser drawers emptied and the mattress split open.

"And I complained," said a shaken Caroline in a hushed voice, "when you made me pack up all my stuff, and put the mattress back on the bed." She looked around in dismay. "Where did you hide our things that they didn't find them?"

Jeff tucked away his Beretta before replying. "Rolled 'em up in one of the quilts and hid it all behind the head … you know, the 'outhouse'. I figured nobody would ever look back there." He paused, looking around the room. "Thank God I did or we'd all be dead."

By the time everything was cleaned up it was mid-afternoon. Other than the bullet holes in the gate and walls, it was as though nothing untoward had happened. Ali and Jeff had dragged the Taliban bodies to the fighters' truck. With Ali driving and Jeff following in their own pickup, they had dumped the bodies in a dry and deserted ditch, then abandoned the truck on a side track several miles away. At the compound, the women of the house had returned to their interrupted work in the kitchen. While the men were away, Caroline straightened up their rooms. That evening dinner was a simple, somber affair. Everyone seemed wrapped in their personal, private thoughts.

7

OVER THE NEXT three days, the interrogation of Red Beard progressed slowly. The details of the local supply and distribution system came easily. The acreage of poppies, the number and names of the many small growers were listed. The location of the local "laboratories" where the sticky poppy paste was turned into heroin took more persuasion. It was when they tried to piece out the upper layers of leadership that fear clouded their reluctant captive's eyes, and he closed up like a proverbial clam. Caroline and Ali conferred frequently. It was imperative that they learn the names and whereabouts of the Americans who seemed to be directing the sales to the military. Unfortunately, their captive appeared to know only a few Americans: Sergeant Jenkins and the other Marines he met in the bazaar and the civilian Jenkins had met from whom the Afghan took orders. Red Beard was only a mid-level player. It was clear the Taliban was the controlling organization extending throughout Helmand and Kandahar Provinces and directing all phases of the process. The drug lord, once paramount in the southwest provinces now took orders from the Taliban. The heroin flooding out of the many labs made its way to Pakistan, Iran and Kazakhstan and in return the money poured back into the treasury of the Taliban. This was a strange reversal as it was well known that in the years of Taliban rule, Afghanistan had almost eliminated the growth of opium poppies. Now opium money had become the main source of insurgency funds for guns, food and medical care. That did not include the riches flowing to the Americans, the corrupt Afghan officials, police and the Taliban leadership.

It was on the third day of questioning that finally a significant gem of information came to light. About fifty miles south on the fertile irrigated plain along the Helmand River, was a large fortified compound hidden in the grape vineyards. This was the meeting place of the Taliban, the Helmand and Kandahar drug lord and the Americans. It was here Red Beard reported to his superiors. Even more important: the next meeting was to take place in just four days.

Later in the morning, back at Ahmed Kahn's compound on the far edge of town, Jeff, Caroline and Ali met to discuss their next steps. In the privacy of Jeff and Caroline's "suite", with a fresh pot of tea at hand, the three arranged themselves on the floor. Caroline was the first to speak.

"What a break! With luck we could nail this whole Helmand operation in one stroke."

"Maybe," replied a more cautious Jeff. "But that kind of operation is out of our league and we have damn little time. Ali, you're the soldier, what do you think it would take?"

The Afghan Captain took a long sip of tea, taking time to think before replying. "Yes, if they have not been warned it is a perfect opportunity — but that is a big 'if'. He paused. "They will be heavily armed and the compound strongly protected. I agree, this is far too big an operation for the 6 of us. We would need to have help, including aircraft, but how to manage all that in such a short window of opportunity? It will be a very risky operation. We also need to know a lot more about this place and its defenses."

The more the three talked the more difficult and dangerous any kind of raid appeared. Surprise was the only hope of success. "I wonder," said Jeff. "Could an air strike take out the entire compound? We could follow with a small team of Marines to clean out what's left of resistance. If any leadership is left alive, we could air lift them out along with our ground team. Jesus, we've only got 72 hours to line this up. It would have to be very quick and very dirty."

Ali listened quietly to Jeff. "It could be done," responded Ali, "We've used this same technique up north with success once or twice. It all depends on how fast we can get authorization for an airstrike and if the aircraft are available. How high is our priority?"

"It comes from the top and I mean Washington. The only way to find out about the aircraft is to get the hell back to the base. We'll have to sell the brass on the importance and tiing of the raid tonight. What's your take on getting authorization, Caroline?"

"We won't know 'till we ask, but my guess is if they can spare the aircraft they'll go for it. It's too great an opportunity to miss."

"O.K." responded Jeff as all three sat cross-legged calculating what would be needed in the next 24 hours. "I'll get our Brigade Major to call the 1st Marine Command at Leatherneck. They'll have to authorize aircraft and the raid. Commander Williams should be able to get a quick Navy approval from Bagram, those people are just waiting for the word. If we're lucky, we could have a 'go' by tonight. As for manpower, it shouldn't be too hard to round up a platoon from the brigade. Captain, you and your guys are going to have to find this place fast. We need on the ground intelligence right now. You'll also have to find a landing area for the choppers and guide in the aircraft."

Ali, who had been making notes, looked up. "The directions we got from Red Beard sound accurate. It's only a couple of hours southeast, getting close will be the tricky part. I'll take my two sergeants. We can put on a pretty good Taliban act and that should let us work our way in close. I'll take the satellite phone, it's harder to intercept." He looked at his watch. "I'll check in by phone at 1900 tonight. When the fighter-bombers are on the way, I can direct them with my VHF radio. I've done that before."

Over the next hour the trio talked over each move and coordinated their actions. There was a lot to do in a very short time. Excuses were made to the family for their sudden departure. The two Americans would be back the next day but Ali and his teammates would be away for a few days. Most of their gear would be left behind to further obscure their departure. By now it was late morning - time to get started.

Jeff walked out to the truck with the Afghan soldiers where he quietly shook each hand and wished them all luck. As though returning to the family farm to continue the interrogation sessions, Ali and his two sergeants loaded into their beat-up old pickup and took off.

Moving fast, Jeff and Caroline were quickly ready to return to the base. Ali's older cousin would drive them back to the tea shop where their mission had begun just a short week ago. From there they would walk the rest of the way to the Base entrance, still posing as an Afghan husband and wife with employee I.D. passes hanging around their necks. With luck they would be back at the compound by midafternoon without arousing suspicion from the inevitable Taliban spies around the base.

Just four hours after leaving Ahmed Kahn's compound they were sitting in Commander Williams' office. Hands crossed before him, a relieved expression on his face, the S..M.O. sat staring at the two apparent Afghans for a few moments, then let out a long sigh. "Thank God you're both alive." He spoke with visible emotion. "We heard there was an abduction in the bazaar. I thought it must be you two … and then not a word. No ransom demand, no bloody clothes. The M.P.'s tried to get information but nothing came from the local police. What the hell has happened … no, hold your story, Major Radcliff from Brigade Headquarters is on his way. You'll only have to tell your story once".

"We'll hold the details, Dave, but we've got to move real fast. If we're lucky we just might close down their entire Helmand operation, or at least set 'em back a longtime. But there's a big 'if', our window of opportunity is less than 72 hours …."

Jeff was cut off as the office door banged open and a tall, harried looking Marine Major barged in. "72 hours? What 72 hours?" Coming to a sudden stop, he stared suspiciously at the two Afghans siting in front of the Commander's desk. "What the hell are these two doin' in here, Dave?" Not waiting for a reply he leaned over, stared hard at Jeff for a moment, then broke out in a laugh. "Well I'll be damned, I do believe that's our very own Dr. Thomas." Then turning, he looked Caroline up and down. "And this exotic an' charmin' lady must be that agent you've been talkin' about." He stood back staring for a moment, then with a bemused smile on his face, he turned to the Commander. "Well, Doc, I gotta say these two make quite a pair." Pulling up a chair, his face and voice turned deadly serious. "72 hours? O.K. Mister, lets hear it."

Over the next 30 minutes Caroline and Jeff recounted the events of the past week. From the capture of Red Beard, the attack on the compound and the revelation of the high level meeting about to take place. For another quarter hour, rapid-fire questions went back and forth between Jeff and the two officers. As they finished, the Commander turned to his telephone and began hurried conversations with his superiors first at Camp Leatherneck and then at Bagram. The Major took particular interest in Captain Ali and his background with the British Special Forces before he, too, began a series of calls.

The Major was the first to re-start the conversation after the Commander finally put down the phone. "I've got one rifle platoon in reserve at the moment. I could spare them for a few days. "Lt. Ed Fuller is in charge, he's young but good." The Major pulled a map from his jacket and reached again for the phone and punched in a number. "I need him over here right now. We've got precious little time. By the way," he smiled at Caroline and Jeff, "You people must have some real pull. As of right now, the strike has been given a green light." He turned back as the phone rang. "Fuller? ..."

"Here's the area you're talkin' about." The Major continued after replacing the phone. "Flat, mostly vineyards... looks like not many structures but a lot of irrigation ditches comin' off the river; they're hell to get past, they can hide a whole company; blast the hell outta you before ya know what hit you."

They all leaned over as the Major pointed out various features of the terrain. While all were intent on the map, the door opened and a young lieutenant walked in. Looking up briefly, the major acknowledged the officer's presence before looking back at the map. "We gotta talk to your A.N.A. man on the ground, hopefully he's got some good intelligence for us …he can guide you in." Looking at Jeff, he spoke brusquely, "When's he supposed to report?"

Jeff looked at his watch, the hands stood at 1857 hours. "If all is going according to plan he'll be calling on his sat phone in about three min…." The phone rang even before Jeff finished his sentence. "Ali?" There was an instant affirmative response. "Good. I've got Major Radcliff and Lieutenant Fuller here." He glanced at the Major and nodded. "Ali, I'm putting you on the speaker."

"This is Major Radcliff, Captain. Where are you and what are the coordinates."

Ali rattled off some fast figures and the Lieutenant quickly pointed down at the map. "He's right there by that slight bend in the river."

"Gottcha." responded the Major, head bent over the map. "O.K. Captain, what's doin' there on the ground?"

The responding voice was loud and clear. "The main compound is about a quarter mile due east – should show up on satellite pictures. It's a large, two storied concrete building, looks like a warehouse with offices. A dozen guys on the roof. There are six outbuildings. Maybe fifteen vehicles parked around. Several with mounted 50 calibers. There are three Land Cruisers," There was a momentary pause. "No. four. Another just arrived. Maybe 50 - 60 Taliban in positions around the big buildings and on picket." He paused for a moment. "Hold on … here comes a big Mercedes, looks like a couple of Caucasians getting out."

Over the next couple of minutes Ali described the area in detail: the defenses and the location of doors and windows and possible escape routes from the buildings. "This place looks perfect for an air strike. A few well placed rockets or bombs could take out the larger buildings. The big ditch just east of the building is going to be a main defense zone. It'll need attention before your Marines rush the place. Can't see the others. You can chopper in your Marines. There's a pretty good landing spot on the road just north of the track leading to the compound." There was a break in communication before Ali returned with a whisper. "Patrol coming. Gotta disappear. Will call in one hour if …." The line went dead.

"I like the sound of that man." Said the Major. "Knows what he's doin'." Turning he spoke to the lieutenant. "Alright, Fuller, you've got about 36 hours to get your platoon ready and over to the airstrip. Maybe we can get lucky and lasso a Sea Stallion for the lift. We're promised an 0800 strike in 48 hours by two AV-8B Harriers. The chopper'll have to be landing at the same time. The Harriers should be able to knock down that warehouse in short order, then pour some 20 mm fire into the big ditch. Maybe we can find a Cobra or two to hose down those other irrigation ditches" He paused considering his next move. "I'll take the Captain's call at Brigade headquarters - pass the word if anything's new. Your job is to move in fast and secure the place after the flyboys finish and then get the hell out." He paused. "And, don't forget, we sure would like some prisoners."

Chairs were pushed back and the Lieutenant took off on the run. The rest remained to get Captain Ali's next report. During all the discussion and Ali's call, Caroline had remained silent. Now she turned to the Senior Medical Officer and spoke urgently.

"Commander, Jeff and I need to go in with those Marines. With Ali's help, we can go through the wreckage while the Marines are cleaning out the compound. We need every scrap of intelligence we can find to wrap this up. I need to photograph and get prints from the bodies. I will also need some DNA samples. We can do the identification later at Bagram or Kabul. If we're lucky we might even be able to interrogate some of the survivors on the spot."

The Commander looked at Jeff and Caroline and then raised his eyes to the Major. "Whatta you think, Tom?"

"Whatta I think? I think they're both crazy!" He snapped. Turning to Caroline, his eyes carefully assessed this strangely garbed woman. "With all due respect, Ma'am, this is a job for professionals – Lt. Fuller and his Marines and that Captain Ali and his sergeants. If you need to have a look around, maybe we could helicopter you in the next day."

"No, Major." Interrupted Jeff. "The whole purpose of this operation is to stop the heroin getting to your Marines. We can't miss this opportunity to close down these bastards. Of course there are risks, but this can't wait." Jeff paused, looking directly at the tall Marine. "Major, unless I get orders to the contrary from Leatherneck, we're going in with Fuller."

There was a long pause. Visibly angry, Radcliff, glared at Jeff. Opening his mouth to speak, he stopped, made a conscious effort to relax and turned back to his counterpart. "O.K., Dave, I'll let 'em ride with Fuller if you agree ... but by God, it's your damn responsibility." Without further discussion he picked up his helmet and marched out the door.

"Well now," said the Commander with an amused shake of his head, "I gotta say, Jeffrey boy, you've got balls. I don't think you made our Major a very happy camper. In fact, it's my personal judgment, that our Major Radcliff is mighty pissed off right about now." He paused. "This operation of yours better be a success. I wouldn't want to be in your shoes if it's blown!"

All three were silent for a moment as they digested the implications of these words. Not good, seemed to be the general consensus. Caroline let out a long sigh. "Commander," She said, changing the subject, "We have to meet Ali's cousin in just two hours ... and I need a shower really bad before we go back."

"I'd say you both need a shower," responded the commander, making motions of sniffing the air. "I agree, you'd better spend the night there if they're expecting you. You'll have to let them know you'll be going back to the base for a couple of days but be very careful – any leak of what's planned would be a disaster. Jeff, check out an M-16 and some ammunition in case you have visitors again tonight. "They all let that unpleasant thought linger for a moment. "If you're back by mid-afternoon," he continued, "You should have plenty of time to get ready, catch a few hours sleep before you meet Fuller at dawn." He smiled. "And in your Marine utilities, helmets and body armor, if you please."

Jeff put out his hand. "Thanks for everything, Dave, we'll do our damnedest to finish the job. Wish us luck!"

It was a quiet evening at the compound on the edge of town that night. Only family and the two Americans were present and conversation was less formal. As talk ebbed and flowed, smoke from Ahmed Kahn's cherished hookah curled lazily in the air. Between puffs the older man attempted to make conversation. Politely, no questions were asked about Ali's whereabouts or their own comings and goings. Ahmed talked about his hopes and fears for his country's future and what might happen when NATO forces withdrew. Would Afghanistan once again be abandoned by the West? What would be Pakistan and India's role?

After the simple dinner of rice, vegetables, yogurt and fruit was cleared away and the men were deep in conversation, the young women not so subtly took Carolyn aside. Accompanied by much giggling, there were questions about Carolyn and Jeff's relationship. Were they really married? What was her real job and what did she do at home in America? It was almost as though they were spending a pleasant evening with friends back in California were it not for the exotic setting, the strange language and the undercurrent of anxiety that seemed ever present. Jeff noticed there was no longer any attempt to conceal the AK-47 standing by the door. Finally, as the moon began to rise, the two guests effusively thanked their hosts and took their leave. Before they left, arrangements were made to have cousin Hakim drive them back to the base in the morning.

Their small house across the courtyard was dark when they entered. Soon Jeff had turned up the wick, struck a match, their only light that flickering kerosene lantern casting it's faint shadows on the white washed walls. The only sound, the distant clamor of a howling dog. Finding two pillows, the two sat quietly as Jeff, arms holding Caroline close, at last began to speak. "It's going to feel strange leaving this country. I know we'll be stuck wrapping up this business, but, dear God, I'm ready to go home ... and Caroline," he turned, eyes pleading. "You've got to come with me."

"You know I will, Jeff." Caroline whispered, her thoughts drifting with her dreams. "We could move to the country … maybe buy a few acres in the wine country." Turning to the dimly seen figure beside her, a smile lighting her face. "Don't forget, mister, you and I still have time for a batch of kids." She paused, "Oh, Jeff, I want your children so much."

He smiled thinking of his own childhood. "Maybe we could raise our kids on a small vineyard the way you and I grew up not so long ago." Jeff leaned over and gently kissed her lips. "But mostly, I just want you."

As the hours drifted past, they talked of dreams, their hopes, what the future might hold. As the moon made its way across the star-lit sky, the coals turned to gray flecked ash and the lamp flickered ever more faintly. It was long past midnight when Jeff and Caroline crawled into their comfortable nest of quilts. There in the soft hush of that distant Afghan night, the two lovers came together again in a slow and passionate embrace.

8

JEFF AND CAROLINE were airborne at 0600 the next morning. Around them, sitting silently on metal bucket seats were Lt. Fuller and his platoon. The billowing sand created by the big Sea Stallion's rotors as they rose from the airstrip was soon left far behind. Visibility, now unlimited, revealed a wide swath of green vegetation along both banks of the sluggish river below. Beyond, stretching to the far horizon, a vast expanse of empty desert shimmered in the morning sun. Cruising at a steady 120 knots with the silver ribbon of the river to guide them, the Sea Stallion would be over their target in a short 30 minutes. Crew members, manning machine guns mounted in the open doors, stood scanning the ground. The noise of the wind, the constant roar of rotors and whine of the turbines was deafening, speech impossible. Dressed like their counterparts in full combat gear, Jeff and Caroline sat side by side.

Peering over the right gunner, the crew chief suddenly yelled "Look!" Ahead jarring flashes illuminated the morning sky. "The Harriers." he shouted in Jeff's ear. At the same moment, two red flares could be seen signaling below. "There, by the river..." pointed the Lieutenant, "Our landing site ..."

As Fuller spoke, the big aircraft tilted sharply to the left and began a rapid descent. Ready lights blinking, the Marines stood quickly, unhitched seat restraints and picked up their M-16's and packs. Fuller, holding onto the overhead straps, watched the huge rear ramp slowly descend as they neared the ground. With a jolt the big craft struck and the Marines poured out onto the road. Even as Jeff and Caroline jumped down to join the fast moving men, the whine of the blades overhead increased their tempo and with a sudden lurch the Sea Stallion rose rapidly into the sky. Ahead on the road, standing in billowing dust, red flares still held in his hands, stood Captain Ali Mohammad. Glancing up, Jeff saw the two Harriers wag their wings as they flashed past heading home. Above, a lone Super Cobra attack helicopter hovered, protecting the cluster of Marines as they fanned out on both sides of the road.

Guided by Ali's two Afghan Sergeants, the Marines rapidly moved forward. As they ran towards the crumpled buildings, they could see burning cars and a few bodies on the ground. Suddenly a burst of automatic fire erupted from a shed ahead. In a perfectly choreographed move, two Marines, crouching low, zigzagged rapidly forward, ducked momentarily behind a burned out truck, then from each side, fired two long bursts from their M-16's. Not waiting for the dust to settle, they moved closer to examine the now silent shed before waving their comrades forward. As Ali huddled with Fuller, six men were sent to the right and others to the left: their job, to flush out the Taliban fighters in outbuildings on either side. Shots continued to come sporadically until a sudden concentration of machine gun and RPG rounds exploded from behind the banks of the irrigation ditch ahead.

"Is that the main irrigation ditch?" called the tense Marine officer, dropping behind a low brick wall.

"Yes, the other is over behind the big building."   Both men peered over the makeshift barricade and surveyed the scene. As they watched, Fuller motioned his radioman close and grabbed the mike. "Cobra! Clean out that ditch behind the wreckage."   Bright muzzle flashes of the AK-47's could be seen up and down the embankment and airburst RPG rounds erupted above the crouching men. "The big ditch!" yelled Ali over the Lieutenant's shoulder. Even as he spoke, the AH-1 Super Cobra swooped down and multiple heavy caliber machine guns under the nose fired in one long continuous burst as it passed low overhead. Climbing swiftly skyward, like an avenging angel the deadly aircraft swung back and dispatched a succession of rockets into the smoking ditch. Making one more run, guns blazing, the fast moving aircraft climbed skyward, banked sharply and swept down to repeat its path of destruction on the other ditch. After one last pass, the Cobra, its hour and a half fuel supply depleting fast, climbed away from the smoke and destruction below. A lone side gunner waved to the men below as the fast disappearing aircraft headed back for Camp Leatherneck.

As the helicopter completed its final run, Fuller, with a shout of command, jumped to his feet and raced forward. The Marines, crouching low as they ran, closed rapidly on the few remaining buildings and the smoldering irrigation ditches. Intense automatic fire came from a half demolished building on the left and as quickly two men dashed forward, lobbing grenades as they rolled to the ground. As the explosions erupted, several Marines ran forward firing short bursts through the windows and now demolished door. There was no return fire. Arriving in two's and three's at the ditch, the Marines poured over the low embankment, firing as they ran. Aside from a few dazed, blood and dirt covered Taliban fighters, there were no survivors of the Cobra's attack.

"Jesus!" exclaimed Jeff, peering from behind the outer compound wall. "How could anyone survive that attack?" Smoke and the acrid smell of cordite permeated the air as Caroline and Jeff watched the action unfold before them. "Get your God damn head down, sir!" yelled one of the two Marines detailed for their protection. "We don't have an all clear!" By some fluke of battle, the black Mercedes and one of the big SUV's parked just ahead had survived the bombing unscathed. As the four watched from behind the wall, two figures staggered from the smoldering concrete wreckage, looked wildly around while blindly firing their AK-47's and ran for the surviving vehicles. Not 30 feet in front of Jeff and Caroline, both were cut down in a hail of fire. Ahead, Marines quickly combed the broken, smoldering, buildings for other survivors. They found few. In less than five minutes, a smoke smudged Lt. Fuller appeared in front of the main building, looked carefully around, then holding his M-16 in one hand, pulled out his whistle and gave three sharp blasts, the "all clear".

"O.K. Doc." Called one of their Marines picking up his assigned equipment and starting towards the buildings. "We don't have much time, Let's get goin'!" Jeff, motioning Caroline to stay still, stood and quickly scanned the court-yard and saw no sign of danger. As he bent down to pick up his camera, he sensed a blur of motion out the corner of his eye. Even as he shouted a warning, two bearded men, once white robes flying, jumped from the shrubbery bordering the road. Screaming for vengeance, knives flashing, they ran straight for Caroline only yards away.

"Run!" Jeff yelled as he turned to intercept the killers, his only weapon, the combat knife strapped to his leg. In one motion, he pulled out the long blade and threw himself at the first bearded fanatic. Colliding with the Taliban fighter, he stabbed up under the man's ribs and into his chest. As quickly, he gave a sharp twist and yanked the knife free from the dying man, then rolling to his side he drove the bloody weopon up into the second warrior's groin tearing through his aorta. Jeff hardly felt the Afghan's knife as it sliced into his arm.

"Jeff!" screamed Caroline, staring at the bloody carnage tangled together at her feet. "Jeff!" she cried again as she knelt at his side and frantically tried to pull him free.

The two Marines had turned at Jeff's first yell. Pushing Caroline aside, they quickly separated Jeff from the two dead

Taliban. Holding pressure on his bleeding arm, they propped him up against the low wall just as their lieutenant arrived on the run.

"I thought you said 'all clear', Boss." said Jeff looking up with a sarcastic grin.

The lieutenant stood speechless, looking first at the man siting in front of him and then at the two figures crumpled dead at his feet. "I'll be God damned!" he finally exclaimed as he took in the whole blood soaked scene. "Doc, I know you're a surgeon, but where in hell did you learn to use a knife like that?"

Over the next few minutes a corpsman examined Jeff's wound and declared it not as bad as it looked. A QuikClot bandage was applied and some of the Taliban blood wiped from his face and arms. Kneeling beside Jeff, Caroline's heart began to slow and her fear to abate.

"Oh, Jeff," she whispered, tears coursing down her cheeks. "All that blood … I thought they'd killed you!"

Without thought of their audience, Jeff pulled her tight in his arms and to the accompaniment of much applause, gave her a very big, very long kiss.

Caroline, her shaken composure slowly regained, rose to her feet. Pointing to the smoking buildings, she turned and called to Jeff who appeared close to normal except for his bandaged arm and blood stained armor and utilities.

"Hurry, we've got to find their records and papers before they're all incinerated in that fire." Starting to run, she yelled over her shoulder. "Check all the bodies. We'll identify them later." The two Marines, carrying the blood draw kits and camera equipment, followed close behind. The stench of high explosives and burning flesh made the two flinch as they got closer to the two wide ditches. In the absence of wind, the now blazing sun and the pall of smoke had them gasping for breath. Arriving at what had once been the front entrance, they found a small collection of men huddled on the ground. Dazed, deafened, staring vacantly ahead, blood seeped from a variety of wounds. Already, the three corpsmen were hard at work in an effort to keep their captives alive.

Jeff, with the help of one Marine, began carefully photographing each of the dazed men. Ali and Caroline, with the help of others, searched the wreckage. Every scrap of paper had to be retrieved. Several metal attaché cases were found in one of the rooms and quickly removed. As bodies were found, they were unceremoniously dragged out to the clearing to be photographed, fingerprinted, and blood drawn for future DNA study. The A.N.A. sergeants searched all the shattered vehicles, collecting any scrap of evidence left behind. The Lieutenant, with a squad of his men, quickly examined each of the outbuildings for signs of life. None was found. The whole operation took little more than an hour. Their only casualties: six Marines with non-lethal wounds, all from the airburst RPG rounds.

"Hurry up you two," yelled the Lieutenant. "I've called for our pickup, they'll be here in 20 minutes." As he spoke, a team of Marines could be seen outlining a landing target for the choppers in the big cleared area in front of the buildings. Working quietly and efficiently, the corpsmen soon had the casualties ready to go. The surviving Taliban fighters from the air attack and those few from the main building were collected nearby.

For the first time since the attack began, Caroline and Jeff had a chance to talk. "Think we lucked out?" asked Jeff to the dust and soot covered woman beside him.

Pulling off her helmet momentarily, she brushed the hair out of her eyes while assessing the collection of evidence stacked up beside them. "I think we may have hit the jackpot, Jeff. Did you see that trunk full of American greenbacks? Must be a couple of million dollars stacked up in there." Turning, she pointed to the body bags lying on one side of the landing target. "I'm sure I spotted the body of Mohammedzai Kahn, the Drug Lord of these southern provinces. We'll know for certain when we examine him back at Kabul ... if it is, this would be doubly worthwhile."

"One of those bodies looked like a Caucasian." Jeff pointed to the body bags and at the circle of men crouched miserably under the relentless sun. "He, and one of those bastards, are dressed like Americans." He paused staring at the survivor. "Look at the classy outfit that guy's wearing ... the son of bitch!" Contemptuously, Jeff spat on the ground.

"Maybe Ali and his men can squeeze some useful information out of those Taliban fighters." Caroline smiled at the thought. "As for the others, my people should be able to identify the important ones."

Even as they spoke, the thumping sound of multiple rotors could be heard approaching. Lieutenant Fuller walked over as they searched the sky. "Sounds like our Stallion and a couple of Cobras." He yelled, cupping his hands to be heard. "I requested extra choppers to help us with the prisoners, those bodies, and all this stuff you've collected." The exhilaration of combat still evident in his face, the young officer looked at Jeff and Caroline standing beside him. "You two 'bout ready? It's time we got the hell outta here before we have company".

9

COLONEL JOHN SAMPSON, USMC, had flown in from Camp Leatherneck. Major Radcliffe of their own Marine battalion and Dave Williams, their S.M.O. all sat attentively around the big table. Lieutenant Fuller, had just completed his terse, clipped, account of the firefight. The room was stifling in the afternoon heat. Every window shut tight against the dust swirling outside, the only sound was a large black enamel fan slowly oscillating in a vain attempt to stir the hot, stagnant air. The rattle of those bent and rusty blades was the only sound as Lieutenant Fuller took his seat.

Major Radcliffe broke the silence. "How many wounded, Fuller?"

"Six, Sir, none incapacitating. The Taliban RPG's with their airburst rounds were our biggest problem — caused all our injuries except one broken ankle." He laughed. "Corporal Leddy stepped in a rat hole."

"Sounds like that Cobra saved a lot of lives," cut in the SMO. "How many Taliban do you estimate were protecting that meeting?"

"We counted 45 dead, Sir. Then there were the seven we captured more or less alive and brought back for our ANA friends to interrogate. Some escaped into the surrounding vineyards, perhaps another 20."

"A damn well-executed operation, Fuller." Interjected Col. Sampson. Reaching over, he picked up a folder while looking across at Jeff and Caroline. "We've all read the first draft of this remarkable report." Becoming aware of Jeff's heavily bandaged arm he turned back to the lieutenant with a frown. "I didn't hear anything about the doctor getting wounded?"

An embarrassed Fuller looked first at Jeff and then at his superior officer. "I'm sorry, Sir, Doctor Thomas requested that I exclude his personal actions from my report."

"Fuller, *nothing* gets left out of an Operation Report." The Colonel spoke sharply. "What exactly are you talking about?"

Without looking at Jeff, the young lieutenant quickly summarized the attack on the two non-combatants under his charge. Briefly but vividly he described Jeff's astonishing struggle to protect Caroline and the bloody deaths of the two Taliban fighters. "Sir," he continued in an excited voice, "I've never seen anything like it. I didn't think it was possible for anyone to act so fast or be so deadly. I wouldn't have believed it if I hadn't seen it!"

The Colonel stared at Fuller for a few moments. "Lieutenant, every incident goes in an Operation Report." He then turned deliberately and looked Jeff up and down as though recognizing his presence for the first time. "Doctor Thomas, where, " he paused and tapped his pencil on the table. "Just where in hell did a Navy Medical Officer learn hand to hand combat?"

It was Jeff's turn to be embarrassed. He got no help from Caroline or his S.M.O., both of whom were smiling at his discomfort.

"Sir," Jeff shifted uncomfortably in his chair, "There is no big story. I did what I had to do. Like many of your Marines, I just happened to grow up on the wrong side of the tracks. You learn early how to survive."

With his bushy eyebrows knotted together in a frown, the Colonel turned towards the S.M.O. now contentedly blowing smoke-rings toward the ceiling. "Damned good thing this crazy plan of yours succeeded." He paused a moment, tight lips relaxing in a faint smile. "Damn good thing!"

"Sir," Jeff addressed to the Colonel. "I want to make special note of the crucial importance of one man, Captain Ali Mohammed of the ANA. Without his assistance before and during our raid, we would never have gotten this operation off the ground." Sitting on Jeff's right, Lieutenant Fuller nodded in agreement. "Sir, I certainly second that!"

"I met your Captain Ali Mohammed this morning, Doctor." The Marine Colonel smiled thinking about his interaction with Ali. "A remarkable man, even with that astonishing beard and his unusual British accent. Gives you hope these Afghans can hang together after we're gone."

For the next half hour, first Jeff and then Carolyn described their findings and their implications. The death of Mohammedzai Kahn, the king-pin of the drug trade in southern Afghanistan. The capture of one and the death of a second Caucasian, both now identified as the Americans responsible for directing the epidemic of heroin taking such a toll on the Helmand Marines. The killing of a senior Taliban commander and the discovery of documents listing the major dealers, growers and laboratories. Last but not least, the recovery of a huge cache of money destined to fund terrorist activities. It was an amazing success story.

Later in the afternoon Jeff and Carolyn met in Dave Williams' office. The S.M.O. was in an expansive mood. "Who would have thought that you two could pull this thing off? Jeff, you ranch hand posing as a doctor, we had to order you to take the job … then, damned if you two didn't know each other! What an unlikely string of events. I still can't believe you did it. … we thought you were both dead after those first reports from the Bazaar." He sat back, flicking the ash off his cigar, before looking back at the two with a smile. "Guess I'll have to send you both home before the Taliban track you down. Ms. Smith, I know you've got to go back to your office in Kabul but Jeff here is overdue for his rotation." He stopped and made some notes. "Jeff, we should have your orders cut by morning. Hell," he laughed looking up. "You must already be packed. You were ready to bail out before I ruined your plans. Think of the fun you'd have missed!" He paused, reaching for a loose page on his desk. "I picked up tomorrow's weather report … it says here this damn dust storm," he turned and glanced out the window at the half-obscured sun. "The report says it's only going to get worse over the next few days. Visibility down to near zero, only emergency flights going out... if any. Maybe you and Ms. Smith could join tomorrow's convoy to Leatherneck and Ms. ....." Caroline stopped him in mid-sentence.

"It's still Caroline, Sir." She said, wagging her finger. "No more of this Ms. Smith business. And yes, I'm pretty well wrapped up here. The three bodies were packed on ice along with the blood samples and a flash drive of digitalized fingerprints. They were all sent to Leatherneck yesterday on the last flight to get out. I'd like to ride with the convoy – with this weather, that seems to be the quickest way back to Kabul." She turned to Jeff. "If you're ready we could travel with the convoy together."

Jeff nodded in agreement. "It'll be a miserable drive in this storm, but it should be safe." He smiled. "Maybe tonight we can put up our feet up at the bar and relax for the first time in the past month."

The Commander looked reflectively at the couple standing across from his desk, his eyes turned quizzical. "Is there something going on here I don't know about? Hmmmm, wouldn't that be interesting!" He laughed aloud as he walked around the desk and held out his hand.

"Jeff, I've already taken you off duty, but young man," his voice turned serious. "I wish you would reconsider your decision to resign from the Navy, these Marines need you."

Looking at this man he admired so much, Jeff noticed for the first time how the streaks of gray above his temples had spread and the lines on his face had deepened over the past two years. For a moment there was stillness in the room as each looked into the other's now familiar face.

"No, Commander." Jeff replied, gripping the S.M.O.'s hand. "You've been a wonderful mentor and I'll never forget my time here with you and our Marines – but it's time for me to move on." Then the seriousness vanished and he laughed aloud, "Don't forget, boss, I'm still just a grape growin' dreamer from California. Who knows, maybe someday I'll send you a case of my own rot-gut wine!" Jeff gave a snappy salute and with that final gesture, the two turned and took their leave. Standing in front of his desk, the S.M.O. picked up his half smoked cigar and with a bemused smile shook his head. "Well, it was worth a try!"

Outside, the two walked in silence for a few minutes when Jeff turned abruptly to Caroline. "Where are we gonna crash tonight? I refuse to sleep alone on our last night at Quah-ye-Gaz. There's not one place on this whole damn base where two singles can bed down together."

Caroline reached over and took his hand. "Someday, Jeffrey, you'll learn how resourceful we women can be. At exactly 1600 hours, you and I are going to be at the front gate in our full Pashtun regalia. That remarkable Saire and her daughters have everything arranged, in fact, it's all really their idea. Haadiya's husband will meet us with his pickup.

We're to arrive in plenty of time for a simple family supper and then Haadiya and Hakeem's house will be ours again for the night." She squeezed his hand and smiled sweetly. "Will that fit in with your plans, Doctor Thomas?"

10

PROMPTLY AT 1600 hours a shabbily dressed Afghan couple carrying a large, tattered valise passed through the gate. Without ceremony, they had climbed into a beat up Ford pickup waiting outside. As would be expected, the man got in front with the driver, the woman, a shawl covering her head and face against the blowing dust or stray glance from a man, climbed into the open back. The always-present Taliban spies, beggars and fruit dealers loitering at the gate took no notice as the truck pulled away

Sand and dust gusted across the road as they bounced down the rutted streets. Jeff watched with growing nostalgia as small boys ran towing bright colored kites and veiled mothers walked small children. Through the open window he inhaled the dusty, pungent air so full of memories. His eyes took in the human dramas flashing past and he realized how much he would miss this exotic land and its amazing people. Caroline, hanging on in back, found herself think of Jeff, to their unlikely meeting again half way around the world and of the intensity of her love for this man she'd thought gone forever.

At checkpoints, lounging Afghan soldiers gave them only a cursory inspection. Glancing over his shoulder, Jeff saw Caroline hunched up close to the cab, body bouncing hard as Hakeem took each pothole head-on in true Afghan fashion. Jeff closed his eyes a moment in reflection. It seemed a lifetime had flown by in these past two weeks. God had somehow brought Caroline back into his life. How he yearned to take this bright, beautiful, woman home with him forever.

Jeff was awakened from his brief reverie by a pounding on the back of the cab. "Hey, you big bozo," yelled Caroline through the half open rear window. "It's your turn to eat this dust!" Hakeem, glancing back through his mirror at the angry face, laughed loudly and yanked hard on the emergency brake. Afghan drivers seemed to know only two speeds: full power ahead or a sudden jarring stop. The brake pads on most of these ubiquitous pickups had long since worn to the hub with no thought of replacement.

With the seating re-arranged, they were off again, Jeff now sitting on the truck's rusty steel bed, feet jammed against the flapping tailgate and with both hands hanging on for dear life. Up front, Caroline chatted happily with Hakeem. At last the vehicle came to a halt at the compound gate. Jeff and Hakeem swung the heavy gates open, Caroline rolled the truck forward, and the two men secured the gates. Haadiya and her mother appeared instantly at the door. Their relief at seeing two alive was made clear as they gave a brief Namaste and then threw their arms around Caroline.

In minutes, the two had been escorted to the guesthouse, a large pitcher of hot water provided and with much giggling, the two had been left to change and clean up. Unusual in desert country, the wind and dust did not abate at the end of the day. Dust and sand still obscured the late afternoon sun.

That evening, with only their two Americans as guests, the scene was much less formal than on the previous occasion. Saire had removed her Burka and was dressed in a flowing maroon gown of silk with gold stitched in an exotic design around neck and wrists. With her once long black hair now an attractive gray; her serene, mature face without a trace of makeup, this was a beautiful, ageless, woman. The two young women, equally attractive, were dressed in simple western style. Sitting cross-legged at the end of the room, the Patriarch of the family sat contentedly smoking his hookah. He also had dressed for the occasion. A long white linen shirt reaching down over white pants, a black vest covering his chest and with a karakul cap on his head, Ahmed Kahn looked every bit the patriarch of this remarkable Afghan family.

As each sat on the intricately patterned, hand-woven Persian rug, a linen tablecloth was brought out and placed over the center and tea was served. Each steaming cup was carefully poured, a bowl of sugar passed and everyone relaxed. Once again Jeff had to depend on Caroline for translation. For the first time, Jeff realized that both daughters spoke some English and both understood more than had been previously apparent. The Americans quickly learned that the local rumor-mill had been buzzing about the American attack on the drug lords and Taliban. Although many miles away, the implications to the citizens of Quah-ye Gaz were serious and recognized by all the inhabitants. Too polite to ask questions, the family well understood that Cousin Ali Mohammed and the two Americans were active-ly involved. The family also recognized that this put them all in no small jeopardy. That being said, the only evidence of concern was the presence of now two AK-47's standing ready by the door.

Conversation, unconstrained by formality, wandered from the future of Afghanistan as the Coalition forces began withdrawal, to the plight of women should the Taliban regain ascendancy. The latest hairstyles and western fashions were not neglected. All took part as the far-ranging discussion ebbed and flowed. Finally, Haadiya and her sister, Mahnaz, left to bring in a large basket of the always delicious, *Naan*. Returning to the kitchen, the two carefully carried in what would be the main course. Although it was out of season for this usually winter dish, a steaming platter of *Kichrei* was placed before the guests. Here, rice had been cooked with beans, onions and topped with melted *qurot,* a thick sauce of garlic and yogurt. Jeff felt his taste buds begin to tingle as he inhaled the tantalizing aroma of spices and garlic. On either side was a long oblong platter arranged with many pieces of *Tandoori Chicken*, carrots and turnips. After these wonderful Eastern dishes had been consumed, *Shomleh*, a cool drink of yogurt, mint leaves and water shaken vigorously together plus a bowl of fruit with nuts concluded the repast.

Caroline sat staring incredulously at what little remained of this once steaming, aromatic feast. The air was still redolent with the scent of spices. . "Saire, I thought you said this would be a simple family dinner."

The proud, stately, woman sitting erect next to her husband slightly inclined her head. "No, no, This meal is in honor of your last night in Quah-ye Gaz and of your stay with our family in this house." Saire indicated with a slight motion of her hand the room and all those within. "We know you will be returning soon to your homes in America." Her eyes looked directly at her two guests. "We do not want you ever to forget this Afghan family."

As Caroline translated, Jeff, looked at this dignified man and woman putting their lives and all their family at such risk. That this remarkable Afghan couple sitting so calmly should welcome these two foreign strangers, into their home; not only welcome them but treat them as part of their family ... he searched for words to express his feelings, but Saire came to his rescue. In halting English she said, "You Americans have come here to protect us from our enemies. Many of you have died in our country." Her face was serious. "How else can we thank you?"

Without thinking, Caroline and Jeff brought their palms together with a slight bow of their heads. Caroline spoke slowly and formally in their language. "Dear family, may Allah protect forever this house and all those who dwell within these walls. You have treated us with love and caring as if you were our parents, our brother and sister. We will never forget you."

Jeff bent his head to his hosts for a moment. "Thank you so very much for all you have done for us. May God bless this family", then with effort, "Thank you dear friends, '*Daera Manana*'", he said in his decidedly poor Pashto. His discomfort broke the ice; everyone laughed at his embarrassment.

For a few moments nothing was said as the seven people, two Americans and five Afghans, sat reflecting on this unusual evening and its many implications. Finally Saire stood gracefully and with a mischievous smile and a twinkle in her dark eyes spoke quietly. "I believe it is time for our guests, this distinguished American couple," she hesitated for a fraction of a second as though searching for the right word, a smile spreading over her face. "This distinguished *married* American couple, to retire. They have a long day before them."

—⸱∞∞⸱—

Caroline and Jeff, a borrowed lantern in hand, made their way toward the small house. It was warm and the wind and dust had almost died away. Above, the heavens were now bright with stars and the moon was just rising over the ancient compound wall. Walking slowly, Jeff took Caroline's arm and steered her to an old stone bench beneath the flowering apricot trees. His arm around her waist, he held her close. In the peace and solitude of this starry night, the two lovers stared into the dark sky, each filled with his own thoughts and dreams.

"To think," whispered Jeff, "Two thousand years ago, Alexander the Great watched these same stars at this same place. I wonder if it was here, under apricot trees just like these, that he set up his tents?" He paused looking around. "The Greeks called this land Paropamisus. It was a great center of civilization in that ancient world." He turned to Caroline. "What shall we name this magic place?"

Above them a shooting star suddenly flashed across the night sky, then flamed into oblivion. Caroline, watching the dying meteor, shivered in his arms. "Jeff, could that tiny star be the two of us, just a moment of shimmering light and then nothingness? Oh, Jeff," She whispered as a tremor of dread ran through her body. "Never leave me."

Jeff held the trembling woman tight in his arms and as time passed the moon rose ever higher in the dark distant sky. As shooting stars came and went, Caroline's anxious heart slowly calmed. It was well past time for bed and soon the two rose hand in hand and walked to their small quarters. In minutes, both were settled into their comfortable quilt cocoon. Without the impediment of clothing, nothing separated their warm bodies and fast pulsing hearts. Caroline, still shaken by her premonition, pulled Jeff close. Although his strength and warmth encompassed her being, she still felt an inner chill.

"Darling, don't be afraid." Soothed Jeff in a whispered voice. "We're safe together tonight." As his hands gently stroked her neck and back, he comforted her. "You and I will always be together."

"Jeff," she hesitated and then, rising up on her elbows, stared straight into his eyes, "I want to get married as soon as we get back to California."

"Why, Madam, is that a proposal?" He teased trying to lighten her apprehensive mood. "I'll have to think about that." After a wait of about 2 seconds he issued his reply. "Hmmmm, unusual as your request may be, Madam, I accept your proposition with pleasure! Shall we seal it with a kiss?"

Lifting himself up, Jeff held her head between his hands and softly kissed her open lips. "Oh, Caroline, I have missed you so much."

As the two nestled contentedly together, Caroline suddenly broke free and pulled him to her breast. "Jeff," She urgently whispered in his ear. "I need you... I need you now!"

It was well past midnight when the two lovers, still entwined in each other's arms, closed their eyes and drifted off in a dreamless sleep.

The raucous crowing of a cock in the courtyard and the dim light of dawn just visible through the solitary window brought Jeff back to consciousness. He felt the warmth of the woman sleeping curled into his body. "Good morning, sweetheart." he whispered in her ear, holding her close and kissing her neck. A mumbled, incomprehensible response filtered up from under the quilt now pulled tight over her head.

"Time to wake up, you sleepy head," he spoke loudly. She wiggled contentedly as her head emerged and turned to look up at his stubbly face. "I had the most wonderful dream last night. There was this amazing man ... a regular old goat. He ravished me unmercifully. Mmmmm, it was so nice." As she spoke she pulled his head down for a long kiss. "Please, just once more, kind sir?" There was no need to repeat the question.

Half an hour later, Jeff was up. He had pulled on his baggy pants and long blouse, his gray *pakol* perched squarely on his head. Reaching down he slowly extracted Caroline from her warm nest while each inch of the way she objected vociferously in quite unladylike language. With a sour expression, she pulled on her long, colorful skirt and tunic, and angrily wrapped her *Hijib* around head and shoulders. "O.K. buster, outta the way. I've got business in the garden."

The sun had not yet risen when they made their way across the courtyard. Already, the sand and dust laden wind was blowing hard. With their few belongings packed and ready for travel, they met Haadiya at the door. Hands on her hips, she looked them up and down, then nodded her head with apparent satisfaction. With a smug smile on her face, the young woman pulled them in out of the storm.

"Does it show <u>that</u> much, you beast?" Said Caroline to her companion with a contented purr.

Tea was ready, a stack of warm *naan* on the small table and a bowl of fruit stood under the window. The rest of the family were already drinking their tea and talking rapidly as the three entered the big room. "Good morning my friends," said Ahmed Kahn, rising in greetings. "I am sorry, but we must hurry. Hakeem rose early to assess the situation in town. Even at this early hour the Taliban are already questioning people in the bazaar and the weather is very bad. We will have to get you back to the base the long way around the town … but we must hurry."

"Not until they have their tea, *naan* and some fruit," interjected the matriarch of the house, once again in full burka. "They will be safe in their clothing." She turned and carefully inspected the couple. "Haadiya, pull up Caroline's scarf on the left side. Too much hair is showing."

In a few hurried minutes the couple said their farewells. Caroline took Saire aside and whispered, "I will send you our wedding announcement very soon. Thank you, mother, for your understanding." The small woman, eyes barely visible behind the gauze screen, beamed in pleasure. "I am so happy. You both have become a part of this family forever."

Ahmad, standing by the door, yelled loudly. "The truck is ready. Hurry, the wind and dust are getting worse every minute. We must leave immediately." Jeff couldn't understand the words but the meaning was clear.

The small pickup took the long way to the base, avoiding main roads, constantly weaving in and out of town. Visibility was limited in the wind and flying sand and driving was slow, often only a crawl. Jeff and Caroline lay on an old mattress that had been placed on the hard metal bed in back, a flapping piece of malodorous canvas and old grain sacks were tucked over and around their bodies. It was suffocating in the heat and dust. At the last checkpoint there had been a near catastrophe. A soldier had jabbed the butt of his rifle into the lumpy collection of canvas and sacking in back. Jeff almost cried aloud when it slammed into his ribs but managed to choke back a yelp of pain. His faint grunt went unheard over the throaty growl of the long suffering engine and the whistling of the wind. Even so, the truck's occupants breathed a collective sigh of relief when they were finally waved on. The truck, gears complaining loudly, carbon monoxide laced smoke belching from the dangling exhaust pipe, inched its way back to the road and moved slowly on towards the base.

It took more than an hour to make their way around town in what should have been an easy 20-minute drive. The growing, sun obscuring dust storm had now engulfed the town. Doors and shutters were tightly closed and few vehicles braved the roads. Even so, they passed more than one pickup crammed with bearded, AK-47 carrying men heading down the streets. The Taliban were on the hunt and the nervous towns people were in lockdown. Arriving finally at the base main gate, they found an extra detail of Marines standing choking in the wind and dust but no sign of the usual Taliban spies to scrutinize the truck and its occupants. It took the arrival of an officer to convince the Sergeant in charge and his trigger-happy crew that this dirty, unappetizing Afghan couple might be a Navy doctor and a civilian specialist returning to base. "God damn Navy!" growled the sergeant keeping a suspicious eye on Caroline and Jeff as they unloaded their few belongs and said their goodbyes to Ahmed Khan and Hakeem. Leaning into the wind and flying dust, the two walked in haste past the barrier and the watching Marines as they made their way towards the medical unit.

The Commander met them at the Trauma Unit's door, pulled them in and quickly closed the door against the howling elements. "There'll be absolutely no flights out of here for the rest of the week. I've checked and you're cleared to join the convoy leaving at noon." He stopped and laughed out loud as he took in the full picture of the dirt-encrusted pair. "You've just got time for a shower and clean utilities." He said, looking at his watch. "Remember, you'll be wearing full armor and helmets on this little excursion. With luck, you'll be able to catch a flight from Leatherneck to Bagram in a few days. We're sending three ambulances with you — some of our more urgent wounded plus a platoon of rotating Marines." Turning to look over his shoulder, he called to Madge Walker, the Chief Nurse who had just emerged from the operating room. "Hey, Madge, look what the cat just dragged in."

The woman, dressed in scrubs, gown, cap and mask walked slowly over. Pulling the mask down, she stared unbelieving at the two filthy Afghans standing in her ward. "Well I'll be damned, Commander, if it isn't young Dr. Thomas and Ms. Smith." She scowled, taking in their unkempt clothes and dirt caked faces. "Well, you two just get the hell outta this surgical ward and clean up. You'll contaminate the whole unit!" As she spoke her face lit up in a broad smile and she took both Caroline's hands. "I'm so glad you're both back safe and sound. We've been worried sick with all that's been going on." She looked at Jeff with a sigh. "We're going to miss you, doctor. Thanks for all you two have done for our Marines." Looking at the strangely dressed, disheveled, pair she shook her head in disbelief. "Who would have thought …"

Jeff blew Madge a kiss, shook the S.M.O.'s hand for the last time and the two headed once more out into the storm. With heads down and scarves pulled over their faces, Caroline and Jeff ran for the B.O.Q. and a long hot shower.

11

As Afghan roads go, the occasionally two-laned lane track from Quah-ye-gaz to Highway One was not bad. Asphalt in places, gravel in most, the trip could usually be made in three hours. But not today. The unrelenting, still raging storm kept the convoy at a snail's pace. The billowing, gusting sand had the drivers cursing as each attempted to stay centered on the road and close to the vehicle ahead. Radio communication was spotty at best. The always present threat of improvised explosive devises and the constant hazard of ambush only added anxiety as the convoy vehicles slowly made their way south.

This small procession was led by three MRAP's, the just deployed Mine Resistant Ambush Protected, armored trucks. Next came three MRAP's converted to ambulances, each carrying four wounded men back to Leatherneck and their next level of care. In the center were five Humvee's, lightly armored but fast and maneuverable. The rear guard consisted of three armored trucks, each carrying eight rotating Marines plus their belongings on the first leg of their long road home.

At one of their frequent stops, the frustrated convoy commander, Sgt. Stepfield, stood beside his command vehicle, goggles pulled down to protect his eyes, yelling up to his radioman. "Somebody get this God damn radio fixed." He banged the mike on the door. "I gotta talk NOW to those engineers down this fuckin' road!"

"It's not the radio, Sarge. It's the storm." Called back the radio operator over the constant rumble of the sand and dust laden wind.

"Shit, we can't stay here." The sergeant muttered. "This is perfect ambush country...we gotta move!"

As he talked the vague outlines of mud walls and low buildings appeared through the blowing sand. "Jesus H. Christ!" He shouted, scrambling up into the high cab and slamming shut the blast proof door. "We're in the middle of a God damn village. Get this truck movin'."

In their Humvee, Jeff and Caroline could catch snatches of the radio conversation ahead. Positioned in the center of the convoy, they were belted into the middle seat, their gear and duffels jammed in the back. The hot, desiccating wind, the layers of clothing, body armor and helmets only added to their misery. "That is one unhappy camper," Jeff muttered, peering out the dust-covered windscreen, unease apparent in his voice. "We've been crawling along this God forsaken road forever. When in hell are we getting to Highway One?"

"Not yet, Sir," said the driver over the crackling of radio static. "I recognize this place. We've got at least 10 miles to go. This hilly stretch ahead is the hairy part." As he spoke, the corporal peered forward, slamming his Humvee into gear as the red lights ahead began to move away. "The boss must be nervous." He laughed. "He's really pushin' us." Outside, they could occasionally make out gray, rocky hills and empty, barren fields extending as far as their limited visibility allowed.

"Dammit!" swore an apprehensive Jeff. "Why didn't we stay at Shinvaki?" Jeff let loose a string of time-honored Marine obscenities as the Humvee bounced and shuddered over the washboard road, "It's my own miserable fault. We should have waited for this storm to blowout."

"Oh, stop beating up on yourself, Jeff." replied Caroline. "We both decided to take the risk. Quit worrying! We'll be at Leatherneck soon and you can relax. Besides," she continued, "Those combat engineers are not far ahead. We'll be fine. "

Unfortunately, that was not quite the case. Deprived of communication much of the time, the combat engineers were having their own problems. At that moment the sappers were at a complete stand-still waiting for visibility to clear. There had been a string of moderate sized I.E.D.'s found and exploded some way back. Now in the hills, and with visibility so poor, they worried that they could miss other well-concealed bombs or be caught in an ambush. With ground penetrating radar on booms protruding out front, converted MRAP's had worked well in the blowing sand but today the usually reliable TV cameras scouring the road's surface were almost blind. At times they had to depend on a heavily armored "Buffalo" truck pushing rollers well ahead to explode pressure sensitive bombs. Sometimes, it required men on the ground, handheld metal detectors slowly, methodically, scanning the road. It was hot, difficult and very dangerous work. The hardest to find and the greatest threat were large I.E.D.'s buried deep and connected with wires or by radio signals that could be detonated from hundreds of yards away. With these monsters, Taliban teams could pick and chose their target.

Well behind schedule, a full five and a half hours after leaving Quah-ye-gaz, the convoy finally ran into the engineers. Lined up on the road was a collection of large, specialized trucks and a cordon of sappers all facing down the road. The lieutenant in command, standing high on his MARP, yelled back to the newcomers just one loud word as he pointed ahead. "Bomb!" Knowing what to expect, everyone jumped out of their vehicles, ready to watch the sound and light show. Almost immediately, not far ahead, the sky erupted in an enormous crimson ball of flames while a mushroom cloud of smoke and dust rose high into the sky. The concussion wave quickly followed as the ground heaved and shuddered below.

"Dear Mother of God," whispered Caroline, as she grabbed Jeff's hand and held tight.

"Son of a bitch, that was a big one." muttered their driver. "Thank God they found the damn thing before …." His sentence went unfinished. Automatic fire erupted from a grove of ancient fruit trees on their left and bright muzzle flashes blossomed through the haze and smoke. Everyone dove for the protection of their trucks. Ahead, the gunners in their turrets atop the MARP's, swung their big 50 calibers and let go a long burst that almost mowed down the small orchard.

In spite of that impressive display of firepower, the convoy did not escape unscathed. Even as they watched, there was a sudden flash and explosion just ahead. A stricken Humvee, smoke pouring from its side, careened off the road and toppled on its side. An RPG round had found its target with devastating results.

For once the radio worked. Jeff and Caroline could clearly hear Sgt. Stepfield yelling to the Lieutenant. "My Humvees are sittin' ducks. I gotta get this convoy outta here."

"Agreed," answered the young engineer. "Pull back a half mile and get turned around. We'll clean out this mess of vermin and then you can follow us to the Highway. I have to get you guys outta here before dark." There was a pause and they could all hear faint talking just out of mike range. "Now here's some good news." he called, coming back on the air. "There's another team of sappers headed our way from the Highway. We'll have you off this miserable road in less than an hour." Again there was a pause. "I'll give the high sign when we're ready to move."

"O.K., Lieutenant. We're pullin' back." With two acknowledging clicks with the mike button, the sergeant replaced the microphone on its hook and simultaneously signaled his driver to move out.

With the exception of one ambulance left to care for survivors, the rest of the trucks, one by one, turned and cautiously moved back down the road. As they passed the wreckage, they could see corpsmen already caring for the wounded. At what was now the back of the column, one of the MARP's peeled off to shield the medics while the other two became the new rear guard of the fast retreating convoy.

Watching the dust-shrouded disc of sun now low in the hazy sky, Jeff could see it was already getting late. Each hour of delay increased their vulnerability.

"What a way to spend a day." Jeff, with a slight smile, took Caroline's hand in his. "Dangerous as hell, hot as hades, and really romantic."

Caroline laughed and smiled in return. "Don't you worry, Doctor Thomas, It may not be romantic but I'm with you and I still love you … that's all that counts!" She squeezed his hand and leaned over to give him a dusty kiss.

In that split second of time, with Caroline's lips still against his cheek, an enormous explosion shattered their world forever. Like a child's toy, the Humvee was flung into the air and torn apart. In a macabre twist of fate, the middle seat remained intact and the two occupants, still strapped to the frame, were hurled into the roadside ditch like two rag dolls.

Jeff's mind, returning from a blur of pain and darkness, was aware of a searing agony in his back and legs. Then, in his dazed and semi-conscious state, he realized he was still clutching Caroline's now bloody, lifeless hand. "Caroline!" He screamed, staring at her torn and broken body, "Oh dear God, Caroline …."

Part Two

Carmel Valley
Northern California

2011

12

"OK, MISTER, THAT'LL do for now." Standing back, the tall, green-clad doctor admired his handiwork. The jagged wounds on the motorcyclist's face and scalp were neatly sutured; only long lines of neat blue stitches remained. The once shaggy hair and large scraggly beard had been unceremoniously shaved away and the now alabaster skull glistened under the intense light of the surgical lamp. The rest of the biker's anatomy had miraculously been spared major injury thanks to his heavy blood spattered, biker's leather jacket and pants.

"Sorry about the beard and hair but that'll all grow back. Next time don't argue with a truck when you're riding your hog and for God's sake wear a real helmet - not that two-bit little beanie!" Patting the big man on the back, he tugged off his gloves, pulled down his mask and took a last critical look at the maze of stitches covering the motorcyclist's very bald cranium as he wound foot after foot of gauze around and around the man's head. "Yeah, not bad. You'll be good as new in a couple of weeks."

"Thanks, Doc!" Came a muffled response through a blanket of gauze and tape.

"Wait'll my old lady see's what I done to myself this time!".

With a last wave of the hand, the doctor, a smile slowly spreading over his craggy, once youthful face, left the trauma room, walked down the hall and into the nurse's station.

"Finished! Done! Kaput! I'm outta here!" he shouted, a broad smile on his face, mask still dangling from his neck.

"You lucky bastard," called a fellow ER physician from across the room, "Didn't think you'd have the nerve."

Jeff smiled and gave a quick thumbs up. Throwing his cap and mask into a bin, he picked up his small duffle from under the desk and blew a kiss to a couple of nurses standing nearby.

"Way to go, Jeff. Have fun!" called a good-looking red-head glancing up from her charts.

Visions of torn and bloody bodies, sick kids, angry drunks and over fed golfers hauled in from Pebble Beach flashed through his mind. Still smiling, he waved goodbye and pushed open the Emergency Department doors for the last time. Two years in Afghanistan and this – there had to be more to life.

Dr. Jeffery Thomas, now pushing 34, had enjoyed the adrenaline rush of working in a busy ER, but broken, sick and drunk humanity had begun to drag. There was never time to talk with patients, to get to know them, to understand them. No time for anything. He was sleep deprived, lonely and often depressed. He needed a change. Two weeks ago he had made his decision. He'd walked into the Administration of-fice and turned in his resignation. He'd quit the madhouse.

As always, his worn old pickup was waiting patiently. The Duchess was a legacy from his years growing up on a Sonoma vineyard. She looked like a refugee from a wrecking yard, but under that scarred and wrinkled hood was an engine that purred like a finely tuned Swiss watch. Jeff had used that ancient truck as a substitute for human companionship and he'd nursed the old lady like the royalty she once was. With strange and always changing hours he was too wired or too tired for friendships, male or female. He longed for some-thing more. Climbing into the battered cab, he looked back one last time, smiled to himself and turned the key.

"OK girl, let's get outta here, I'm as shot up and beat up as you. Life's too short for this crap – it's time for a change." The engine coughed a couple of times, then came to life with a self-satisfied, deep and throbbing rumble. Letting out the clutch, Jeff and the Duchess pulled out of his reserved space for the last time. That stenciled name on the pavement, "Jeffery Thomas, M.D." was history.

Decrepit as she seemed, the still proud Duchess purred along like a debutante on her first date. Turning onto Highway One they headed down the hill. When the signal turned red at Carpenter, she came to a sedate stop at the white line. Beside her, a hot looking Mustang pulled up with a load of kids on their way down to Carmel High. They gunned their engine a few times, then made the fatal mistake of yelling and hooting at the testy old dowager. Fuming quietly, when the signal turned green, that frumpy old lady transformed into a raging lioness. Off in an instant, she roared down the hill leaving the astonished Mustang and its young occupants choking and coughing in a vast cloud of blue-gray exhaust. "That'll teach the little bastards," chuckled Jeff.

Reaching the Carmel Valley turnoff they took a left, then sedately preceded up the road. It was time for their after-shift ritual, breakfast at Joe's Valley Diner. As usual, the parking lot was crowded at 7:00 AM. Pulling in, Jeff turned off the ignition, climbed wearily out, slammed the door shut and walked in to join the warm, inviting crowd. "Best Breakfast on the Peninsula" was no idle claim, and the full house gave proof to the words. Jeff liked this funky eatery. The tired, exhausted young man in green hospital scrubs was a frequent visitor. Edith, a woman of uncertain age, known to one and all as Edie, was hostess, waitress and cashier. Joe ran the kitchen.

"Rough night, Doc?" queried Edie with her usual big smile. "Havin' the usual?" She had already put a steaming cup of coffee in front of the young man and with his nod of assent, she gave a signal understood only by Joe and the order was underway. In minutes it was all there. Two flawless fried eggs, a stack of Frisbee sized pancakes browned to perfection with melted butter oozing over the top. A pitcher of "Maple Syrup" stood at the ready. This impressive testimonial to masculine digestion was made complete by three crisp, thick, slices of bacon. A tall glass of fresh orange juice stood nearby, rivulets of water snaking down the frosted sides. Empty stomach growling in anticipation, his taste buds twitching and his salivary glands primed and pumping, Jeff was ready. Picking up his knife and fork he dug in before embarrassing himself by drooling.

Pausing while savoring a heavenly mouthful, Jeff looked around at the other customers contentedly consuming their breakfasts. Feelings of failure and fatigue slowly dissipated as he listened to the happy voices of these hard-working men and women enjoying the simplest of pleasures. The day came alive. The long smoldering ache in his soul seemed to fade and for the first time in over three years he felt he could let down his guard and relax.

Gazing out the window, Jeff could see the beautiful valley now sparkling in the early morning sun. Watching this fresh, bright panorama his face broke out into a broad smile and soon he couldn't help laughing out loud. It was infectious. First, the two guys sitting at the table on his right joined in. In seconds the whole room was laughing. Joe, greasy 49'er cap perched on his sweaty, bald head, peered out the kitchen pass-through. Looking quickly around he spotted Jeff's usually somber face creased in a happy smile. Shaking his head in amusement, he turned back to his smoking grill.

Sighing with satisfaction, Jeff finished his last sip of coffee. Stretching, he stood and paid his bill. With a wave to Joe in the kitchen and blowing a kiss to Edie, he walked out into the sunshine and to what he hoped would be a new life.

It was eight miles up to the village and for once he was in no hurry. Feeling totally free was a new experience and he was savoring it by the minute. He found himself looking at sights barely noticed in the past. Nurseries with row on row of trees, shrubs and colorful plants, a small shopping center, a golf course and further on a resort surrounded by grapevines. Slowing, he watched a group of beautiful horses in a large paddock and was reminded of the gentle old mare he'd ridden each day as a kid. The long procession of cars heading into town and the frequent sight of large, imposing homes behind locked gates all offended his sense of space. After the constant turmoil of the emergency room, he longed for a place where you could look out over uncluttered vistas and feel the solitude of emptiness … where you could smell the aromatic scent of chaparral covered hills and the musky dampness of the river below.

Jeff had found a small reminder of his dreams in a tiny cottage high above the village. It was a compromise, not too far from the hospital but just far enough to see and smell the open country. A one-room studio, it suited his simple needs. What really sold him was the view. On the hillside below, a vineyard nestled on the slope. The rows of vines contouring around a small knoll reminded him of his father's vineyard. Finishing a long 72-hour shift, he would relax in an old wicker chair sitting under the canopy of an ancient Live Oak. Sipping a glass of wine in the leaf-filtered sunlight, he would watch hawks soar gracefully on the thermals or a family of deer daintily nibbling among the vines.

13

J EFF DIDN'T DO much cooking; it was easier to go down to the village. Tonight, enjoying his newfound freedom, he checked in at his usual choice, the Branding Iron Saloon and Cafe, a local watering hole. The high decibel noise of loud voices, a few neon beer signs over the big mirror behind the bar, it was a friendly place that welcomed the world. He liked listening to the ranch hands, motorcyclists and the loud, colorful women who frequented the place. With the crowd yelling around him, a ball game blaring on the big TV, he never felt alone. Tall and muscular, he looked like he belonged outdoors, not in hospital corridors. His Marine's close-cropped black hair had begun to show a few flecks of gray. With dark, inquisitive eyes and a lined angular face, he looked older than his 33 years. Dressed in a shirt rarely visited by an iron, worn jeans and scuffed cowboy boots, he could well have just left his horse at the bar room door. Absent his ever-present glass of wine and his quiet, withdrawn demeanor, he was just one of the crowd.

Sitting alone at the end of the bar, he found himself thinking back over the past few years. College followed by medical school and a residency courtesy of the Navy. Then came Afghanistan, his wounds and always the memory of Caroline. Discharged finally from Navy hospitals and VA rehab programs, he'd become an emergency room physician … probably too soon after all the mental and physical trauma he'd survived. Now he was free for the first time in years. Jeff knew the euphoria of this new found freedom would soon wear off, but it had been the right decision, at the right time. Curiously, It was tonight of all nights that he met Pierre Vaillard.

Jeff had often noticed the tanned, heavily built old rancher with his bushy tobacco stained mustache sitting alone. It seemed each Saturday night there was a table in the far corner with a red checkered table cloth, a mason jar full of fresh flowers and two empty wine glasses. Once seated, Pierre seldom looked at the menu. Unlikely though it might seem, the Branding Iron was well known for its Snapper, Calamari steaks and Bouillabaisse. That seafood reminded the old Frenchman of growing up among the vineyards of Languedoc not far from the Mediterranean Sea. Pierre had come to Carmel Valley many years ago and here he had planted his vineyard on the rocky, limestone laced hillsides. The gravely, chalky soil, the warm days and the cooling fog of summer nights, all blessed his grapes. He loved his adopted country, Carmel Valley, and the vineyard that had become his life.

Pierre made his own wines and always brought a bottle or two on his weekly visits to the Village. Coming from the south of France, eating seafood without a Rosé would be an unforgivable sin. As in Languedoc, his wine had a lovely pale pink hue, was very dry and had a seductive fruitiness in the mouth and nose. As any proper Frenchman, Pierre never hurried his meal. His still muscular frame, his sun and wind weathered face were softened by blue twinkling eyes. His ever-present smile attested to his long pleasure with food, wine, and a good life. As he ate, Pierre often cast his gaze over the happy crowd drinking their beer and whooping it up. It took him back to the bistros of France and the bars of Saigon. The two of them, the young doctor at the end of the bar and the weather-beaten old Frenchman sitting quietly at his table seemed a world apart from the boisterous crowd.

Quietly sipping his wine this evening, Jeff watched the old rancher sitting alone at his table. Guessing his age to be somewhere in his late seventies, Jeff was drawn to this solitary man who, like Jeff, was alone in this room of noisy, happy drinkers. The two men seemed kindred spirits. Without further thought, Jeff picked up his half empty glass, stood and with his slight limp, walked over and introduced himself.

"Jeffrey Thomas," he said, extending his hand.

"Pierre Vaillard," was the prompt response with a slight French accent and handshake surprisingly firm.

"As the only wine drinkers around," said Jeff smiling. "I thought it was time we met and shared a glass together."

With a sparkle in his eyes and a slight bow of his head, the older man quickly replied, "That would be a great honor, my young friend." With a sweep of his hand he indicated the chair next to his own. "Please, won't you sit down?" Resting his glass on the table, Jeff pulled up a chair as Pierre continued. "I would like you to taste my wine. I believe it will be a considerable improvement over that thin, watery red I've watched you drinking tonight."

Jeff carefully dumped his glass in the empty pot on the table, rinsed it with water from the carafe and emptied the remains into the jar of flowers. "Keeps 'em fresh." he said, drying the glass with a corner of the tablecloth.

Smiling with amusement, the Frenchman replied, "Now taste my little Rosé" and with that he filled the now sparkling glass just 1/3 full.

Gently swirling the wine, then nose deep over the rim, Jeff inhaled deeply. "Mmmm, wonderful bouquet." he murmured. Then taking a sip, he rolled the wine around in his mouth and over his tongue before slowly swallowing. Fresh and fruity but still quite dry, the wine had just the right acidity and a lingering finish as it slid softly down his throat. Putting down the glass, Jeff slowly smiled as he looked up at Pierre. "This must be what summer tastes like in Provence— it's delicious! Grenache and a hint of Syrah. ... but there's another grape?"

"Ah," breathed Pierre as he watched the brief ritual and listened to the description with quiet approval. "That is Cinsault, rare here but a work horse in the south of France near the border of Spain. It loves the heat of our valley." Saluting Jeff with his glass he continued. "I was sure you knew something of wine!"

"I should," laughed Jeff. "I grew up in vineyards and put myself through school working with grapes and wine."

"The waitress tells me you are a doctor," said Pierre. "That's a strange background for medicine. And why are you always sitting alone? At your age there should be a beautiful woman at your side."

Eyes clouded in memory, Jeff stared into the distance, his thoughts far away. Looking back slowly, he quietly responded. "There would have been, Pierre, but a roadside bomb in Afghanistan tore my love and my heart away."

Pierre said nothing for a few moments, eyes looking into Jeff's face. "I'm sorry, my friend. They said you had been away in the war but I didn't know…."

"It seems a lifetime," Jeff spoke slowly, "You'd think I could let go. It was so very hard…." After another long pause, Jeff looked over at Pierre with a wry smile. "It's high time I got my head screwed on straight and looked at the present! I started today — I stopped playing doctor for awhile."

Pierre poured the last of the wine into Jeff's glass. "I see you driving up in that ancient pickup and I say to myself, 'he's a doctor, where is his red Porsche?' First the vineyards, then medicine and war. Now you've retired? For one so young that is rather unusual, I suspect an interesting story." Pulling a second bottle from an ice bucket, he carefully set it on the table and smiled. "We have plenty of wine, I'm an appreciative audience—what better time to bare one's soul?"

Jeff laughed. "O.K., you asked for it—here's a short version of a short story." Taking a sip of wine, he launched into his tale. "I was born on a vineyard up in Sonoma County. My father was a vineyard manager and my mother was a teacher in the local elementary school. When I was five, my mother died and our neighbor Juanita, a wonderful Mexican widow came to take care of me. I worked every day after school in the vines with my father and his Mexican crew. I grew up with their kids. Hell, I thought I was Mexican." Jeff laughed. "We fought each other and together we fought the rest of the world. In school we were the poor dumb ranch kids - we hung together to survive and did I ever learn to fight dangerous and dirty!" He paused thinking back to those happy days. "We were one tough bunch of delinquents. I spoke Spanish better than English, much to my father's dismay." He was quiet for a moment. "How I love those wonderful people!" Then smiling he continued. "With grapes and wine in my blood, I put myself through college working in the vines and at wineries. I even managed a vineyard part time." Jeff stopped, eyes far away. "My father was killed in a tractor accident while I was in high school. That old truck, my boyhood saddle, my Dad's hunting rifle plus a lot of useless knowledge about grapes and wine are my legacy." Jeff took another sip and looked over at Pierre. "I always thought I'd like to make a good wine someday, but I also discovered science and medicine. The idea of becoming a doctor won out.

I also knew that making wine takes a lot of money (which I didn't have) and with medicine and hard work I could maybe make a lot of money (which I sure did need). I was going through college on a shoestring — didn't see how I'd ever make it to med school. Then the Navy came along with an offer to pay my way through school and residency with a guarantee to see the world when I was finished." The young man smiled in recollection. "Guaranteed and required! It was an offer I couldn't refuse."

As Jeff took another long sip, he wondered why he was suddenly pouring his life story out to this Frenchman he'd only just met tonight. Looking at the older man, he wondered if it was the warmth of the smile or the questioning twinkle in the eyes that had unlocked his usual silence. "Are you sure you want to hear the rest of this sorry tale?"

Pierre smiled. "I still haven't heard why you don't have that red Porsche."

"O.K.," laughed Jeff, "I'll make it brief. I went off to U.C. Davis Med School and then a Family Practice Residency in Salinas courtesy of the Navy. It was while I was at Natividad Hospital that I fell in love with this part of the world. I always wanted to come back some day." He was interrupted by the arrival of a noisy group of bikers piling up at the bar. "After my training," he continued when the room quieted down to its usual roar, "I put on my uniform and reported to Camp Pendleton and the Marines. A few months later I was shipped out to Afghanistan. Boy, was that a learning experience for a young doc! I was there two years. Unfortunately, as I started home on my rotation, a roadside bomb, an I.E.D., put a rather spectacular end to my Navy career." His voice trailed off. "And destroyed all my hopes and dreams." Jeff stopped for a moment, then quietly continued. "They didn't tell me for a week, but that blast instantly killed my Caroline. She had also grown up in the wine country and we were planning to be married, set up practice, maybe even buy some land." It was several moments before he continued. "I was pretty messed up. They flew me to Germany where I spent a couple of months at Landstuhl Hospital and had multiple surgeries to put things back together more or less like they used to be before the bomb. When they thought I was ready, I was flown home to Bethesda Naval Hospital in D.C. I was there for another three months before they gave me my purple heart and kissed me goodbye."

Pierre raised his eyebrows in question. "They couldn't just dump you out on your own after all that?"

"Never!" laughed Jeff. "I did lose my uniform and Navy paycheck but they sent me west to the Palo Alto VA hospital. Those surgeons and neurologists worked on me for over a year before they declared me fit to go back to work, said I needed to start doin' something useful again. That's how I ended up here in Monterey County. There was a vacancy in the ER at Monterey Community Hospital. I loved this part of the world and trauma surgery was right up my alley. It was exciting, It kept my mind off my troubles, but I never seemed to have time to ...."

Jeff was cut short by the noisy arrival of a couple of wild looking motorcyclists who were greeted by shouts and jeers from their friends at the bar. One of the new arrivals, head swathed in bandages, spotted Jeff and walked over. "Remember me, Doc? You did a great job sewing me up— my old lady says I look better'n ever. Shit, maybe I outta go to Hollywood! Didn't have a chance to really thank you." Then he gave Jeff a clap on the back that almost knocked him off his chair. "Damn nice job—thanks Doc!" And off he strode to claim his beer.

Jeff laughed. "Now there's a good ending for my story! I know how to patch these guys up but I can't seem to fix up myself." He looked over at the old Frenchman and laughed ruefully. "And that, Pierre, is why I just walked out of the hospital, why there's no girl sitting next to me and why there's no red Porsche out front."

During the time Jeff was speaking, Pierre was studying this complex young man intently. Behind that smiling face there was way too much pain for one so young. "I'm no psychiatrist," he mused to himself, "but if ever a man needed to get back to the soil and sweat out his demons, this is certainly one … and wonder of wonders, he knows about grapes and how to make wine. God above must have sent me this lonely young man." In those moments he made up his mind. Looking directly at Jeff, Pierre began speaking quietly. "Jeffrey, I want you to humor an old man for a moment and listen carefully. Tomorrow I would like you to visit my ranch, walk the vineyard and see the winery. There is a small trailer near the barn, which is vacant. It is completely private but is close enough to the house for meals and talk. From what you have told me tonight, I believe you need my ranch as much as I need you—your knowledge of grapes—maybe even your Marine training." Pausing briefly, the Frenchman concluded, "This is a very serious invitation, Jeffrey, you will learn why when you visit."

14

DRAGGING HIMSELF OUT of bed the next morning, head throbbing to some exotic jungle beat, Jeff headed for his tiny kitchen. He felt an urgent need for coffee ... lots of coffee. Plans to work up a good sweat in Garland Park were quickly dismissed. The tom-tom pounding in his skull suggested a quieter start to the day. Two glasses of wine at the bar plus two bottles of Pierre's wonderful Rosé had him whimpering "Never again!" Jeff went in search of coffee beans, then through bloodshot eyes, he managed to fill the coffee grinder. The instant roar and crackle of that demonic machine ripped and tore at his poor suffering brain. Moaning pitifully, he pulled the plug. With shaking hands he poured the slightly ground coffee into the pot, flicked the switch and tottered off to shower. Most days after a run, Jeff looked forward to a long, hot, shower. Today he turned on the cold and soon the frigid stream restored some semblance of order. Dried but still shivering, he pulled on his jeans to the happy sound of coffee burbling in its pot. Clutching a mug, he filled it with that steaming restorative and enveloped in a cloud of heavenly aroma, he cautiously sat and let out a deep sigh of contentment. The day could now begin.

It had been an evening to long remember. Sitting in the morning sunshine, head still throbbing from the night before, Jeff ruefully reviewed the evening. "I talked too much and I sure as hell drank too much!" He muttered to himself. "That Frenchman is one tough old bastard, it didn't seem to faze him." As he looked out over the hillside and the row on row of vines, he wondered what Pierre's ranch was like and what the mysterious problem might be. Jeff stopped to sip his coffee while talking to himself. "The 'Pierre Vaillard Vineyard'… said I'd see the sign … twenty-four miles? Jeez, I better get movin'. "

Jeff found a clean shirt and pulling on his boots, he was ready to go. He'd slept late after that long night with Pierre. The sun was well up and the morning sky was the perfect blue of a Chamber of Commerce Post Card. With one last sip of coffee, he closed the door and climbed into his truck.

Sunday morning was quiet in the village. The parking lot at the Branding Iron was empty save for a lone woman sweeping up last night's illicit cigarette butts. Turning up the valley, the few cars moving were headed for church. "Dammit," he grunted angrily, slamming on the brakes as he took a turn too fast. "Pierre was right! What I need is a woman sitting beside me. Admit it, you dumb bastard, you're scared to try again!" Memories of Caroline came flooding back. It seemed only yesterday that the two were together in war-torn, far off, Afghanistan. "Stop it!" he muttered to himself. "That time's gone forever. Get on with your life!"

The road twisted and turned following the slow-moving trickle that was the Carmel River. About 3 miles out his spirits began to revive. Passing the Cachaqua turnoff, the ribbon of asphalt now followed Tularcitos Creek up into the Santa Lucias. In the narrow canyon the white-barked Sycamores arched over the slow moving stream and moss draped oaks crowded the shade. As the road climbed higher, the shadows gave way to sunshine and a broad expanse of rolling savannah opened before him. Every few miles a road would lead off to some ranch and he could see small groups of cattle grazing on the distant slopes. He was aware that he'd not passed one car since leaving the village; not seen one house in miles. With the wind blowing in his face and the golden hills above, he reveled in his newfound freedom.

Passing the Tassajara junction, he started looking for Pierre's sign. Not one vine, much less a vineyard had come into view. "Where does he hide those grapes?" he mused. "Must be tucked behind some ridge." As the road twisted on toward the skyline he wondered if he'd missed the gate when, without warning, there it was on the left. A worn and bedraggled sign, "*Vaillard Vineyard*" hung precariously over the old ranch gate. He could also make out even more faded printing above. "*Nacimiento Rancho.*" To the right of the entrance was a bright, obviously new, metal sign: "*Private Property - No Trespassing*". Stopping, he swung open the big ranch gate, pulled forward, then closed the gate behind. Looking at the sign as he drove past, he wondered aloud, "Hmmm, that warning is brand new, wonder what that's all about?"

Slowing, he navigated the rutted entrance and continued up the dirt and gravel road, following a small stream that had no business in these dry and desiccated hills. Up and over a low divide about a half-mile farther on, he passed a good-sized pond behind a low dam, ducks paddling peacefully on the calm surface. Winding on down the road, he rounded a bend and there, unbelievably, was a verdant paradise. Before him was another larger lake with grassy pastures on its banks. Bright poppies and blue lupine were splashed on the hillsides where moisture had collected in earlier spring rains. A dozen horses were standing in swampy ground across the lake, ears up, warily watching his arrival. "Where in hell could all this water be coming from? It hasn't rained in months, this place should be dry as a bone".

Not far from the lake, well sheltered in this small, secluded, valley was a large rambling ranch house plus two red barns with attached corrals. Some distance away stood a smaller home and near the lake, a small cabin and a nearby trailer beneath a spreading oak. Pausing for a moment as he passed over the rise, he took in his surroundings. What he saw seemed unbelievable, a Garden of Eden hidden here in the hills. Rolling on down the gentle slope, he pulled the old truck to a stop on the grass in front of the house. It was from another time. The mortar free rock foundation, the irregular handmade brick chimney and the ancient, lichen encrusted stonewalls surrounding the house were signs of a time long passed. The house itself was painted white, the roof of hand-split redwood shakes. A broad verandah circled the front and sides. Before the steps going up to the porch was a neatly trimmed lawn with a huge California Live Oak providing shade. Bright flowers grew by the walk and clusters of red roses arched over the gate. Off to one side was a patio with a large stone fireplace. Within the gaping, smoke blackened hearth, was a heavy iron grate that hung above the ashes. Jeff could almost smell huge slabs of ribs slowly grilling over glowing coals. Above the patio was a vine covered arbor and to one side a wall of the house was decorated with rust encrusted branding irons. This pastoral scene was made complete by a large weathered bronze bell, perhaps a relic of some long forgotten sailing ship. In his mind he could hear that deep, sonorous peal calling the Vaqueros in from the range.

As he stepped down from the truck, a smiling woman, clearly of Mexican descent, appeared at the door. "You must be Jeff," she called "Welcome! I am Maria. Señor Vaillard is out in the barn, he'll be here in a moment. Please come in!"

Jeff was halfway to the steps when a remarkable projectile of hair, muscle and bone came flying around the corner and nearly knocked him off his feet. About the size of a full-grown grizzly, the mud splotched, once white dog had a tail like a furry baseball bat, alternately whacking the gate and Jeff's right leg. The gate was mute—Jeff gave a startled, "Ouch!" With a deep and guttural rumble that emanated from some place deep within, the beast delivered his personal greeting. Catching a closer look between blows, Jeff, took note of a broad collar around the dog's neck. Once the color red, a name was woven in large black print. "Bruno" it proudly proclaimed.

"Good morning, Jeffrey," came a booming voice from behind. "I see you've met Maria, my keeper and helper par excellence. It seems you've also met another of my companions." He laughed, "Don't worry, the mud washes off and the bruises will heal." Hearing that voice, the dog went bounding over to sit at Pierre's feet. Tongue dangling from one side of its mouth, a smile on its face and a tail still wagging some ninety miles an hour, the bear-like carnivore looked up at its master and barked a joyous, "What's next, Dad?" As if on cue, Maria came rushing down the steps and tried in vain to wipe the mud from Jeff's pants with her large floral apron. Walking over, Pierre extended a well calloused hand.

"Welcome to our ranch, Jeff." Pierre released the young man's half crushed hand and gestured towards the house. "It's cooler inside and I know Maria has brewed us fresh coffee. Last night you told me something about yourself. Now it's my turn to tell you about myself, this ranch and why I need you". With that, the smiling, heavy set man turned, walked up the steps and into the cool, inviting house.

15

MOVING THROUGH THE entrance hall, the two men turned left through an open door and entered a large welcoming kitchen. Making his way to a broad, well-used pine table, Pierre pushed aside a pile of papers and motioned Jeff to sit down. Sunlight streaming through the large windows flooded the cheerful room. The delicious scent of bread baking in the large black oven brought back long forgotten memories of Jeff's second mother, Juanita, and another wonderful ranch kitchen. On a smaller table against the wall were stacks of bills, letters, old newspapers, an open laptop and a telephone. It was clear this cheerful room was the business office, dining room as well as busy kitchen — the center of ranch life. As they were getting settled, Maria came bustling in through the patio door, changed her muddy apron and busied herself with the coffee.

After taking his place, Pierre looked at his young visitor. "You may remember the history of the French in Vietnam. About Saigon, 'The Paris of the Orient', and how after a century of colonial rule we were defeated by Ho Chi Minh and his Vietnamese Communists back in 1954. Thrown out would be a better word. I was a 24-year-old French soldier, an electronics specialist, which means I set up and repaired our primitive electronic gear. I was wounded and captured at Dien Bien Phú, and finally got home in 1956. That was well before your country made the same disastrous mistake."

He paused to take a sip before continuing. "I came home to our family vineyard in the south of France and spent the next year regaining my health. It was working the land that saved me, not doctors or medicine." Pierre stopped to sip his coffee.

"In France, by law the older son inherits the land. Since I was the second son, and because I had learned some English while in Saigon, I decided to try my luck in America. I still had some money saved from my Army days and knew just two trades: electronics and vineyards. I decided to start in California because of the grapes. I arrived first in San Jose to begin my search — it was a very lucky time for me. A new kind of company was just starting and they were desperate for electronic technicians. One of those new ventures was Fairchild Semiconductors, and I was fortunate enough to land a job. In 1968, two of the brightest men I'd ever met, Bob Noyce and Gordon Moore, broke away to start a new venture. They called their company 'Intel' and I was persuaded to come along." Pierre stopped to pick up his pipe and tamp down a fresh clump of tobacco. "Jeff, every single day was an exhilarating, challenging, experience! There were only a few of us at the beginning and we worked like lunatics—often slept in the lab. It was one of the most exciting, creative, times of my life. There wasn't much money but we were given stock, quite a lot of stock, long before it went public ... and I expect you know what happened with Intel".

Jeff watched as Pierre struck a match and held it over the scarred briar bowl of his well-worn pipe. When ignited to his satisfaction, he returned to his story. "Intel made this ranch possible. I had always wanted to get back to the land and when the company went public, my stock suddenly was worth a small fortune and I went looking for my vineyard. Every day I could get free I drove to the wine country of Napa, Sonoma and finally Monterey County. There were only a few grape growers down here in those days. I fell in love with these warm, dry hills so like the south of France. One day, exploring dusty back roads, I came upon this hidden jewel. One square mile in size, it had everything. South facing hills, plentiful water, two small lakes, even a legend of Spanish gold." He laughed. "The gold we have is the land and the water!"

Maria interrupted Pierre to pour more coffee. "It had been part of a large Spanish Land Grant that once covered about four square miles of these rolling foothills of the Santa Lucia Mountains. As happens over generations, the original grant had been divided, then divided again among children and grandchildren. The owner of this portion had just died and his only child, a daughter, had no interest in a cattle rancher's life. All 640 acres were for sale. Land values in these dry hills were nothing back in those days. In 1972, I bid *adieu* to my friends at Intel, purchased the ranch and have never looked back." Pierre leaned back with a smile. "You must excuse this long history—you will be bored to death before I get to the important part, but you need to know the background!"

Jeff was fascinated by the Frenchman's tale. "So what happened next? As you remarked about me, there should be a woman in your life."

Pierre laughed. "I was in my late thirties, a few years older I think than you. My family thought I was going to be a permanent bachelor. That's when I met Annetta and my life changed forever. She was the daughter of a neighboring cattle rancher and was helping her widowed father run the place." Pierre, his mind far away, paused before picking up his story. "We fell in love and were soon married. The next year Annetta became pregnant and to our joy delivered a beautiful baby girl we named Samantha. I was never happier in my life."

The Frenchman paused briefly to introduce José, Maria's husband who had just come in from the vineyard. With a powerful frame, a face etched a glistening bronze by years in the sun, and a warm and welcoming smile, the big man leaned across the table to shake hands as he pulled up a chair. When all were settled and José was given his coffee, Pierre continued. "Not long after that these two wonderful people came to live on the ranch." Pierre extended his pipe pointing to the big cheerful Mexican and his wife. "José and Maria brought their baby, Carmen, and the two little girls grew up together." He laughed thinking back. "Carmen couldn't quite get her mouth around that big name 'Samantha' and soon shortened it to 'Sam.' My Samantha has been Sam ever since. We were one big happy family." As Pierre paused again, Maria moved silently behind him, placing a hand gently on his shoulder. "Then my life fell apart. Annetta found a lump in her breast one morning and despite everything doctors could do, my dear wife was gone in a year. I was broken hearted … didn't care if I lived or died. Sam was just two. If it hadn't been for these two," He gestured at José and reached up to hold Maria's hand, "I would never have survived." He paused, wiping his eyes "Please excuse an old man's tears. It was so very hard for all of us. Having Sam to take care of was a great challenge but it also saved my life. I had to go on."

Pierre stopped and stood up, wiping away a last tear. "Now enough of the past," he continued, "I know Maria is preparing one of her special salads for lunch and I can smell the baguette in the oven. Before we eat, let us walk out to the vineyard. On the way, we can visit the *cave* and pick up a bottle to go with our meal. We'll stop first at the small trailer up by the lake — it is my hope you will honor us by joining our small family for dinner and spending the night."

Leaving the kitchen, the two men walked quietly up to the trailer parked under a spreading oak. With all four corners resting on concrete blocks and a large propane tank standing on the far side, the still shiny aluminum box looked ready for occupancy. "It is very comfortable for one person." said Pierre. "As you can see," he said pointing under one corner to a wire and a pipe coming up from the ground, "we've run electricity and water over from Sam's cabin. There's no connection to the septic tank, you can use the bathroom in the house – and for us men," he chuckled, "there are plenty of bushes outside. By the way, our telephone is in the house, there is no cell-phone reception up here in the hills and canyons."

Opening the door, Jeff saw the standard small trailer floor plan. A table surrounded by a U-shaped settee up front. There was a minute kitchen area across from the door with a two burner stove, sink, and a tiny refrigerator. A double bed and very small bathroom took up the back. The trailer was spotless and with its large windows, quite light and airy. The green canopy of the ancient oak provided shade from the midday sun. Not far away was the simple cabin where, as Pierre explained, his daughter Sam and grandson Peter often spent vacations. A short distance further and closer to the lake was the home of José and Maria. Turning to Jeff, Pierre cocked his head. "What do you think, my friend, can we entice you to spend a night or two in our expansive 'guest house'?"

With a nodded positive response from Jeff, the two walked on up past the big red barn and its outbuildings for a quarter mile up the gentle valley. Pierre again noted his young visitor's slight limp but asked no questions. Rounding a last bend the vista opened and there on the hillsides ahead lay the vineyard. The two men stopped as Jeff took in the miracle spread out before him. "My God, Pierre, I would never have guessed such a vineyard could be hidden in these hills. This is unbelievable!" In front of them on the south facing hills, row on row of vines wound in and out following the soft contours of the land. The exposure was ideal, taking full advantage of the sun and the dry rocky soil. Pierre swept his arm in a half circle. "There they are", he said with obvious pride. "The reds struggling for existence above and the whites enjoying the gentler slopes below".

Jeff was astonished. He had expected to find a small three or four acres of grapes but here on these hidden hillsides were at least 20 acres of vines winding over and around the gentle slopes above the broad valley floor. "Pierre, it's beautiful." Shading his eyes, he looked at the expanse of vines spread before him. "What an amazing vineyard — why isn't everyone beating a path to your door?"

"Ah, that is the problem! I doubt it's the grapes and the wine that has a moth circling our flame. It's probably the land and the water—but who knows." They both stood silently for a few minutes before Pierre spoke again. "Let us go down to the *cave*, it's cooler and I think you will find it interesting. We'll sample a bottle and I'll tell you what's happened and the other reason I invited you to join us today."

Turning, Jeff looked back towards the lake and the houses beyond. As they walked down the narrow tractor path, he became aware of a break in the hillside he'd not noticed walking up the valley. There, hidden by the leaf-covered branches of several large Valley Oaks was a brick-faced opening in the hillside. An apron of concrete lay before the entry. Close by was a small red barn-like building, further shielding the area.

"That *cave*," gestured Pierre, "was tunneled into the hill more than one hundred and fifty years ago when wine was first made on this ranch. I am told it was dug by some of the same Chinese coolies who built the railroads in California. I sell most of my grapes to my fellow wine-makers over the hill in the Arroyo Seco. Of the rest, we hand select the very best and with those we make about eight hundred cases each year for our friends and ourselves. I sell none of my own creation. One of these days I hope to enlarge the vineyard and make a good mid-priced wine, both white and red." He gestured towards the concrete pad in front of the cave. "We wheel the equipment out onto the apron during the harvest. Inside, the *cave* is perfect for blending, aging and storing the wine."

As they walked closer, Jeff could see more clearly the large opening tunneled into the hill. The concrete and brick wall covering the entrance seemed as old as the *cave* itself. In the center, two large double doors had been constructed, big enough to allow a small tractor, the crusher and other pieces of machinery to be moved in and out as needed. Pulling wide the doors, the two men walked into the cool darkness. Reaching over, Pierre switched on lights to illuminate the deep interior. Rack on rack of barrels lined each side and cases of wine could be seen stacked towards the back. "Amazing!" Exclaimed Jeff, as two stood enjoying the coolness of the *cave*. "You'd never dream this existed if you didn't see it with your own eyes."

"Yes, now that you have seen my vineyard and this *cave*, you can understand why I love this place and why I hope never to leave." Pulling a bottle from an open case tipped on its side, the Frenchman walked over to a table where a half-dozen glasses stood upside down on a tray. Pulling out a couple of chairs, he motioned Jeff to sit down. "Let's relax for a bit, taste my wine, and I'll tell you the rest of my story."

Deftly, Pierre uncorked the bottle and carefully poured out two glasses, handing one to Jeff. "Two years old, but this Claret is still young— it should only get better with more time in the bottle—what do you think?"

Holding the glass up to the light Jeff could see the dark crimson of the wine. Gently swirling the glass, he watched red "legs" glide swiftly down the inner surface. Bending forward, Jeff inhaled slowly several times taking in the faint aroma of cherries and currents. Raising the glass to his lips, he slowly savored a mouthful. The wine was young but the depth of tannins and the acidity promised a wonderful future as the wine reached maturity. Eyes wide in wonder, he whispered, "It's absolutely delicious!"

Pierre beamed. "First it is the land. These dry, flinty hillsides are what make it unique. Without *le terroir,* you have nothing. We are very careful with the vines and even more careful with the grapes. With the help of Jose's friends, we carefully pick each bunch and each grape by hand. We use only French Oak for our barrels, never more than two years old. And here," he gestured around, "In this peaceful place the juice of my grapes becomes wine." Sitting quietly while holding his glass, the Frenchman returned to his story.

"Two weeks ago a man and his driver came calling. He arrived unannounced in a large black Mercedes. The driver, a tall Asian, knocked on the door and his appearance was enough to alarm Maria—and she is not easily frightened. We have an intercom to the *cave* and she called to tell me of the two men. They were walking around and taking notes when I arrived. The smaller man, a Caucasian, was all smiles. Handing me his card, he introduced himself as Mr. Antonio, Attorney at Law. He went on to say he represented the Asia-American Development Company. He then proceeded to tell me that his principles had been seeking a small but quality vineyard in California to purchase."

Pierre stopped to savor a sip of his wine. "It seems the demand for 'high-quality wine', as he called it, is unlimited among the *nouveau riche* in China. His principles were intent on satisfying this demand. With no response on my part, the attorney continued to speak. 'We've been talking to experts and have decided on Monterey County. Not long ago, we heard very good things about this little known but excellent winery." Then the man extended his chubby little arm to encompass all the ranch and said: "And that led us to you and your vineyard. You have everything we want.'

Pierre stopped and looked up from his glass. "As you might guess, I was dumbfounded. 'Just what are you suggesting, Mr. Antonio? It is well known in Monterey County that our vineyard is not for sale. It never has been and never will be for sale.' "

"Mr. Vaillard," The little man responded, "Everything is for sale if the price is right! As always, we've been doing our due diligence: checking deeds, permits, County records, old ownerships, even Spanish Land Grants. Can't be too careful, you know. We found quite a few irregularities—always are if you look deep enough—nothing too serious, if you know what I mean."

Pierre stopped to look at Jeff. "This was one of the strangest conversations I've ever had. The man was either deaf or didn't understand the English language. Jeff, I pride myself on having an even temper, but I could feel my annoyance beginning to show. 'No.' I responded, 'I don't know what you mean and I definitely don't like your innuendo. I'll repeat one time more. This vineyard and ranch are not now and never will be for sale. I am flattered by your interest but I think it's time for you leave.' Well, that attorney seemed unfazed by my words, just kept that silly smile on his face, tried to shake hands. Then, as he and his driver walked back to their big Mercedes, he called back one parting shot: 'Better think carefully, Mr. Vaillard, don't want any trouble you know ... you'll hear from us soon.' "

Pierre picked up the bottle and refilled their two glasses. "Jeff, I was very angry but also worried by this so-called agent. I called Tom DeBeers, an old friend who has been my lawyer for years. He checked his Bar Association directories and couldn't find this man's name under any listing. That doesn't prove anything, of course, but it was strange. Tom told me he'd check over at County Records and see if anyone had been nosing around. He called back the next day to say he and the clerk checked the files and damned if they didn't find half the ranch papers were missing. The only person who'd looked at the files in years was this same mysterious attorney. By now I was very nervous and I bought that 'No Trespassing' sign you saw at the gate."

Maria chimed in, "They were very bad men, Jeffrey, a woman can tell. They frightened me!" José nodded agreement.

Pierre continued, "Last week I received an expensive look-ing letter from this Asia-American Development Company. It had an offer, actually a very good offer, to purchase the ranch. It was also a threat ... suggesting 'We get what we want.' " Pierre paused, and his frown was replaced by a broad smile. "I'll show you the letter after lunch—right now noth-ing should interrupt the pleasure of Maria's food!"

By the time the three men had washed up, the table was set and Maria was busy slicing tomatoes and chopping green onions. An avocado and Ancho pepper lay waiting their turn. The corn chips were broken into small pieces, the sharp Mexican cheddar shredded. garlic, cumin, salt, and pepper were set to one side. Home cooked, well chilled, ranch pin-to beans lay ready in an ancient wooden salad bowl. Crisp, chilled leaves of Romaine rested on each plate. Quickly toss-ing all the ingredients together with a vinaigrette made from what Maria described as the ranch's own home-pressed olive oil plus balsamic vinegar, fresh ground pepper and herbs from the garden, she carefully lifted the salad onto the table. Two baguettes, crusts golden brown and still warm from the oven lay waiting on a heavy wood plank. As Maria put the plates on the table, José poured the wine and Pierre sliced the bread.

Later, relaxed and satiated, Pierre went to a file in the corner and pulled out a letter. Glancing at the envelope, Jeff saw it was postmarked in San Francisco the previous week. The heading was engraved with the company name in English and also below in what he presumed was Chinese. As Pierre had said, there was an offer to purchase the vineyard and winery. Jeff read it with astonishment. "That's some offer! That would be pretty tempting."

"It is a good offer, probably too good an offer," replied Pierre. "But there's something funny about the whole thing. Napa and Sonoma are much better known in the world market. Why are they looking at an obscure place like this? Makes you question what they actually want."

Looking up from the letter, Jeff glanced at Pierre, "Wonder who this bunch really are, just listen to this paragraph." Jeff read aloud: "We trust you will give our offer your most serious and immediate consideration. Our principles are anxious to proceed immediately and we believe our terms to be quite agreeable. Mr. Antonio, whom you have already met, will be in touch shortly. Anything less than a positive response would not be to your best interest. Asia-American Development Company and the interests of those we represent do not make frivolous decisions."

"Just what does he mean by that statement?" said Jeff, "Sounds like a not very veiled threat. No wonder you're nervous! Has this attorney made an appointment to come back?"

"No, and I have no intention of talking to him. I'm taking this letter down to Tom DeBeers tomorrow and have him draft a proper legal response. I want it made absolutely clear that this vineyard is not for sale and to cease bothering us at once."

⚬⚬⚬

Jeff spent the rest of the afternoon walking the vineyards with José. It was a lovely setting and there was pride in Jose's voice as he described each block of vines, the grape varieties and the different soils. Clearly a great deal of effort was spent keeping the vineyard in near perfect condition. The vines were well tended and carefully tied to the heavy supporting wires. Each trellis was straight, tight and true as they contoured around the slopes.

Working up a sweat hiking up and down the slopes, Jeff walked back to the trailer in the late afternoon. José had left early, mentioning something about "another job." Jeff's utilitarian, one temperature only, (frigid), outdoor shower prepared him for the evening meal. It seemed his three hosts each loved preparing food and had over many years developed an unofficial rotation of duties. Once a week the two men alternated preparing the meal of their choice giving Maria a night off from cooking. This evening it was José's turn in the kitchen, which explained his early disappearance.

Jeff arrived in a clean shirt and jeans. Entering from the patio, his olfactory buds were immediately struck by the wonderful odors of garlic and roasting chili peppers. There standing at the stove stood José, a big apron draped over his heavy-set, muscular frame. Having watched this tough Mexican swing a sledgehammer at a post, it was a revelation to see him daintily stirring a variety of colorful ingredients into a large cast iron receptacle. José didn't look up from his task but called a welcoming greeting as he bent over to inhale the steam rising from the simmering pot.

"Come in, Jeffrey," called Pierre from the far side of the room where he was nursing a frosty bottle of Corona. "We all like a cold beer with José's cooking. Find a bottle in the refrigerator and come watch a master of Mexican cuisine at work."

Maria shooed Pierre and Jeff out of the way and set the table while José produced a large bowl of Guacamole and a plate of fresh tortilla chips. Loading a chip with this classic Mexican appetizer, Jeff immediately recognized that this was like no store bought mix. Lime juice, fresh minced garlic, a chopped Serrano pepper, a hint of cumin, all melded into perfectly mashed, sun ripened avocadoes made Jeff smile with pleasure. The main course, which had been simmering in the big pot when Jeff arrived, was now ladled out on a large platter. Piled high was recently barbecued and shredded chicken that had been cooked in sour cream, Chilquiles and Salsa Verde. Chopped Cilantro with goat cheese sprinkled over the top completed José's south of the border creation. The cold Mexican beer was the perfect liquid accompaniment.

At last, the main course was completed accompanied by many sighs of satisfaction. The chef now rose from his chair, opened the refrigerator and carefully brought forth four ramekins of traditional Mexican Flan. With great care, each was inverted onto a small plate, the homemade caramel sauce, once at the bottom of the ramekins,now coating the top and oozing slowly down the sides. It was the ideal conclusion to a marvelous meal.

It had taken almost two hours for the four to work their way through José's culinary triumph. By the time the dishes were washed and dried, the four contented participants were ready for bed. Before adjourning for the night, Pierre rose and proposed a toast to the Chef who bowed low in response.

"Jeffrey," The big Frenchman sighed, loosening his belt. "Now you can understand why there are no thin people on this ranch."

It had been a long day, a huge soul-satisfying meal, and Jeff was ready for bed. Accompanied by Bruno, he walked back to the trailer in the darkness of a night illuminated only by the dazzling Milky Way high in the sky above. Arriving at the trailer, Jeff opened the door and both man and beast crowded their way into the dark interior. Turning on the light, Jeff and Bruno then discussed who would sleep on the bed and who would curl up on the floor. They both slept on the bed.

16

JEFF AWOKE TO the sounds of morning on a ranch. He heard the whinnying of horses across the lake. Nearby a cock was loudly announcing a new day. From the barn came the muted voices of two men, the stuttering cough followed by a throaty growl issuing from a tractor as it came to life. Bruno had already gone on his morning rounds. It was way past time for Jeff to rise and shine! Quickly he slipped on his shirt, stepped into his jeans, then pulled on his boots. The slanting rays of the early sun were just kissing the hilltops, the air was calm and a faint mist rose silently from the placid surface of the lake. Horses walked slowly along the far shore and in the tall reeds a solitary Blue Heron stood, unblinking eyes fixed on the surface. Turning, Jeff looked down at the house and the sight of smoke lazily drifting up from the kitchen chimney. His stomach growled in anticipation … no question, it was time for breakfast.

As he approached the kitchen, he was greeted by a roaring noise that sounded like some terrifying prehistoric monster moving back and forth inside the room. Cautiously opening the door, he found Maria noisily moving back and forth over the floor with a remarkable marvel of chrome plated steel: an ancient Kirby vacuum cleaner. Jeff thought these beauties long extinct, but this elegant specimen was clearly alive and well. Seeing Jeff enter, Maria flicked off the switch and the great beast wheezed to a stop. Bruno, smiling ear to ear, came bounding over from his place in front of the stove. Maria, indicating the floor with a sweep of her hand, exclaimed, "You men and your dog—just look at this mess!" Parking the Kirby in one corner, Maria leaned up and gave Jeff a hug and a kiss, laughing at his startled expression. "We're all family here at the ranch. You'll have to get used to our old-fashioned ways. Now then, is it coffee or tea? Most of us drink coffee, Carmen and Sam always have tea."

"Coffee for me — and tell me about Carmen and Sam."

Pouring a steaming mug of coffee, Maria placed it carefully on the table. "While I fix your breakfast I'll tell you about the two little girls who spent their childhood on this ranch." As she busied herself over the stove, she continued to speak as she worked. "First there is Carmen, our daughter. Carmen was just a year old when José and I came to live on the ranch. She grew up with the vines and the winery. She spent hours after school and most summer days tagging along after Pierre and José. She did well in school, but Carmen's real interest was always wine and before long she had a job at a wine shop. Then she decided she wanted to try something new; she found an opening at a fancy restaurant in Carmel. Soon she knew more about wine than her boss. To learn more, she went to Fresno State and studied wine. After college she moved to San Francisco and now, believe it or not, our Carmen is a real wine specialist, a *Sommelier* (did I say that right?), the youngest one in the City. I'll tell you about Sam while you're eating your breakfast."

Tantalizing smells were emanating from around Maria as she moved rapidly between stove and sink. In a few moments she turned to the table with a large plate piled high with succulent scrambled eggs and slices of crisp bacon. Returning with toast, butter, and jam, she sat down with her own mug of scalding coffee and picked up her story

"Our life at the ranch started a long time ago. As Pierre explained yesterday, he married a beautiful girl from a big ranch down the road and it wasn't long before Annetta was pregnant and in no time they had the baby girl they named Samantha. Then Annetta got a very bad cancer." Maria's eyes dimmed as she stared through the open window, voice now barely a whisper. "She died when Sam was just two years old. Pierre was heart broken." There was a long pause before Maria looked back at Jeff, her voice now a more normal tone. "Carmen is just a year older, so those two little girls grew up together. Samantha is like my second daughter."

Maria stopped to refill their cups. "Sam was a very good student. She'd visited France many times with her father and loved the language – she could speak almost as well as her dad. After Carmel High she went up to Stanford, even got at Ph.D. and stayed on to teach French. Now comes the sad part. Sam met a handsome, very smart, investment man named George Segovia. He really went after her and she fell for his charm. We were never comfortable with George. He always seemed to have a lot of money but we couldn't see where it came from. You could never pin him down, we knew something wasn't right. Then before long, Sam became pregnant and soon she had a wonderful little boy they named Peter. We were all so glad, but our happiness didn't last long—we began to hear bad things about George. This man lost all Sam's savings in some shady deals and he tried to borrow a lot of money from Pierre. He was always talking about the ranch and what he would do when it belonged to Sam. We began to feel that was why he had married her. The worst was when we saw bruises on Sam and found out he was beating her when he was drinking, and he did a lot of that. It got worse and worse and finally Sam filed for divorce. George was furious and she had to call the police a couple of times. He threatened to take away Peter and tried to get her fired from Stanford. That was when her father stepped in. Pierre hired a very expensive San Francisco lawyer to help and they found all sorts of bad things about this man."

Maria stopped to push Bruno off her feet and shift her ample frame. "They found he was running investment scams tied up with a lot of crooks from Hong Kong. They also discovered he had a made a lot of money in Afghanistan, but no one seemed to know how. It was so bad that the judge granted Sam complete custody of Peter. Sam took a leave from Stanford and stayed with us at the ranch while all this was going on – in fact, she's coming down to the ranch in a couple of days."

"Some story!" said Jeff, taking his last bite of toast. "I can see why Pierre's so nervous about this outfit nosing around."

"That's why we're all nervous." said Maria, putting the dishes in the sink. "And now," she turned with a feigned angry frown and pointed to the door, "it's time for you and that lazy dog to get out and do something useful! You're supposed to be learning about the ranch!" With those last words, she grabbed the Kirby by its handle, flicked the switch, and the monster came back to life like a rocket on lift off. Jeff and Bruno barely escaped through the door.

Jeff spent the rest of the morning in the village collecting his meager belongings, notifying his landlord that he'd be away for awhile and loading the truck. Next stop was his storage locker to pick up the saddle he'd had since high school; it had become his talisman and he often dreamed of riding again on a ranch of his own. Closing up the locker he saw the dusty black doctor's bag he'd been given when he was still a resident. Next to the bag was his Dad's old hunting rifle and on the spur of the moment, he added these both to his stash Next stop was the hardware store for some fresh 30.06 ammunition and it was time to fill the truck's tank and head back up the valley.

"Bruno's been looking all over the ranch for you!" Pierre called with a mock frown as Jeff parked the old truck by the barn. "You're stealing my dog's affections!"

"He's a great dog," replied Jeff, kneeling and scratching the thick fur behind the big mutt's ears. "I used to have one almost as big when I was a kid."

Helping Jeff unload, Pierre noticed the rifle. "Not much hunting this time of year but that saddle we can put to use this afternoon."

"Wasn't planning to hunt—it's just for show in case those friends of yours get unpleasant."

"Speaking of which," said Pierre, "I got a message on the answering machine from that attorney—said he'd be dropping by again soon. There was no answer when I called back."

"Hope you don't mind if I tag along when he comes. I'll just stand in the background and keep my mouth shut."

Pierre laughed "Not only do I not mind, I was hoping you'd be there, see what you make of the man." Looking over Jeff's meager possessions, he shook his head. "You travel light! That old saddle, your truck and that rifle look like the only permanent part of your life."

"Yeh, I've been travelin' light ever since I left home. No roots except these reminders of my family and that hardly used doctor's bag ... not much to show for 33 years."

Pierre looked quickly at Jeff. For one brief moment the young man's guard was down and in that instant he saw the same emptiness he'd seen that night in the village. "I wonder...." he mused, but then spoke quickly again. "Looks like you're finished for now. Let's head down for lunch. After we eat we can saddle up and ride through the vineyard, you can inspect the vines, the soil and the miraculous source of our water. We'll stop at the *cave* if there's time. I'll show you our small wine making operation ... maybe open a bottle."

Lunch was simple but delicious. Maria joined the men, and together they talked about the ranch and the extended family that lived here. José had come in from working on the trellises. It was going to be easy working with this big, cheerful man, thought Jeff. When they were finished, the three men plus Bruno headed up to the barn, picking up Jeff's saddle en route.

Pierre pointed to a small, mud caked all-terrain vehicle loaded with rolls of trellis wire. "When we're really working we use the ATV. It can go almost anywhere on the ranch and it carries two plus whatever we're going to need for the day. These ugly vehicles may be the modern ranch horse but they're never quite the same.

Opening the corral gate, José selected a large mare for Jeff. "This is Sally, you'll like her, she's tough, smart and she knows the ranch." Jeff threw a blanket over the horse's back, slung up his saddle and cinched it tight. "Tighter!" yelled José, "Sally likes to play games!" Jeff nodded, bracing himself, his knee against the horse's flank and with a loud grunt, managed to pull the strap up three more notches. "It's been too many years since I've saddled a horse - I've forgotten their tricks." smiled Jeff.

As the horses made their way up the valley, the men talked about the different soils, the drainage, the clones and how long they'd been in the ground.. Pierre told of his experiments with different grape varieties for each hillside exposure. "The Cabernet and Pinot Noir up there on those dry hillsides really have to struggle, but Ah, the fruit! It just seems to get better each year. We give them plenty of space and thin the clusters—the grapes are small but the concentration is wonderful." For two hours they slowly rode along row on row of vines gently contouring around the rolling hills. Now and then, Jeff would climb down, examine a vine or run his hands though the dry, gravely, soil to smell and feel the earth. It seemed only yesterday that he had been riding through other vineyards with his father performing this same careful inspection of vines, soil and drainage. Pierre watched as Jeff rode his horse along the rows, occasionally stopping to look at the ground or the vines. He well understood the pleasure this young man was experiencing. It was as if he was reliving his youth, riding through the vineyards of Languedoc with his father so many years ago.

Finally, the three came to a halt under a large spreading oak on the crest of a small knoll. The only sounds were their horses nibbling dry grass, the whisper of a breeze and the scolding objections of a nearby crow. Hands resting on his saddle horn, Jeff's eyes roamed over the peaceful scene as the late afternoon sun cast long shadows across the hills. Looking out over his ranch, Pierre broke the silence. "I think you can see why I love this wonderful place. Watching you this afternoon, I believe you felt that same pull of the land on your heart."

Riding back down the slope, Pierre turned to Jeff. "Now I'll show you the miracle that makes this ranch and our vineyard possible." As they rounded a slight bend, Jeff was astonished to see a massive rock thrusting up out of the hillside. Worn almost smooth by time and weather, it was still almost as large as a house. As the men rode closer, Jeff looked with astonishment at the scene before him. Gushing out from a cleft in the enormous rock's base, a torrent of water cascaded into the large pool below. Soft swaths of green lined the pool's banks and at the far end a fast running creek tumbled down the valley. While the horses drank from the pool, Pierre talked about the remarkable spring. "The only thing vaguely like it are the small lakes at the Cienega del Gabilan Ranch, near the top of Fremont Peak, 60 miles away. The experts tell us this spring could have arisen from some long past earthquake cracking the strata of granite and basalt, bringing a subterranean river to the surface at this spot. The rock is just as unusual. There are some similar outcroppings in the Gabilan Range but none have been found here in the Santa Lucia's. Amazing, isn't it?" Pierre climbed back on his horse. "This water irrigates our grapes and fills our ponds. One of the names the early Spanish settlers gave the spring was *Namaciento*, 'the source' or 'the birth'. If the existing Spanish land grant documents are correct, the stream was once called '*Rio del Oro*'. The River of Gold. That was more than two centuries ago. In more recent times we've put in a pipe running underground from the spring to the winery and the buildings below." His eyes looked wistfully at the pool. "That swimming hole was the girls' favorite place on the ranch. I can still hear their noisy yells and screams as they played in that cold water. There was never any question in their young minds that this was their pool and theirs alone." Pierre laughed as he remembered back to those happy times.

Noticing for the first time the lengthening shadows, the old Frenchman straightened in his saddle, exclaiming, "*A bien*! Maria will have a fit if we're late. I'll stop and pick up a couple of good bottles at the *cave* as we ride by, we'll save the winery 'till tomorrow. You two get your horses brushed down and yourselves cleaned up. I'll be right behind you."

Later, after the men had suitably expressed their enjoyment of another wonderful dinner, and appropriate toasts had been made to the chef, Pierre passed out cigars. "I think you can see, Jeff, what a pleasure it is for us to have you here with us. It's been a long time since someone has been on the ranch who really understands what we are trying to do with our grapes. Not to mention that Maria loves having an appreciative guest at her table."

"Oh stop that, Pierre." said Maria testily, shaking her head. "The boy just likes good home cooked food after eating in a hospital cafeteria or down at that noisy place in the village. I just don't understand why a nice old man like you goes off once a week to that loud, awful place."

Pierre laughed, "Maria's constant lament: my visits to civilization. She'll never understand why I enjoy watching all those young people whooping it up while I sit in my corner dreaming dreams of my youth."

"Tomorrow" he continued, "We'll go through the winery ... it's nothing fancy but the results are good ... in fact we think our wine is very good indeed. That Cab you liked so much tonight is an example. Fortunately, I don't have to make money from the vineyard. Those years at Intel and some lucky early investments in Silicon Valley took care of that. Our goal is just to make lovely wine. Carmen is sure ours can stand up to the best and she should know." He stopped for a moment to puff slowly on his cigar. "Jeff, I've never wanted to have a big name, have wine reporters nosing around, a parking lot full of visitors, a tasting room, people wandering all over the ranch. Our joy is the pleasure we've had creating good wine, just the three of us — with help, of course, from José's brother and friends."

Pierre took another long pull on his cigar, tilted his head back and slowly blew the smoke towards the ceiling. "The problem is I'm getting older. The day is coming when I'll have to slow down. We'd always hoped one of the children would come back to the ranch, but you know how that goes."

"I can just see you sitting in a rocking chair," José snorted. "But you're right about the kids. They love the ranch — but they're all too busy with their own lives".

"Oh, you men, always worrying about the future!" chimed in Maria. "I'm worried right now about those people who are after the ranch. And what about Sam and Pete who're coming next week? That's what you should be thinking about!".

"You're right, Maria," said Pierre,   "José and I will deal with this Asia - America bunch and if Jeff stays, he can help. I want you to keep Sam and Peter away when those men come. Maybe you could all three go up to your house and lie low until they've gone. I can't help thinking there's a connection between Sam's snake of an ex-husband and these people."

17

ONE SATURDAY MORNING, a few weeks after Jeff's arrival, Pierre announced at the breakfast table that this was the night the Branding Iron Dinner Group gathered for their monthly feast. "How would you like to join us, Jeff? You would meet some of my oldest and closest friends." That was an invitation Jeff couldn't refuse. That evening, after a quick shower and attired in his one and only jacket, Jeff was ready to go.

Inspecting the two men preparing for their outing, Maria made clear her irritation. "You nasty old man, you should be ashamed taking this nice boy down to that noisy, smelly saloon. What's the matter with my cooking?"

Pierre threw back his head and laughed. "Jeff, don't' pay any attention to that cranky old woman, she's consumed with jealousy. She can't get over the fact that some of us like a night on the town once in awhile."

As Jeff reached for his keys, the Frenchman quickly placed his big hand on top of Jeff's. "Thanks but no thanks, young man. Tonight we'll take the Buick. I'm not riding in that disreputable heap of yours. For this occasion we must arrive as proper gentlemen — I don't intend to show up looking like we just escaped from a junkyard."

So the Buick it was. As they drove down the valley without a trace of shake or a rattle, there was no question the big, black car was cleaner, quieter and rode much more sedately than the Duchess. Jeff shook his head as he muttered under his breath. "Smooth, yes. Clean, sure, but this things got no personality."

Reaching the village, they pulled into a parking space in front of the Branding Iron. Watching Pierre load a rolling cart with multiple bottles from the trunk, Jeff realized this was a serious affair he was about to attend. As they entered the noisy bar, it seemed like old times: the same loud, happy voices, the same blaring TV.

Waving to their friends at the bar, the two men went through a passageway into a smaller, quieter private dining area and closed the door. The others were all already gathered and greeted the old Frenchman with a cheer. Busy hands emptied the cart of its precious cargo placing the winemaker's contributions carefully in the center of the table.

Spotting Jeff, one of the men walked over, hand extended in greeting. "Jeff Thomas! I've been wondering what happened to you. We all miss you at the hospital. What on earth are you doing with this old reprobate? "

"Dr. Demitross …."

Before Jeff could complete the sentence he was interrupted by Pierre, banging on the table, "Quiet down everybody,

I've a guest to introduce." Pointing his finger at Jeff, he loudly announced, "This is Dr. Jeff Thomas, late of Community Hospital and now working like a poor Mexican peon in my vineyard. Maybe he can explain that, I still haven't figured it out … but we're all having fun with the grapes. Jeff, you seem to know our village quack, George Demitross. That ambulance chaser next to him is Tom DeBeers, Esq." The lawyer stepped forward to shake Jeff's hand.

"Next to Tom is Bob Winters, a young man who thinks he knows all there is to know about wine. I make it; he's dying to sell it."

Turning, he cast a baleful eye on the big man across the table. Pointing, Pierre loudly announced, "And there before you is the local law and order, Sheriff Paul Rodriquez. Better be careful, he's mean and tough. He also thinks he's the great white hunter!"

His voice softened as he bowed low before the only woman present, "Standing before you, Jeff, is the most beautiful creature in all of Carmel Valley. Please meet Julia Barnes, the object of all our affection." With that, Pierre stepped forward and gave Julia a loud kiss on both cheeks as any true Frenchman would. Banging the table with his pipe, he sent ashes flying in all directions. "Enough with introductions. Tonight was my night to chose the menu and bring the wine, so I hereby call this meeting to order! Now, who has the corkscrew? I'm dying for '*un verre du vin.*'"

"Don't mind the old duffer," said Bob Winters, chuckling as he shook Jeff's hand "This eatin' and drinkin' society couldn't exist without him. He's our Chairman, C.E.O. and sommelier-in-chief for life!"

When everyone had taken his seat, Tom DeBeers went in search of the waitress while Sheriff Rodriquez opened the bottles. The reds, *Annetta's Couvée*, and a *Vaillard Vineyard Pinot Noir,* (three bottles of each) were opened and set on the table. The three bottles of white, a *Vaillard Vineyard Sauvignon Blanc* were opened and placed on ice to chill. In front of each place setting stood three empty glasses, each with a long stem to grasp without warming the wine and each with a generous bowl to allow air to reach the precious fluid. There was no question; these were serious eaters and drinkers.

All six members plus Jeff now sat expectantly with much smacking of lips. As if on queue, two waitresses arrived with a cart on which stood two baskets of still warm French bread partially sliced, and loosely wrapped in checkered napkins. Long sticks of unsalted butter were next followed by seven plates containing chilled oysters in shells floating on a bed of ice. As these were set in place, Pierre stood, carefully extracted the three bottles of Sauvignon Blanc from the ice buckets, pulled out their corks and poured himself a quarter of a glass. Holding the glass up to the light, then gently swirling the wine, he took a deep sniff and then a sip. "Ah, the acidity is perfect for our oysters." Picking up a bottle he proceeded to pour the clear, faintly yellow wine into each designated glass. Everyone followed his lead, heads bent over the wine in concentration as they slowly inhaled. This ritual was followed by a small mouthful rolled gently over each tongue and palate amid soft murmurs of approval.

The Tomales Bay oysters were consumed with alacrity and the dishes removed. Again with due ceremony, Pierre poured the *Annetta Cuvée*, his remarkable Bordeaux blend. As the wine was poured, the waitresses arrived with the main course: large plates, each with two generous slices of perfectly pink roast tenderloin of beef, a small mound of glazed carrots and several small roasted potatoes. At each end of the table sat a large bowl of homemade horseradish sauce. Aside from the click of silverware and the occasional sounds of quiet satisfaction, peace settled over the table as the seven self-proclaimed gourmands attended to the business at hand.

When each plate was wiped clean of any remaining traces of dinner with the last of the French bread, the dishes were duly removed. This was followed by a simple salad of torn hearts of Romaine with a wonderful vinaigrette which had been made that afternoon by Julia Barnes. This course finished and removed, the waitresses brought the feast to a conclusion with two plates of crackers and cheese, one for each end of the table. Bob Winters did the honors with the Pinot Noir. The crumbly dry Jack, Spanish Manchego and an Italian Romano, all firm, mellow cheeses, made the ripe tannins and lovely fruit of the Pinot Noir explode with flavor. Around the table, contented members lingered happily over their final course. Everybody toasted Pierre for his excellent menu and the marvelous Vaillard wines. It was a pleasant evening and conversation flowed. George Demitross pondered aloud his desire to cut back on his practice and his hope to find a younger doctor to work with him. Looking directly at Jeff he started to speak but Pierre cut him off. "No proselytizing at the table...and anyway, George," he laughed at his friend, "I've got him busy in the vineyard. Ask him next year."

Julia, leaving her place, moved close to Pierre, telling about her flourishing antiques business. More tourists were making their way up the valley, and their full pocketbooks were good for business. She was busy and happy. Her next-door neighbor, Tom DeBeers, often dropped by for coffee as did sheriff Rodriquez whenever he was in the Village. Jeff was struck by the many interconnections between these old friends, how much they supported and cared for each other. Looking around the room, he wondered what chances his lonely life had for the love and friendship so evident in this room tonight.

18

Jeff's alarm went off at 5:00 AM. The night sky was beginning to fade as he climbed over a sleeping Bruno stretched out at the foot of the bed. Leaving the door ajar for the dog, he quickly dressed and was in the kitchen by 5:30. Walking through the door, he promptly had his good morning kiss from Maria. "Amazing," he smiled to himself. "She's just like my old Juanita."

"Morning, Jeff," called Pierre as he filtered a large sip of coffee through his bushy, yellow stained mustache. "Come on in, José and I are just going over the day's schedule. Thought you and I might start up at the *cave* and go over our winemaking set up. . Later you can join José in the vines and work up a sweat."

"You'll find me up in the Grenache," interjected José. "That's on the far slope. Don't waste too much time with the old man - the vines are where the action is this time of year!"

Breakfast was what you might expect on a ranch ... substantial. In the center of the table was a plate piled high with toast along with a dish of butter and a jar of jam. A round container held warm corn tortillas and next to that was a platter heaped with scrambled eggs and bacon. An old wooden pepper grinder, a saltshaker and a jar of Mexican hot sauce stood nearby. In front of each man sat a steaming bowl of oatmeal. All conversation ceased as this mountain of food quickly disappeared.

"O.K. *mes amis,* time to go to work," called Pierre as he pushed back his chair. He gave Maria an affectionate pat on the bottom and pushed open the door. Jeff pulled on his faded denim jacket and followed. The slope was gentle and the pace comfortable as they followed the graveled road to the *cave.* Pierre slowed occasionally to catch his breath or speak to Jeff. Was the Frenchman tired and short of breath or was he just being conversational? Any concern was quickly forgotten when they arrived at the almost hidden entrance.

Dark and cool, the cavern came to life as Pierre turned on the lights. With the barrels on racks and cases stacked high at the back, the large chamber was still half empty. Close by the door was a long counter and sink. Overhead were shelves for glassware. In front of the counter stood two tall stools and, close by, the same table with chairs they had used the day before. This was the "lab" where the fermenting juice was tested for sugar, alcohol and tannins - the alchemy of wine. "Let's take a walk around first". said Pierre, moving over to the first rack of barrels against the *cave* wall. "We only use French Oak and never more than two years old, expensive but we want to give the wine every chance. The temperature here is always perfect—it never varies even one degree." Turning to his right he gestured to the rough ceiling. "With the roof so low, the racks can only stack three barrels high near the center and just two along the sides. We keep the big initial fermentation tanks in the winery across the apron." Walking around a small forklift, they looked at the barrels, each with identifying chalk marks in front. Jeff did a quick count: there were 32 barrels lining each side. That made 1,600 cases, an impressive production for this small operation.

"Here in back we stack the cases to age. Thanks to the size of this place, we've still plenty of room to move the crusher, forklift and the other equipment in for the winter months".

Jeff walked slowly around looking intently at each area of the operation. Everything was clean and neatly in place. There was pride in this winery at every turn. Walking towards the back, he carefully inspected the cases, all the while doing math in his head computing bottle numbers. In the process of peering behind and around the stacked cases, he noticed an almost hidden heavy steel door built into the back wall with a very serious double lock. "Treasure house?" called Jeff.

"*You're* absolutely right," laughed Pierre. "That's where I keep my private collection of really fine wine. Aside from José, Maria, and the kids, you're the first person to notice that door." He laughed. "Nobody ever sniffed around behind the cases before." Moving past Jeff, Pierre carefully unlocked the heavy door. Stepping aside for Jeff, he continued. "When I started this winery, I went back to France almost every year to visit my family and hoping to learn all I could of making a great Bordeaux. That went on for almost 25 years. Usually I sneaked in a suitcase of cuttings for the vineyard and always shipped two or three cases of Petrous, Chateau Margaux or one of the other great estates where I'd spent time with their winemakers. Those cuttings are now growing up on the hillsides and this is the wine I put away for posterity. When Sam was as in school, I would take her along to learn of my heritage and understand my love for France. She was a natural at language and could soon speak French like a native. As I got older and when first my parents and then my brother passsed away, I stopped the annual trips. I haven't been back for several years."

"Amazing!" Said Jeff as he looked at the treasures stacked along the walls. "Did you have any idea what these bottles would be worth when you began locking them away 30 years ago?"

"*Pas vraiment*! It wasn't cheap even then but what's happened since is unbelievable, much better than the stock market! I only knew it was the most wonderful wine I'd ever tasted and that I had to have some for my old age. Each year at Christmas I select two dozen bottles for our *Joyeux Noel* celebration and as gifts for a few very special friends. It only gets better with age. My dream is to someday create something like these. Carmen, our in-house expert and Tom Bradley, my distributor, think we're getting very close – Ah, Jeffrey, how I wish that could happen during my lifetime."

Standing in awe, Jeff almost whispered, "I'm not sure you should have told me about this treasure, Pierre, that's a fortune you have locked away".

Pierre looked over at Jeff for a long moment without speaking, then in a calm voice, he spoke slowly. "I'm not sure why I'm showing you either, Jeff, but for some reason it just seemed you ought to know."

Jeff hadn't expected an answer like that to his half-joking comment. Looking at Pierre in the dim light at the back of the *cave*, he realized for the first time that this remarkable man was treating him as though he were a long lost son.

After a final inspection, the two closed and locked the hidden room and made their way back to the entrance, each lost in thought. Pierre turned off the lights and together they closed and secured the big doors. Walking across the concrete apron, they stopped in front of a small barn-like structure that partially screened the *cave*.

"This building we still call 'The Winery'. Except for the fermentation tanks, we don't use it much anymore except for harvest celebrations and a rare party for friends." The tour finished, Pierre turned and a smile slowly spread over his face. "Now young man, what I want to see are some blisters on those lily white hands of yours. It's time for you to find José and Rivera up in the vineyard and get to work." With that, Pierre headed back to the house while Jeff walked rapidly up towards the vineyard.

When Jeff arrived, he found José hard at work tightening trellis wires with a strainer and heavy iron bar. It was the same two-wire system that he remembered up in Sonoma County. Jeff looked at the solid steel posts angled in at the end of each row. Late in the growing season, those trellises would have to support the full weight of tons of grapes in any wind or weather. Each row gently followed the hillside contours. The spacing looked to be about 10 feet between rows, each individual vine some 9 feet apart - plenty of room for each long, deep, root system to search out what little moisture lay hidden in the hillside's rocky, arid soil. He nodded in approval at the Dutch Clover growing between the rows. That extra nitrogen would strengthen the vines and enrich the fruit. With the gentle slope and this gravely, chalky, soil the drainage was perfect. Looking at the leaf covered branches, he knew the heavy work of the vineyard was about to begin. It would soon be time for the backbreaking effort of thinning the small dark clusters just now beginning to form and to trim the leafy canopy to let in the sun.

"José," he called, "How do you and your brother manage all this? You can't take care of this whole vineyard by yourselves."

"Almost! "replied José, walking over. "When the time for thinning and the harvest arrives, my brother and I call in some of our friends who work over in the vineyards of the Arroyo Seco. Rivera's around the hill today working in the cabernet. Which reminds me," he said as he bent over with a smile, "I brought an extra strainer wrench just for you. How about some help tightening these trellis wires?"

Two hours later they heard the big bell ring for lunch. Jeff had thought he was in pretty good shape but he was soaked with sweat and his shoulders ached. After picking up Rivera, the three men rode back in the ATV, stopping at the barn to wash up. Stripping off his shirt, Jeff put his head under the spigot and let the cold water run through his hair.

"Holy Jesus," exclaimed José as the big Mexican looked with astonishment at the scars on Jeff's back. "You back into a chain saw?"

"You should see my ass and legs." laughed Jeff. "A roadside bomb, an I.E.D., over in Afghanistan did that dirty work. I was luckier than a lot of guys … I'm alive and even better, I still have my *huevos*".

"You are one lucky gringo," said José with a shake of his head, "But cover up! Maria would faint if she saw those scars!" Pulling on their now almost dry shirts, the men headed over to the house.

During their meal, Jeff, José, Rivera and Pierre discussed the vineyard and what needed to be done before harvest. The weather was always the great unknown. From what they could learn from long-range forecasters, it looked like this would be a good year. Not too hot this summer and good weather into the fall, or so they hoped.

After they had all eaten, Pierre needed time in his office, and the three others prepared to return to the vines. "Amigo," said José, "Why don't you finish the trellis work you started this morning. You should be able to get that done today before we go over with Rivera to work on the Cab. I'm gonna see if I can unclog the fuel line on that old tractor of ours."

After Jeff had left, Pierre turned to José. "Well, old friend, what do you think? Was that young man any help? Does he know what he's doing?"

"He's one tough *hombre*! Pierre, have you seen his back? Now I see why he has that small limp. He's a very lucky man. As for the vineyard, he understands the grapes. He listens and works hard. He's not afraid to get his hands dirty … I like him." Taking a last sip of water, José raised his eyebrows in question. "But Pierre, what is a doctor doing working like a poor *peón* in a vineyard?"

"I don't know all the story, José, maybe it's Afghanistan and those terrible wounds. Perhaps it's a broken heart. Maybe it's both. One day we may find out but that troubled young man needs this ranch, that I know. He needs to work in the soil to sweat out his demons. I think we can help him and he can surely help us!"

∼⬦∼

As José had suggested, Jeff took the ATV and driving back up the road he found his mind wandering. He began to think of what he'd heard of Sam and her son, Peter. He was curious to meet this woman who was Pierre's daughter. He was also somewhat apprehensive.

Arriving at the vineyard, he jerked himself back to reality. Taking off his shirt, he pulled on heavy gloves softened by long use, picked up the heavy steel bar and began to work up a sweat. Two hours later, he stopped for a break. Walking back to the ATV with its big orange, insulated, water jug, he pulled off his gloves and filled a cup with the still cool, refreshing water. While he drank, he looked

up at the long rows of vines. He was tired but felt better than he had for months. The sweat, the sunshine, and
the vines seemed to renew his spirits. Memories flooded
back to his teenage years. Of working in the vineyards after
school and during vacations, of listening to his father talk
about the soil, the importance of drainage and always the
grapes. Day after day, he had absorbed the lore of vineyards and the making of wine. He had loved working with
the grapes then and he realized how much he longed for it
now. Leaning on the ATV, he thought also of medicine, his
other love. One way or another he would have to combine
the two, how was another matter. "I'll give Pierre and the
vineyard a few months and maybe I can come up with some
plan." Straightening up, he looked at his watch. "Enough
day dreaming … back to work!"

Later, as the sun dropped over the ridges and the shadows
crept down the slopes, he collected his tools, loaded up the
ATV and headed back to the barn. There was just time for a
shower before dinner. Maybe tomorrow he'd try a dip in that
pool by the rock.

The weeks passed quickly, one day following another. Hard
work, pleasant conversations each evening and to bed early
and long made the time fly. As Pierre and Jeff got to know
each other, a deepening respect and interest developed between the two. Evenings, sitting around the table or out

under the stars, they found how similar were their interests, their likes and dislikes Talking those star-lit nights, they were like two old friends, or perhaps a father and son getting to know each other after a long absence.

José reminded Jeff of the ranch foremen he remembered from his father's vineyard. Strong, proud, hard working men with little formal education but with a vast store of knowledge learned not from books but from the grapes and the land. Maria's sunny smile and gentle kiss greeted Jeff each morning. Much to everyone's amusement, she fussed and worried about him morning, noon and night.

For Jeff, it was a time of re-awakening. Stripped to the waist laboring in the sun, his skin turned from a gray pallor to a healthy brown; his muscles strengthened as he worked among the vines and the callouses on his hands became thick and tough. The greatest change was in his mind. For the first time in many months he found himself enjoying each day and looking forward to the next. He felt alive again.

Many afternoons were spent in the winery with Pierre. It was blending time and Pierre was intent on producing a wine as good as any he'd tasted in France. Jeff thought he knew lot about making wine but working with this old Frenchman made him realize how little he really knew. The hours spent in the *cave* were a revelation about the intricacies and frustrations of making a truly great wine. More than once he asked Pierre why he wasn't selling this superb wine and the answer was always the same. The Pierre Vaillard Annetta Cuvée was his tribute to the love of his life. It would never be for sale. He personally selected the grapes. He alone made the blend. Despite the best efforts of his distributor and Carmen, the Annetta Cuvée was only for family and a very few dear friends. Fifty cases, just two barrels each year. No more, no less. Day after day, Jeff listened and absorbed the vast knowledge stored in the older man's mind. It was the opportunity of a lifetime, almost an obligation to this remarkable man who was sharing his knowledge and opening his heart to a total stranger.

Watching Pierre, Jeff worried about the future of the ranch. The Frenchman was getting older and the task of running a vineyard was daunting at best, even for a much younger man. He was aware of subtle changes in Pierre's health since he had arrived at the ranch. Jeff felt a growing need to help but was it any of his business? And how did this professor-daughter fit into the picture? Was she even interested in the future of the ranch? That Pierre's life work might be lost was unthinkable. Without understanding how or why, he knew he was being drawn into the life of this family. The people, the grapes, the history of this remarkable place all attracted him like a magnet.

19

SURE ENOUGH, THREE weeks later on a Saturday afternoon, they heard from the unwelcome attorney. Yes, he understood the ranch was not for sale but he would be there on Wednesday with an offer you could not refuse. Pierre could feel the aggression and resolve in that suave voice. He'd hung up on the man.

As the four of them sat around the dinner table that evening, they talked about this unknown outfit and what was behind their aggressive behavior. Pierre thought it was the water. "No development could even begin without an ample water supply. This place is the only reliable source for miles around."

Jeff was sure it was the vineyard and the winery. "Getting your hands on a developed and producing vineyard in the best growing region of the central coast isn't easy … and it would cost a bundle if you could find one." He looked around. "But why this place?"

"By the way" Maria called to the men from the kitchen, "Sam called, she and Pete are coming down tonight for a week or two, they should be here soon. As for this crazy business with the vineyard, why don't you call Carmen and see if she knows anything about this Asia outfit?"

Pierre laughed out loud. "First good idea of the evening. Carmen was due home from France yesterday, let's try her right now." Pulling over the phone, he punched in the numbers. In moments Carmen came on the line.

"Hello, Pierre. What a surprise, I was just going to call you. I had a wonderful trip and I brought you some very nice bottles of wine, but you'll never guess what else I have to tell you."

"Wonderful," responded Pierre, "we want to hear all about the trip, but before you tell us, we've got an urgent question for you." Quickly he pushed a button on the phone and moved it into the center of the table. "Carmen, we're all here and I've put you on the speakerphone. Jeff Thomas, that doctor I told you about before you left is also here." As the group chimed in with greetings from around the table, Pierre continued. "We've got an interesting problem and maybe you can help us." With that, Pierre quickly summarized the events of the past month. "Do you know anything about this Asia-American Development Company?"

"Hold on, all of you. Before I answer your question, I have something to tell you first. Maybe they're connected. On the night before I left for France, we had a very exclusive private tasting at the restaurant for some major wine buyers for the Asian market. Just twelve wines – eleven of the finest and most expensive California Bordeaux-style reds. One had a price tag of $1,000 a bottle, you know which. As you'll remember, we always insert one mystery wine. Because I'm so impressed with what you're doing on the ranch and had a bottle saved from Christmas, I slipped in your *2006 Annetta Cuvée*, all identification removed of course. Can you believe it? You won the tasting! They all insisted on knowing who made it and where was the winery? I just smiled and said it was from a small private California vineyard. No names or places. I was as surprised as you probably are—I hope you're not too upset. Pierre, I know I should have asked your permission but I had to leave at dawn the next morning and it was just a spur of the moment thing. I planned to call you the moment I got back into town to congratulate all of you." She paused a moment, then continued, "But there was one other interesting thing about that evening. Sam's ex-husband was there with a wine hot- shot from Hong Kong. Of course he knew me; I wonder if he might have put two and two together?"

There was a momentary silence around the kitchen table, then everyone started talking at once.

"George!"

"I wonder if ….?"

"What did he say?"

"Hold on everybody," said Pierre, raising his hand. "So George was there, Carmen? Did he act suspicious? Did he mention the vineyard?"

"No, we hardly had time to speak, but he did seem very intrigued by the wine … gave me his card and said to please call him as soon as I got back."

"This has got to be more than just a coincidence." Said Jeff. "If this guy is as smart as you all …"

"You bet he's smart. He knows wine and he certainly knows where Carmen came from." exclaimed Pierre.

"The Asian market is red hot for big name, very expensive wines. If he had that great wine of yours," responded Carmen, "there are all kinds of tricks he could play. He could foist it off as a Petrus or a Lafitte. All it would need is a counterfeit label. The average Chinese millionaire would never know the difference and if he did find out he'd never admit it – loosing face is the ultimate humiliation."

"That just might be the answer to this whole crazy business," said Pierre. "Carmen, why don't you sniff around a little and see if you can find a connection for George and Asia-American. Their man's coming down in a few days to push again for me to sell – more of a threat than a request. This gets more interesting every day!"

The conversation drifted off into talk of Carmen's trip, Maria wanting to know all the places she'd been and what she had worn…woman talk. Pierre had to hear about his gift of wine. They wound up the conversation with a promise that Carmen would do some quick sleuthing and get back to them as soon as possible.

"Well now, isn't that an interesting turn of events!" said Pierre after he'd hung up. "If George is involved we will have to be very, very careful. He's a dangerous man and has some very unsavory friends."

"When did you say this attorney was going to show up?" asked Jeff.

Before Pierre could respond, the kitchen door flew open and in ran a small boy followed by a very attractive young woman carrying a small duffle bag that she promptly dropped. Running across the room, the boy leaped joyously into Pierre's arms. "Grandpa!" he cried as he flung his arms around the old man. Smiling, the woman walked to Pierre and planted a tender kiss on the top of his head, blew another to José and gave a huge hug to Maria who was standing arms extended. "Sam," cried Maria, "You didn't call!"

"I didn't have time, Maria, I couldn't wait to get here, hope there's something left around here to eat – we're starved!" But Maria, anticipating her request, had already turned back to the stove. Having greeted the family, Sam turned to Jeff who was looking at her transfixed. "No staring, it's not polite" she smiled, "You must be Jeff."

"Sorry! Please excuse my dumb look, but you look astonishingly like someone I once knew." Still staring, he tried to hide his embarrassment. "You must be Sam and I suspect this young man is Pete." He forced himself to look down at the boy now wrestling joyfully with Bruno.

She laughed, "Yes, I'm Sam, and that's my boy Peter." Maria, busy at the stove, looked with approval at the two standing smiling at each other. "Yes!" she thought as she dished up a platter of the evening's left-over casserole.

Pierre broke the spell. "Pull up a chair, Sam. Tell us how you are and what's happening in your life—but before you start, there is something important I have to ask, have you heard anything recently from that ex-husband of yours?"

"Strange you should ask. Yes, George called last week, angry as ever. He had a lot of questions about you and the winery. I listened for a minute and then hung up on him. Why?"

"Well now, isn't that interesting," said Pierre. "First Carmen and now Sam. I think it's all coming together."

While they were speaking, Maria placed a platter of warmed over dinner on the table. Bringing a glass of milk for Peter, she served up a plate for each while Jeff poured wine for Sam.

"What are you talking about? What about Carmen?" asked Sam between bites.

"While you eat your dinner we'll tell you an interesting story", said Pierre and with that he scratched a match under the table, lit up his pipe, and launched into his tale.

It didn't take long to re-tell the happenings of the past few weeks "What a strange business" said Sam. "I'll bet George really is behind all this ... but right now Pete and I are pooped." She said with an expansive yawn. "It's been a long day and I'm falling asleep, is the cabin still mine? I can get our suitcases in the morning."

"Your room is always ready," said Maria. "I put fresh flowers in the room this afternoon hoping you'd come. Now you and Pete get off to bed; Jeff can carry your duffle." Getting up, Sam hugged her father again and gave José and Maria a kiss. Jeff slung the duffle's strap over his shoulder and carefully picked up the now sleeping boy. With Sam leading the way, the three went out into the evening darkness lit only by a canopy of bright stars and an iridescent half moon. As they walked along, Sam said quietly, "Coming home to this ranch is like a return to paradise. I always feel safe here ... feel unconditionally loved. I don't think there's another place like it in the world."

Arriving at the cabin, Jeff opened the door and turned on the light. He carried the sleeping boy to one of the twin beds and gently laid him down. Leaning over, he whispered, "Sweet dreams, Peter, sleep well." He then unslung their bag and placed it on the table before turning back to Sam. Unable to help himself, he looked intently at this woman now bending over her son. "Good night Sam, it's been nice meeting you after hearing all Maria's rave reviews ...see you in the morning." She smiled a thank you as he closed the door.

Walking slowly over to the trailer, Jeff stopped and looked back. "Dear God, it seems impossible. From that first moment when she walked in I could have sworn it was ...." His voice trailed off, his eyes in a far off, distant place.

20

I N THE MORNING, Jeff was in the kitchen at five thirty having coffee with Maria and José and planning the morning's work. Jeff would finish the trellising on the upper slope before joining José in the Cabernet. It looked like another hot day and they wanted to start while there was still some cool air in the vines. Maria, a big smile on her face, served their breakfast, humming a tune to herself.

"Why're you grinning like a Cheshire cat, Maria?" asked Jeff.

'What's a Cheshire cat?" She laughed as she pushed them out the door. "I'm smiling," she called, "because I'm happy and it's going to be a beautiful day. Now you mind your own business and go to work!"

The morning moved by quickly. The sun rose over the Santa Lucia's and the day warmed. Working on opposite sides of each row, the two men went through the block of grapes. The gnarled vines, now almost thirty years old, and the dry rocky soil gave off a faint, earthy scent, the perfume of a vineyard. Tiny clusters of grapes were beginning to form. It would soon be time to start the thinning process.

"What about this ex-husband of Sam's?" said Jeff across the vines. "Why are you all so worried about this guy?

"It's a funny story, well, maybe not so damn funny. George is a good-looking man ... real smart. Smooth would be a good word." He stopped for a moment to tie back an errant branch. "He was a hot young investment guy in San Francisco. He really went after Sam and she fell for it. They got married right here on the ranch."

The tall Mexican looked over at Jeff. "He and Sam used to come down a lot. George tried real hard to get his hands on the ranch. Really turned on the charm. It was almost like he wanted the ranch more than he wanted Sam."

"How did that go over with Pierre?" asked Jeff.

"Pierre didn't fall for it and it really upset Sam. You couldn't trust anything George said. It seemed he was always angry, always dissatisfied. It wasn't much later we learned he was cheating on Sam."

The two men worked silently for a few minutes, then José picked up his story.

"The next year Sam was pregnant and little Peter was born. We hoped that now things would be different. I think he really loves that boy but their marriage just got worse. He'd yell at her all the time, then he'd get drunk and take off ... hardly spoke to Sam. It broke our hearts".

Pausing at the end of the long row, José looked back along the vines. "When Peter was almost four, she threw in the towel ... filed for divorce. That was a terrible time for Sam, for all of us. I don't think she's recovered yet".

"Do you think he could possibly be behind this Asia-American business?"

José stood thinking for a minute.. "It sure wouldn't surprise me - they say there are a lot of really rich *hombres* in China and we know he's been doing deals over there. He's tricky and goes hard after what he want, look what happened to Sam. Yeah, if there was big enough money, it sounds like his sort of thing."

When the ranch bell rang at noon, the two men drove back, washed up and headed for the kitchen. Peter, racing around with Bruno on the small patch of lawn, stopped when he saw them walking over from the barn. Running up to Jeff, he blurted out, "Are you really a doctor?"

"Peter! "cried Sam from the kitchen door. "That's no way to talk to Dr. Jeff. I told you, he's on vacation. Now go wash your hands and get ready for lunch."

"He's right, Sam," laughed Jeff. "I don't look much like a doctor and right now I sure don't feel like one."

Sitting down at the lunch table together, Peter plunked himself between Sam and Jeff and proceeded to pepper Jeff with questions. "What kinda doctor are you? Do you really sew people up? Where do you live?" Are you married? Do you have kids?"

Sam blushed. "Peter, stop that right now! Eat your lunch. No more questions."

"That's O.K., I don't blame him, I'd be curious too about some new guy showing up at his grandpa's ranch." Putting his arm around the boy, he whispered in a loud conspiratorial voice so Sam could hear, "After lunch lets take a walk around the lake and I'll tell you all about me and you can tell me all about you. O.K.? "

"Yes! Let's go right now. Can Bruno come too?"

"Of course Bruno can come, wouldn't go without him, but not untill after your plate's clean and we get your Mom's permission."

Finishing, everyone helped Maria clean off the table, then Pierre and José took off for town to pick up a missing part for the tractor. Sam stayed with Maria to help in the kitchen and Jeff and Pete started off on their walk. Looking out the window at the retreating figures, Sam was joined by Maria.

"What's he really like, Maria?"

"Jeff's only been here a few weeks, Sam, but he's become almost part of the family. He doesn't talk much about himself. We know he was badly wounded in Afghanistan and his fiancé was killed but he never mentions it. We heard from Doc Demitross that they have a lot of respect for him at the hospital. A fine doctor, he told us. He didn't know why he'd just walked away. Your Dad loves talking with him … about the ranch, the winery, even about growing up in France – things we've never heard before. It's almost like he's talking to a son. We've never seen Pierre act like this before."

Maria turned back to the kitchen. "He's been working hard with José. It's not easy to impress my husband, but he says Jeff knows almost as much as he does about the grapes and works just as hard. He likes him." Looking out the window at the retreating figures, she spoke quietly. "Me? I think he's the best thing that's happened on this ranch in a long time."

"It's funny, Maria, Pete couldn't wait to come to lunch today. He wanted to sit by Jeff … hoped he'd play with him this afternoon. It makes me uncomfortable—I wish I knew more about him."

"Well," smiled Maria, watching the young woman looking out the window at the man and boy talking and walking along throwing sticks in the lake. "There's no time like the present. You can still catch up with them."

And so she did.

—⁂—

Sam found Pete and Jeff sitting on a large boulder at the edge of the lake busy skipping pebbles over the quiet water. Approaching quietly, Sam watched as Jeff began to show Pete how to make a whistle from a blade of grass. Reaching over, he picked out a flat, firm, blade and placing it tightly between his thumbs, pursed his lips and blew a piercing blast.

"Let me try!" cried Pete finding his own blade of grass. Jeff put both arms around the boy holding his small thumbs tight together and said, "Blow hard!" Pete took a deep breath, puckered up his lips and blew. It worked, perhaps not very loud, but a definite whistle.

"Mom!" cried the boy, spotting his mother. "Look what Dr. Jeff showed me," and he gave another bigger, harder puff. This time the shrill whistle was loud and clear.

Sam took a seat beside them on the rock watching her happy child intent on his grass whistle and this gentle man holding her son. Pete seemed happier than he'd been for a long time. It was catching. As she leaned back, she felt the tension of the recent months drain from her body. Looking up at puffy clouds drifting across an azure sky, feeling the warmth of the afternoon sun, she felt her life awakening once again. Was it the magic of the ranch or was it the presence of this stranger? Sitting forward again, she was aware of Jeff's penetrating eyes staring intently into her face. Laughing, she returned his gaze, "What's the matter, doctor? Never seen a contented woman before?" But the spell was broken.

"I'm sorry Sam … I was in another world." As he spoke his half-smile faded. It was as though a dark veil had dropped between them. Confused, she could only mumble in reply and soon got to her feet, taking Peter's hand as the three started walking back towards the house. The only sound was the crunching of shoes on the damp ground and the faint buzz of bees in the last of the summer flowers. In the distance, Maria occasionally looked up from her work to watch the three walking in silence. "Why are they walking so far apart?" she wondered aloud.

Returning to the kitchen, Peter had a glass of milk and lay down on his grandfather's bed for a nap. Sam sat quietly at the big table shelling peas for dinner. Maria asked no questions, and Sam volunteered no explanation for the change now so evident between these two young adults.

The afternoon passed swiftly. The sun was hot. Jeff, stripped to the waist, was dripping sweat as he slowly made his way down the rows. It was hard work but didn't require much conscious thought. As he twisted, tied, and trimmed the young shoots, he found his mind wandering over the past few years. With each passing day, a weight seemed to lift from his shoulders but with the arrival of Sam and Pete there was a new dimension he didn't quite understand. He was aware of his rudeness at the lake. He knew it wasn't Sam's fault she bore such a striking resemblance to Caroline. "Jesus, Jeffery Thomas," He muttered. "It's been almost three years. That's past history."

As the sun dropped over the ridge tops, Jeff collected his tools and headed home. As had become a habit, he stopped first at the spring with its cold, restoring pool. A quick dip finished each day's work. Back at his trailer, he took a real shower with plenty of soap before putting on a clean shirt and jeans to be ready for dinner.

As he dressed, his thoughts returned to Sam. He remembered as yesterday the pain and sadness he'd known when Caroline had been taken from him. He sensed the same feeling of loss in Sam. "What an insensitive bastard!" he said pulling on his boots. To complicate matters, this was Pierre's daughter.

The days went by rapidly. Life at the vineyard was busy and uneventful. Pierre had gone off to San Francisco on business and hoped to learn more about Asia-America. Some mornings Jeff took Peter for a ride on his horse before joining José in the vineyard. Pete would sit in front of Jeff's waist, wedged in by the horn of the saddle while holding tight to the reins. They would walk the horse up to the winery and then wander around the lake. When they reached the road they would gallop back to the barn. Sometimes after lunch there was time for a walk, often joined by Sam. Evenings were relaxed, talking around the big table while Peter fell asleep on the floor, head cradled in Bruno's soft flank. Later, Jeff would carry the sleeping boy up to the little cabin. As the nights went by it became harder to say good night and turn back to his dark trailer. He found himself wanting to stay, to sit quietly and talk

When Pierre returned from San Francisco he was full of news. Finishing his business, he had spent two days with Carmen talking about wine, about George and also about Asia-America Development Company. He had traced down Asia-America, found its address and as they had guessed, learned that George Segovia was very much involved. Pierre had tried to laugh it off but now he knew this was a real threat to the ranch. Jeff's guess had probably been right, almost certainly they were after the winery and its vineyard. He had also learned that the company was exporting wine to

China—not cheap brands for the mass market but the most expensive and sought-after wines of France and California.

"I asked Carmen why would they want our unknown wine?" Pierre began. "We're not a big name; in fact we're not a name at all!" He paused for a moment to re-light his pipe. "Carmen had been shocked when George walked into the tasting event that evening escorting one of Hong Kong's biggest dealers. Our problem seems to be that my Annetta's Cuveé was as good as the best, maybe better - or so Carmen says."

"Did he get in touch with Carmen after she got back from her trip?" asked José.

"You bet! When she wouldn't return his calls, he walked into the restaurant just at opening time, demanding to speak to her."

"Sounds like George," said Sam, "Poor Carmen!"

"She told him she was very busy; to please leave. He got angry and belligerent—any vestige of charm vanished. Her boss had to threaten to call the police before he would leave."

Jeff had been listening quietly, but now he spoke up. "If George had control of your wine from vine to bottle, he'd have a lot of options, legal or otherwise. Pierre, you need to know a lot more about what is going on. Somebody, maybe your lawyer, needs to talk to this guy and find out exactly what he wants and why. You've talked to Carmen but I think there's a lot more to this than just the vineyard and wine. You need much more intelligence – and soon."

Pierre looked over at Jeff and took a long pull on his pipe. "Maybe you're right. I'll get Tom DeBeers to come over. Let's see what he thinks we should do next."

Pausing, he looked at his daughter sitting listening across the table. "Sam, do you think you and Peter should stay while George is nosing around? Is it safe?""

"You bet we're staying." retorted Sam. "Father, I'll never run away from that man again."

"I hope it's not that serious. George may get very angry but in spite of the bitterness between you two, I know he loves Peter. He would never do anything to harm that boy."

"You may be right about Pete, but past that he will do anything to get his way." Sam replied quietly. "If he decides he wants the vineyard, he'll use any tactic, including violence, to get what he wants. I know that man from bitter experience."

Maria, holding Jose's hand tightly, spoke up. "Sam, Pierre is right. You should take Peter and leave. You could stay with Carmen in the City. She's got plenty of room. It's just not worth taking a chance."

"No, I will not let that man drive me away from my family. If you are all so worried, Pete and I can move into the guest room here with Dad".

After further discussion, it was agreed that Sam and Pete should move down to the house. The *cave* seemed safe. Those massive doors would take dynamite to blast open. As for the small winery and barns, they'd just have to hope for the best.

That night in his trailer Jeff cleaned and oiled his father's old rifle. "So much for a nice relaxing interlude working in a vineyard." said Jeff to the dog stretched out on his bed, "This just might get exciting. Bruno, if this guy wants to get rough, you and I can also play that game."

21

It was late the next afternoon when they gathered again at Pierre's home. Seated around the big pine table were Sam, José, a space for Maria now busy passing coffee and tea, then Pierre, Jeff and finally, attorney Tom DeBeers. Pierre was occupied extracting a large kitchen match from the blue box in the center of the table. With a swift flick of the wrist, he ignited the match on the side of the box and soon pungent smoke from the well-used pipe drifted toward the ceiling. Looking at the expectant faces around the table, he called the meeting to order.

"Alright, everybody, let's get down to business. Jeff is right; we need to know what we're up against before we have any more visits from these people. As you all know, I asked my friend here to do some research." He gestured to the lawyer. "Tom, the floor is yours."

Tom DeBeers was a gray-haired, cheerful and undoubted permanent bachelor. Tom had retired 15 years ago from a very successful law practice in San Jose. Coming to Carmel to escape the rat race of Silicon Valley, he'd opened a small office in the Village and pretended to work. He came to work late, enjoyed a long lunch and left well before five. He'd never been happier, never regretted his move. Enjoying food, wine and good conversation, Tom had been drawn to Pierre and the two men had become fast friends. In addition to providing occasional legal advise, Tom often drove up to the ranch for Maria's wonderful cooking and to sit on the porch Sunday afternoons with a glass of wine over a long, intense game of chess. Tom was almost one of the family.

Looking seriously at Pierre, the lawyer pulled a folder from his well-worn briefcase. "After your first call I looked into this crazy situation. First, as Pierre has already learned, Asia-American Development Company is for real. They have offices in San Francisco, Hong Kong, and Mexico City. San Francisco is their headquarters. Although most of their business is in China, there is a strong link to Mexico that isn't quite so clear. There are also rumors of a connection to Afghanistan and drugs. The official story is they're exporting high-priced wine to Hong Kong. Whatever they're doing, it's a very lucrative business." Tom stopped, looking directly at Pierre and Sam. "There is one other very interesting bit of information. The head honcho is an old friend of yours — George Segovia."

"I knew we were right." exclaimed Pierre.

Watching the four anxious faces looking at the attorney, Jeff was aware of the tension permeating the room.

"Yes, George." smiled DeBeers taking a sip of his coffee. "Thought you'd all find that interesting, but I gather you've already figured that out."

"George is still after the ranch," Pierre declared.

"You're probably right again." smiled DeBeers, "George does put a whole new perspective on the problem. It probably explains the missing documents from the County Recorder's archives, the pressure tactics you've all been feeling, even the Asian thug Maria told us about." He picked up the letter Pierre had received and admired the expensive engraved piece of stationary. "That is a very fancy address in the City." He paused for a moment and looked at his host. "Putting this all together, Pierre, I agree, it's time somebody sits down and talks directly to George."

"Oh, I know what he's after," replied Pierre. "His obsession with this land never stops. But why now and why this round-about way of getting to me? "

Tom raised his hand to quiet the buzz now bouncing around the table. "The problem we have is that all of you except Jeff and perhaps me, have a very bitter history with George ending with Sam's divorce and the battle over Peter's custody. I don't see how any of you can effectively meet with this angry, hostile, man. I could probably go. I was only peripherally involved in that mess, but I'd rather not go alone. I thought I might recruit one of my old partners in San Jose …."

"Pierre," interrupted Jeff who had been listening quietly and watching the nervous faces around him. "I don't know this man and he doesn't know me. It makes sense for Tom to go; after all, he's your attorney. I could go as your proxy. Also, I keep picking up interesting vibrations that I don't quite understand. I'd very much like to meet this George Segovia."

The attorney looked thoughtfully at the young doctor. "I'm sure George will have been told by his watchers of your living here. But as a new face on the ranch, he may even want to meet you. What do you think, Pierre?"

Pierre took a long draw on his pipe and slowly exhaled as he considered the suggestion. "Yes, that could just be the solution. Jeff, you know a good deal about this ranch by now and Tom certainly knows about the past legal issues." The old Frenchman carefully put down his pipe. "I think that just might work."

Sam had been carefully following this exchange between her father, the attorney, and Jeff. Why would this stranger be so anxious to meet George, she wondered? Did he know something he wasn't revealing? Looking at the pleased smile on her father's face as he looked at Jeff made her feel even more ill at ease. As Maria had said, this young man and her Dad were acting almost like father and son. Looking from one to the other she wasn't sure what to think. "Should I be concerned … or am I just being silly? Either way, I need to know a lot more about this Dr. Jeffrey Thomas … and soon."

Jeff and Tom made good time to the City. Driving from the quiet roads and blue skies of Carmel Valley into the traffic, smog, and confusion of the Bay Area was a jarring experience.

Jeff was acutely aware of the dramatic change from the peace and tranquility of the ranch to the constant din of packed humanity, the blaring of horns and the all-pervasive stench of exhaust.

It hadn't been hard to find the Transamerica Pyramid, a San Francisco icon for over 40 years. With an appointment at 11:00 AM, the two arrived in the vast underground parking garage with time to spare.

"Pretty classy building." observed Jeff, attired in his one and only Navy blue blazer and gray slacks and the tie he'd had to borrow from Pierre. Silently they were whisked to the forty-first floor.

"An office in the Pyramid must come at a pretty fancy price," wheezed Jeff as he waited for his stomach to catch up after the heart-stopping ascent.

"You're so right," smiled DeBeers. "One of my old law school classmates has an office here and it costs him a small fortune each year."

Moving down the hall, the two men soon located an impressive appearing door with the name Asia-American Development Company meticulously stenciled in gold letters. Entering, they found themselves in a tastefully appointed waiting area, one entire wall of which consisted of a large picture window. "Now that is a million dollar view!" Jeff exclaimed, stopping to gaze. It was a perfect, cloudless, day and in the distance stood the Golden Gate Bridge with the Pacific stretching to the horizon. Nearer, the water glistened in the late morning sun. Sausalito and Angel Island were clearly visible beyond Alcatraz and a multitude of white sails danced on the blue surface of the bay.

Spaced around the room were a half-dozen comfortable chairs, each placed with spectacular views across the water. Three low tables stood nearby, each crowned with a lovely floral arrangement. Soft music played quietly through hidden speakers and a hint of lilacs perfumed the air. Walking in on the thick cushioned carpet, they were greeted by a beautiful Eurasian woman who stood and gave a small bow in greeting.

"Mr. DeBeers and Dr. Thomas?" Perfectly sculpted eyebrows were raised in question as she spoke in a low, well-modulated voice. "Won't you be seated? Mr. Segovia will be with you in just a few moments."

After a suitable time admiring the employment taste of Mr. Segovia, Jeff's mind turned to this man who had made life hell for Sam and who seemed such a nemesis to the whole family. As they sat waiting, a tall Asian man came into the reception area. With a black turtleneck shirt, black blazer and slacks, his lean, muscular frame seemed wound like a tight spring. His eyes, devoid of all expression, took in the room with a quick glance, then briefly but carefully inspected the two visitors. Turning to the receptionist, he murmured an inaudible question. The young woman, busy at her computer, turned slightly and gave a faint nod in their direction. Without another glance, the man sat in the empty seat just to the right of an impressive walnut door where burnished brass lettering announced: "George Segovia, President".

Looking at the erect, impassive Asian staring into space, Jeff was aware of the faint outline of a holstered gun tucked under the left arm of his jacket. "A bodyguard, no less." Jeff mused to himself. "Interesting!"

After a few minutes of silence broken only by soft music and the muted sound of typing, the imposing door at the end of the room swung silently open and Jorge Segovia stepped out. As Jeff stood, he quickly assessed the man standing before him. About his own height and weight, he seemed of similar age. There was a hint of bronze in his handsome face, perhaps from his Spanish-American heritage. His jet-black hair had been styled by a professional; his attire was straight from Brooks Brothers. On his face was a slight smile but the eyes were glacial cold. An aura of suppressed danger seemed to follow him into the room.

"Mr. DeBeers, we meet again," Segovia said with a tight smile, "and this must be the Dr. Thomas that my Attorney mentioned." As he spoke, his dark eyes locked on Jeff. They shook hands with a mutually crushing grip.

"Nice to meet you, Dr. Thomas. You'll have to tell me how you've come to be living on Pierre's ranch. That old man is pretty choosy about who he invites," he spoke with a wry smile. "I know from bitter experience!" Turning, he motioned to the adjoining room. "Shall we step into my office?" As they moved into the room, the phone softly rang.

"Excuse me for a moment, gentleman, I have been waiting some time for this call." As he picked up the phone and turned toward the windows, he motioned to the seats facing the desk and expansive windows. Jeff took the moment to inspect the handsome office. Located in one corner of the building, two of the walls were entirely of glass. A handsome walnut desk stood midway between each, facing into the room. Furniture was sparse, elegant and matched the desk. Against one wall was a credenza on which stood several bottles of what Jeff recognized as very expensive French wines. Above was a framed coat of arms and on the floor a beautiful Persian rug. As he glanced to the right, he saw mounted on the wall a remarkably preserved *Jezebel*, the ancient musket of Arabia and Afghanistan. The long barrel was engraved with intricate designs and the beautifully carved stock was inlaid with mother-of-pearl. It was a classic example of the famous weapon that twice drove the British from Kabul and back through Khyber Pass to the plains of India. Beneath this museum piece was a narrow ebony-black table of a kind found only in Central Asia. On the polished surface stood a single, framed, photograph of a young man. Staring, Jeff's eyes widened in recognition. He had seen that face before, a face he well remembered.

As Segovia replaced the phone and saw Jeff looking at the photograph he spoke softly. "My brother, assassinated three years ago by American Marines in Afghanistan." He stared at the handsome likeness for a long moment then with an obvious effort pulled back to the present.

"May I offer you gentlemen a drink?" he queried, opening a panel in one wall to reveal a small wet bar.

"Not before lunch," laughed Tom, taking a seat, and ever the lawyer, pulled a yellow legal pad from his briefcase. He hoped that keeping this meeting business-like might avoid acrimonious accusations and threats.

"What we hope to accomplish this morning is an understanding of Asia-American Development Company's interests in the Vaillard Ranch and Vineyard. "Looking directly at Segovia, he continued. "To tell you the truth, George, we were all very surprised to know of your involvement in this affair. Perhaps you could tell us a little about Asia-American and why you have selected this ranch to purchase out of all the better known vineyard properties in California."

Segovia sat back at his desk and smiled. "Perhaps, Mr. DeBeers, you and I should cut the bull shit. DeBeers, you know well enough my history with the ranch and the reasons for my interest."

Sitting forward, the smile vanished from his face and any pretense of cordiality disappeared. "The *Sierra de Santa Lucia Rancho* has belonged to my family since it was given to them for service to the Spanish crown in 1795. You Americanos stole that Rancho from my ancestors in the 1850's, divided it up and sold it again. I intend to return this Rancho to my family." Standing, he moved to the wall and from a hidden recess pulled down a large map depicting Monterey County. On the map had been outlined the historic Spanish and Mexican land grants of the early 19th Century. Shaded in red was a large tract in the Santa Lucia Mountains. "There is the Sierra de Santa Lucia Land Grant, and that," Segovia used his pen to circle a significant area of the huge Rancho, "is the portion occupied by your friend Pierre Vaillard, the heart and soul of my ancestral land."

Holding up his hand, Tom calmly responded. "Yes, George, no one disputes the injustices of those days when the United States annexed California. But that was 1851 and this is now. That land has been sold and resold under the laws of this country. George, Pierre Vaillard is the indisputable legal owner of that ranch."

As their reluctant host slowly retracted the map into the ceiling recess, Jeff and the lawyer watched with concern the evidence of his escalating anger. Turning back, he shoved aside the few papers on his desk and sat carefully and deliberately on the edge. "I know the Frenchman bought the ranch. Legal is your choice of words." George paused and looked directly at DeBeers. "I have made Pierre Vaillard an offer to buy his land, a very substantial offer. He has refused even to discuss the matter." With his striking features pulled tight over high cheekbones and his eyes flashing, George stabbed a finger straight at the attorney's face. "DeBeers, you know and I know, that ranch is rightfully mine and I intend to have it back by whatever means necessary." George stood, this time speaking to Jeff. "You tell that old Frenchman and his darling daughter they had better take the money. It is my only offer and if he doesn't …" The angry man's voice trailed off, but they all clearly understood that statement as a declaration of war.

Staring coldly at the two seated men, Segovia abruptly stood, walked to the door and swung it open. As Jeff and

Tom made their exit, George spoke again. "You know my offer, it's my only offer and time is running out. See that Pierre gets my message." With that, the door swung shut.

Walking back into the reception area, the two found the Asian bodyguard now standing unsmiling across the room holding open the handsome office door. "Muchas gracias, Senor." smiled Jeff to the black clad figure as they made their way into the hall.

22

THE FOLLOWING MORNING broke bright and clear. Outside worries were put aside. The routine of vineyard life and the soon approaching harvest were now the daily priority. At the end of the day working with Maria, Sam walked up to the spring with its nurturing pool for a late afternoon swim. With Pierre reading a story to Pete, she was free to enjoy this long cherished end of the day ritual. Skinny-dipping here since childhood, she considered the pool her personal domain. Arriving wrapped only in a colorful beach towel and wearing sandals on her town-tender feet, she became aware of Jeff and Bruno yelling and playing by the water. Although angry at this intrusion of her private space, Sam also knew how strongly attracted she was to this young doctor whom her father seemed to trust so much.

Approaching quietly and standing in the shelter of the great rock, she watched Jeff throw a large stick into the pool as Bruno jumped and dove for his trophy. Sweat stained clothes were thrown carelessly on the grass. The muscles of his strong, wet body glistened in the late afternoon light. "Oh God, it's been so long … "she whispered.

Watching, she found the jagged scars on his back and thighs strangely exciting. When he raised his arm to throw, he turned and his body came fully into view. Mesmerized, her eyes never left his rugged frame. Bruno, spotting Sam standing by the rock, dropped his well-chewed prize, and came bounding up the path in greeting. Picking up the stick to throw, Jeff became aware of Sam's silent presence. Eyes fixed on each other, neither moved nor spoke. With no conscious thought, Sam slowly released her covering towel. The two stood immobile, staring unashamed.

In that moment when time stood still, two loud cracks from a high-powered rifle shattered their trance. Splitting the air, the bullets exploded on the rock above Sam's head. Jeff dove forward, visions of Afghanistan swirling through his mind. Roughly shoving Sam into a crevice of the sheltering rock, he grabbed Bruno with one hand, clamping his muzzle with the other, and shoved the huge dog in front of Sam as protection. "Hold him tight—don't let him bark," he whispered. Putting a finger to his lips for silence, he slowly inched forward, hidden in the shadows. With infinite care, exposing only his eyes, he examined the hillside yard by yard. While he searched, they heard the high pitched, ripping sounds of a dirt bike clawing its way up and over the ridge heading fast towards the road. Waiting another long minute in total silence, he slowly stood, moving cautiously forward. "No!"

whispered Sam, but there were no more shots. Whoever fired had fled the scene.

"Sam, here's my shirt — forget the towel. Take Bruno and run like hell back to the house." He looked once more at the hillside. "Get everybody inside and call the sheriff. I'll check over on the hill… maybe see who that bastard was."

Shakily, Sam slipped on the shirt and clutching Bruno's collar, began to run. "Be careful, Jeff," she called back as she sprinted down the trail.

———∞∞∞———

Three hours later, they were all still sitting around the kitchen table. It was now dark and the deputy had left, taking two spent shell casings, a couple of cigarette butts along with photographs of the scene. Sheriff Rodriquez stayed on drinking coffee with the men while Maria took a still shaken Sam and a now frightened Peter up to her house.

"From that distance and with a scope, that guy coulda put a bullet through your eye." said Rodriquez to Jeff. "Looks like the shooter was just trying to scare you two."

"Jesus!" exclaimed Jeff, "He scared the shit out of us— but what was the point?"

Pierre had been silent as questions flew back and forth across the table. Looking up from his coffee cup he mused aloud, "I wonder if this could be George putting pressure on us in a not very subtle way!"

"Could be," replied the sheriff, "that's one strange story - not like any land deal I've ever heard of in the County. Have you found out anything more from that Asia-American outfit?"

"Quite a bit, actually. I'll fill you in as we walk out to your car. It seems to fit a pattern."

"When did you say that attorney was due back?" asked the sheriff, standing to leave.

"In a couple of days, or at least that was his last message."

"José," said Rodriquez looking across the table, "I know you've got a good camera. Why don't you hang around in the background, see if you can get some telephotos of the car, the license plates and the two guys. Try for some head shots so I can put their pictures on the wire. Never know—might get lucky."

"I'll stick with you, Pierre," said Jeff, "And from what you've all said, we need to keep Sam and little Peter out of sight while they're here. This problem of yours is getting just a little out of hand."

"Damn!" laughed the sheriff as he picked up his Smoky-the-Bear hat. "This is the most excitement we've had up this way since John Tabor shot Gladys Smith's old bull—thought it was a bear. Can't wait to get your next report." Then more seriously he continued, "My guess is we've heard the last of the shooter, but play it safe, boys. Pierre, I know you and José both have rifles, and Jeff, I heard you brought yours up from town … might just keep 'em handy."

After the Sheriff had driven up the dusty road, a shaken Pierre was the first to break the silence. "Gentlemen, this has been one crazy afternoon. I, for one, need a big, stiff drink. Anyone else for a large shot of scotch?"

—∞∞—

Dinner was quiet. Sam and Peter returned with Maria and they all settled for soup and sandwiches; nobody seemed very hungry. Sam and Pete would move to the guest room tonight. They would all feel better with those two secure with Pierre. Jeff and José agreed to split the night keeping a watchful eye on the houses and barns.

At 10 o'clock, Jeff took the first shift. With Bruno, his now usual evening companion, he slowly patrolled the area. First circling the houses, then over by the barns, cabin, and trailer. A couple of times he checked the winery and *cave*. His watch was uneventful; he found no evidence of intrusion or danger. Walking slowly making his rounds, there was plenty of time to look back over the day.

"First Venus steps out from behind a rock and then some nut takes pot shots at us." he told the big dog ambling along beside him. "Boy, do a couple of bullets kill your erotic fantasies in a hurry! Good thing too, Bruno, that could've gotten totally out of control in another couple of minutes."

Sitting on a stump outside the barn, he could watch both houses in the faint light of a three-quarter moon. His mind kept returning to the vision of that beautiful woman standing before him at the pool. Then that picture would fade and Caroline would appear, smiling and holding out her hands.

Resting his rifle on his knees, he looked out into the darkness. "Oh God, Caroline, I miss you so. Why did you have to leave me?"

Watching the moon slowly traverse the star-studded sky, Jeff heard no untoward sounds. There was no movement on the road, no lights, no sign of an intruder. When José arrived at 2:00 AM, Jeff headed back to his empty bed and a few hours of oblivion.

23

FROM THE MOMENT tiny grapes begin to form until the wine is safely in the barrel, there is little time for rest at a vineyard. Everyone on the ranch was up at dawn. Maria was in the kitchen, busy making bread. Pierre, in the winery, was checking on new cooperage that had just arrived. Jeff and José were busy in the vines while Sam was organizing the guest room where she and her son would be spending their nights. Peter was the only exception. He and Bruno were curled up sound asleep in his grandfather's bed. .

"When are they supposed to come?" Sam called to Maria.

"Don't know," came a muffled response from the kitchen. "Sometime this afternoon."

"Well, I'm not leaving this house just because those men are nervous. Nobody's kicking me out." She muttered aloud while hanging up Pete's clothes

Maria, wiping her hands on her apron, walked in laughing at the indignant young woman. "You're just as obstinate as your cranky old father—but this time I'm on your side, I'm staying too."

Like all the meals this past week, today's lunch was simple and quick. Between the work in the vineyards and concerns about Jorge, everyone could feel the rising tension. Pierre paced up and down the kitchen as Maria fussed around her sink. José was the only seemingly relaxed one in the crowd— he was showing his new digital Nikon with its fancy zoom lens to Peter. The boy, putting the camera to his eye, pointed it at Bruno lying splayed out in front of the stove.

"Wow, you can almost see the fleas." he said with astonishment.

"You bet!" whispered José into Pete's ear "And I'm gonna get some great shots for the sheriff. You just watch!"

They didn't have long to wait. Promptly at 1:00 they heard two cars coming down the gravel road to park in front of the house. Jose, camera slung over his neck, left by the back door. Unnoticed, the big Mexican picked up the shotgun he'd hidden behind a bookcase before closing the door. Taking up positions by the front windows and well hidden behind the drapes, the two women prepared to watch and listen.

As Jeff and Pierre walked out into the sunlight, four tough looking Asians climbed out of the second car. Only then did the doors of the front car open and out stepped two men. The first was the lawyer who had been driving. The second was George Segovia. Well dressed in a dark blazer and gray slacks, he stood erect with a fixed smile on his face. The tall, handsome man appeared completely relaxed but for the aura of suppressed anger that seemed to surround him as he walked forward.

"George." said Pierre, conspicuously not extending his hand.

"Hello, Pierre," Jorge replied with a sarcastic smile. "It's been a long time."

"Yes, George, so it has." Turning, he indicated Jeff "I believe you've already met Dr. Thomas."

Jorge slowly turned and his cold, angry eyes bore unblinking into Jeff's face. "Yes, I have met this man before." His bitter voice was as Arctic as his eyes. "I believe he also met my brother in Afghanistan."

Jeff returned the hostile stare but said nothing. If Pierre noticed that brief exchange he made no comment. "So, you really are mixed up in this Asia-American deal! Why am I not surprised? I guess then you're here about the ranch, *my* ranch. George, you know perfectly well it's not for sale."

As though not hearing a word Pierre had said, George, with obvious effort, tore his eyes away from Jeff, and looked straight at the old Frenchman. After a moment he seemed to regain his composure and spoke to Pierre in a low but crystal clear voice. "I know you have refused to sell the ranch but don't be in such a hurry. Pierre. We've had our differences and in spite of your damn daughter, I respect you and what you have done on these hillsides. Because of that history, I am prepared to pay a lot of money for this ranch and vineyard."

When Pierre opened his mouth to speak, George put up his hand. "Before you start objecting, we better talk over your options. Some aren't so good, In fact, old man, I can make a case that you really don't own this vineyard much less the water rights."

"No, George. You may think you can make trouble with my deed but I've had it checked and double-checked. I respect that your ancestors were treated unjustly but the Deed to this property is as good as gold. Now listen carefully, I'm going to say this for the last time: This ranch is not for sale, never has been for sale, and certainly will never be for sale to you. As for your money and those options ... , "he gave a dismissive gesture. "George, I'm going to ask you politely to take your friends and leave before there's any trouble. I've nothing more to say to you or your representative."   With that, Pierre started to turn back toward the house.

Face red and eye dark with anger, the big man quickly stepped forward, thrusting two fingers hard into Pierre's chest, almost knocking the old man over. "You listen to me, you …."

Before George could finish his sentence, Jeff grabbed the offending arm, twisted sharply and sent the tall man crashing into the big Mercedes. In an instant all four of the Asians whipped out their guns. Unfortunately, they were so intent on protecting their boss they failed to see José walk up behind them, his 12 gauge pointed straight at Segovia's head.

"Buenos Dias, George."   José was smiling, but his eyes, cold and unwavering, never left Jorge's face. "I think you heard Señor Vaillard. You got no welcome on this ranch and I've got one real itchy finger." Moving a few steps closer, the big Mexican growled. "If you or any of those thugs mess with Pierre, I'll blow your head off."

Not bothering to look at José, Segovia stood, brushed off his blue jacket, and with a caustic smile, looked at Pierre. "You better put José back in his cage before he gets hurt." Standing by the black Mercedes, he continued, "Take my advice, old man, you better take the money while you can. I don't give a damn if you do or you don't. Either way, this ranch is as good as mine." Looking at the house, his angry voice momentarily softened. "Say hello to Peter, I know he's here, I saw Sam's car parked up by the cabin." Then, bitterness again resonating in his voice, he looked directly at Pierre. "Tell that daughter of yours to get off the ranch now. If anything happens to my child, I'll hunt her down like a dog." After a last venomous look at Jeff, he turned back to the car. The doors slammed, and with wheels spinning in the gravel, the two vehicles headed up the driveway toward the road.

"Whatta son of a bitch!" exclaimed Jeff. "I think that bastard really means what he says."

———

Back in the house, five subdued people considered what had just taken place. One thing was clear, the ranch and the vineyard were in serious jeopardy. Pierre was the first to speak. "Jeff, what was going on out there between you and George? It looked like something new has been added to this strange situation of ours."

"I'm sorry Pierre. I realized when DeBeers and I visited the Asia-American office that I knew about this man. Perhaps I should have told you but I hoped he wouldn't connect the dots ... you've got enough worries without my adding any more. In his office was the picture of a man I recognized from a Marine operation I helped organize. It was his brother, a brother killed in a raid on the Afghan drug lords, their American friends and the Taliban. George and his brother were very involved with the heroin trade. Somehow our friend seems to have learned of my connection to his brother's death."

"Well now, isn't that interesting. You, Sam and I seem to have some common connections with Mr. George Segovia. Heroin ... no wonder that man is loaded with cash."

Sam stared in disbelief at the young man across the table. "What kind of doctor is this man?" She wondered to herself. "He's a good surgeon we know from Dr. Demitross. He knows a lot about wine, he's proven that. Now he tells us he's involved in drugs and Marine raids." She watched fascinated but fearfully as Jeff, her father and José continued their animated discussion of the afternoon.

"I'm calling Paul." Pierre finally declared. "The sheriff has to know what's going on up here. This mess is getting way out of control."

"Dad, all of you are making me very nervous. I don't think any of you realize how dangerous that man can be."

"I'm beginning to understand that, Sam," said Pierre reaching over to gently put his hand on hers. "Furthermore, if you and Peter intend staying on the ranch, there's to be no wandering around by yourself. I think you're safe so long as Peter is with you and you and Maria stick together."

José had been quietly sitting with Maria, but now he spoke up. "I think I'll ask my brother to round up a few of our Mexican friends. They can come over for a week or so, help in the vineyard and patrol the ranch at night. These *hombres* are tough, they know how to use their guns."

"Great idea! We can sure use some reinforcements at night." Jeff turned to Pierre. "I'm worried about the winery. I took a good look at the *cave* this morning. That door could stand up to a bulldozer, but the lock is ancient – any good thief could pick it in minutes. Hell, they could be up there right now for all we know. Pierre, you've got to have some kind of alarm system."

"*Mon Dieu*! I haven't been thinking about the wine! I know that lock's old but I didn't think ... Jeff, you and José get up there and check on the lock and the wine, I've been worrying too much about our family."

Grabbing their guns and a couple of flashlights, the two men took off at a run for the *cave*. One quick look told the story. The massive doors stood slightly ajar, the lock hanging loose from its shackles.

"Shit, we're too late!" exclaimed Jeff quickly pulling open the doors, and flicking on the lights. Moving carefully, the men probed the dark recesses with their flashlights. There was not a sound other than the soft scuffle of their feet on the rough concrete. Nothing seemed to be missing, nothing disturbed or out of place. Jeff walked cautiously behind the three tiers of barrels along one side while José inspected them from the center aisle. They then repeated the process on the opposite wall. No obvious signs of trouble were evident but the open doors made clear someone had entered while they were talking with Jorge down at the house.

"What the hell were they doing in here?" called José in a low voice.

"Damned if I know." responded Jeff from the back of the *cave* where he was peering around the stacked cases of wine. "There's nothing back here."

"They sure as hell didn't break in here just for fun," called José walking back towards the entrance.

Jeff followed, flashlight beam moving from side to side and up and down. "I'll go over this place with a fine tooth comb in the morning, but we've gotta have an alarm up here by tomorrow night. I'll feel a lot better when your brother's friends help stand guard at night."

Later in the afternoon, Jeff and Pierre were ready to start for Salinas to pick up a remote alarm system for the winery and *cave*. As they prepared to leave, they watched Sam and José walking out to the old quarry with two rifles. Pierre smiled. "Sam used to be the best shot on the ranch. An afternoon at the quarry and a few boxes of shells - she'll be the same old dead eye."

"O.K., Pierre, let's get moving, we'll take my truck. It'll take us almost an hour to get over to town." The two men climbed into the old pickup and headed for the gate, the ancient wreck purring like next year's top of the line.

"Amazing!" said Pierre, "It's held together with bailing wire but listen to that engine! Unbelievable!"

Arriving at the gate, they turned left heading up over the low pass. It was quicker to Salinas by cutting over the ridge to Highway 101. In 10 minutes they reached the summit and Pierre motioned Jeff to pull to the side.

"I always stop here for a minute when I go by. On a day like this you can see forever." He let his gaze wander over the dry, oak studded hills and the green fields of the Salinas Valley below. In the far distance, great roiling cumulus clouds dropped rain on the dark jagged peaks of the Pinnacles, an occasional flash lighting up the dark sky as huge thunderheads reached for the invisible stars.

"Jeff, you have no idea how I love this land." He sighed then looking across at Jeff, his voice grew serious. "You've been on the ranch now almost four months. I've watched you sweat in the vineyard, seen your excitement when you are working with the wine. I sense that same longing of mine growing in you." Pierre stopped for a moment, looking at the far horizon. "How I've enjoyed the evenings you and I have spent talking about the ranch, my long life and your future, your dreams, your lost love." Looking searchingly into the eyes of the young man sitting beside him, he said quietly, "You are like the son I never had." He paused for a moment searching for words. "Jeff, you belong on the ranch."

As the two men sat quietly, their thoughts in another world, the only sound was the whisper of breeze gently rocking the ancient truck. "I'm an old man, Jeffrey. We both know my hearts on its last legs. One day before long it's going to stop. I have no regrets, I have loved my life and the people who have shared it with me." He paused, seeing distant images floating before his eyes. "My darling Annetta, Samantha and my little grandson Peter; José, Maria, and their Carmen … these are the treasures of my life."

Turning to Jeff, a smile slowly crept over his weather-beaten, wrinkle-lined face. "Maria and I have been watching you and Sam. Funniest thing we've ever seen. You two act like a couple of old dogs circling a bone hoping for the other to make the first move." Serious again, he continued. "And you know Peter is crazy about you. I think you feel the same about him. Jeff, Peter needs a father."

"Whoa there!" Jeff chuckled, raising both hands in protest. "You and Maria are just a couple of old matchmakers! Sam's been hurt enough. What makes you think she's ready to try again on a burned out, broken up bum like me?"

Pierre laughed aloud. "The signs are pretty obvious to everyone but you."

Glancing suddenly at his watch, the Frenchman jerked back to reality. "*Good Lord*! Look at the time. Get this bucket of bolts rolling. We've got work to do before it gets dark."

24

I T WAS EVENING before they all sat down to eat. There wasn't much idle chatter around the table. Even Peter was quiet, seeming to sense the anxiety of the five adults. After supper Jeff played checkers with Peter—they'd been working on the game all week and Pete was definitely catching on. With Jeff's mind on the winery, Pete babbled with delight as he captured piece after piece.

"Mom, I won! I won! I beat Dr. Jeff." The small boy yelled as Jeff bowed his head in defeat.

Sam gave her son a big hug and whispered in his ear, "Good for you," she said winking at Jeff. "This guy's not so smart after all, is he?" Looking up, she glanced at the clock. ."O.K. Pete, time to brush your teeth and jump into your P.J.'s. It's way past your bedtime."

When Sam came back to the kitchen, José and Maria had already left for their house by the lake; later the two men would split the night watch. Pierre was busy at his desk. Taking Sam's hand, Jeff motioned to the door. "There's still some light in the sky; put on your jacket. You and I need to talk." Taking her hand, they slowly walked up to Peter's favorite rock looking out over the lake, still faintly shimmering in the fast fading light. Sitting together, he took her hand in his and began to speak

"Sam, I don't know much about your marriage except it must have been a disaster. That's your business and none of mine, but that man is bad news. I know more about him than I've told your father; he's even more dangerous than any of you realize. I'm worried about you and Peter but I'm even more worried about your Dad and how this may affect his health. I don't think you're aware that Pierre's heart is not good at all."

"That can't be! He's always been so strong and healthy," exclaimed Sam looking up, her voice filled with anxiety. "Oh Jeff, nothing's ever been wrong with my father!"

"I wish that were true. I took him to a cardiologist a couple of weeks ago. It isn't good news. Your father has a lot of trouble ahead. I've told José and Maria, they know." He turned to face the frightened woman beside him, tears welling up in her eyes. . "He thinks he has to protect you and Peter but the truth is, Sam, you've got to protect him. My job is to protect the three of you."

❦

The next morning dawned bright and clear. The sky was the intense sapphire blue so often seen during Indian summer in this beautiful valley. Jeff had gone early to the *cave* and found nothing amiss. He looked with great care for a timed explosive device. He'd had a very personal experience with those killers; thankfully he found none. Later, he joined José in the vines. The grapes were growing fast and it was time to thin the bunches, to make certain the canopy of leaves let in enough light but prevented the direct heat of the sun from spoiling the fruit. Six more weeks and it would be Harvest time. José's reinforcements due this afternoon would be a big help in the vines as well as on guard.

Sure enough, eight tough-looking Mexican gentlemen arrived after lunch. Jeff and José went out to show them the night routine and to look over the grapes where they would be working during the daylight hours.. All were seasoned vineyard hands and needed little instruction. Pierre had gone up to the winery. It was time to think about blending the wine now aging in barrels. It was just after three when disaster struck.

José, Jeff and the eight new men were walking through the vines when they heard an urgent clanging of the ranch bell, the long agreed emergency signal. Dropping everything, the men ran for the house. As they passed the *cave,* Maria was standing pointing to the entrance and screaming to hurry. Jeff arrived first. After the bright sunlight on the hillsides, it seemed pitch dark, even with the lights full on. As his eyes adjusted to the semi-darkness, he saw

Sam kneeling beside a crumpled figure lying in a pool of wine and blood.

"Jesus! What happened?" he exclaimed as he knelt, looking at the broken body lying before him on the cold cement floor. Pierre was unconscious, one leg twisted grotesquely with a shattered bone protruding through his ripped pants.

"I don't know," said Sam as she cradled the old man's head in her lap. Around Pierre was complete chaos. Two or three of the huge barrels from the top rack were smashed on the floor and wine was everywhere. Even as he did a rapid triage of the inert and broken body, he yanked off his belt and cinched it hard around the top of the compound fractured, profusely bleeding leg.

"Quick, your shirt – mine's filthy ... gotta get pressure on this wound to slow the bleeding." Hesitating only a moment, Sam stripped off her blood-flecked blouse. Snatching it from her hands, Jeff jammed the cloth hard into the wound. Thankfully, the bleeding seemed to slow. Taking time to feel the pulse in the old man's neck with the other hand, he was encouraged to find a faint but regular beat. "Ramon," he gestured to one of the new arrivals, "get down here and keep this shirt jammed tight in that wound—press hard, you can't hurt him!"

Looking up, he spoke hurriedly to José, "Go call 911. Tell 'em to step on it, we've got a badly injured man. And tell 'em to bring plenty of plasma—he's going to need a lot. On the way back, grab my bag from the trailer and get your brother over to the road, that gate's easy to miss."

He barked a quick order to Maria standing wringing her hands, "I need a flashlight — now!" Jeff's Afghanistan experience was flooding back. He found blood in Pierre's throat but it was otherwise clear; his breathing was shallow and labored. Shining the light into the unconscious man's eyes, he found the pupils dilated but equal. Ripping open the blood-soaked shirt, he put his ear to the chest. The left lung was silent. He didn't dare move the neck or spine—who knew what else might be broken. "A rib's punctured his left lung but his heart sounds O.K.," he spoke to no one in particular.

Undoing the old man's worn leather belt, he pulled out the shirttails and unzipped the pants, as he cautiously felt for liver and spleen. The belly was soft. "No sign of internal bleeding, thank God," he muttered as he continued his rapid examination of the mute Frenchman.

When his bag arrived, he used his stethoscope to check the lungs more carefully and got a good listen to the fast beating heart. "That collapsed lung can be treated in the emergency room while they get him ready for surgery; an EKG will tell more about his heart. "Reaching over, he pulled a large sterile dressing from his bag and covered the jagged bone protruding from the thigh. Next, placing his own rolled up shirt on the floor, he very carefully lifted Pierre's head from Sam's lap, laying it on the pad while keeping the neck carefully aligned with the spine. Rocking back on his knees; he looked over Pierre's silent body. "Now comes the tricky part," he muttered out loud.

"José, we've got to reduce this busted leg – pull it back into place before the muscles clamp up." Jeff shifted over and gently took hold of the foot pointed unnaturally to the side. "We usually do this under anesthesia, but don't worry, Pierre's out like a light so he won't feel a thing. I want you to sit down behind his head and grab him under his arms, really hold him tight while I pull the leg out. Sam, get over here and keep his pelvis flat on the floor. It'll take all your strength but do it!" While speaking, he reached for a large pair of bandage scissors and quickly cut off the torn and bloody pant leg.

Positioning himself, Jeff then took hold of the old man's leg and slowly began to pull. "Damn, the muscles are already setting up" he muttered.as he put all his strength into drawing out the leg.

"Here it comes "he spoke in a clenched voice as they all watched the bone slowly start to pull back into the thigh. Feeling the inert body start to slide, he yelled at José, "Damn it, Hold him tighter – he can't slip now!"

Suddenly, with a harsh grating unheard but clearly felt, the two ends of the broken femur met. "You! Hold on to this leg, keep the tension tight." he said to one of the Mexicans kneeling beside him. "I've got to check—see if the ends match up."

With the man's big hands holding firmly, Jeff gently felt around the thigh. "Seems O.K. – now we've got to splint it as best we can." Tossing aside Sam's once white shirt, he carefully pressed more heavy gauze pads over the wound.

As old ranch hands, the Mexicans knew what was coming and already had two boards ready and Maria had found a big roll of duct tape. While Jeff held the boards tight against the leg, the shorter on the inside, the longer on the outside, Maria and Sam wrapped the tape around the leg above and below the wound, then down at the calf and foot. Everyone let out a sigh of relief as they gently set the now splinted leg down on the concrete.

Leaning back, Jeff looked over their efforts. As he was checking Pierre's blood pressure, he noted some flickering of the old man's eyelids and movement of his lips. "Looks O.K. and he's beginning to wake up. Now comes the pain." Pulling a syringe and an ampule of Demerol from his bag, he quickly jabbed a healthy load of painkiller into Pierre's arm. Maria had found some blankets to cover the old man and things seemed stable. Pierre had lost a lot of blood and was certainly in some degree of shock but blood pressure and pulse were steady. It looked like they'd done all that was possible until the ambulance arrived.

"You make a hell of a team," said Jeff in appreciation as he looked up at the faces peering anxiously at the blood-soaked old Frenchman. "Thanks to your help, I think our Pierre's gonna make it to the hospital."

Standing at last, he lifted Sam to her feet and held her close. Suddenly she jerked free. "Where's Peter?" she frantically cried out. "Did I leave him alone in the house?"

"Pete's right here." called Maria. "Miguel brought him up when José came back." Running over, Sam found her boy curled up in the big Mexican's lap, still sound asleep.

"Oh, thank God," she whispered, hugging the boy tight.

With the ambulance on its way, Jeff for the first time could inspect the cataclysmic scene. A broken ladder and pieces of chalk lieing in the bloody muck showed Pierre had been up marking the barrels. But how had they broken loose and come crashing down on the old man?

"José, those barrels were wedged in tight. Not even an earthquake could have jarred them loose." The two men quickly found another ladder and propped it up against the top beam. Jeff climbed up and carefully inspected the heavy steel rails where the barrels had rested.

"I'll be damned!" he called down. "The wedges are gone. The barrels just rolled right off on poor Pierre when he grabbed hold of the butts." Climbing down, he looked at the group gathered around Pierre. "I screwed down those wedges myself," he said, looking at the now semi-conscious form. "That was no accident. This was a pre-meditated murder waiting to happen."

25

THE AMBULANCE, SHERIFF and fire truck arrived simultaneously. Red lights still flashing, they screeched to a halt just
outside the winery doors.

"Hey, Doc Thomas!" called the male paramedic. "We
haven't seen you in a long time – whatcha you doin' way out
here in the boonies?"

Jeff gave them a quick run-down on Pierre's injuries. As
he was speaking, the second paramedic, a short, husky young
woman, quickly got oxygen flowing through a mask, then
they both started I.V. lines, one in each arm. In minutes
plasma was running fast. The big shot of Demerol had put
the old man back in an almost comatose state. With Jeff and
José's help, the two paramedics carefully moved Pierre onto a
spine board, strapping him tight. Before loading Pierre onto
the gurney, they examined the wound in his leg.

"Jees, no wonder he lost so much blood!" said the rangy
paramedic as he peered into the wound.

"Great tourniquet, Doc." laughed the woman, admiring Jeff's blood caked belt still cinched tight around Pierre's thigh. "What's holdin' up your pants?"

Very carefully removing the belt, she allowed the circulation to flow for a few minutes before replacing it with a standard tourniquet ready for the long ride to the hospital.

"O.K., not much more we can do here. Want to ride along?"

"No, his daughter'll want to go with you guys. I'll follow in my truck."

"You still got that old wreck?" exclaimed the young man, pausing to admire Jeff's battered pickup. "O.K., time to get movin', see you at the E.R. Doc." he called, carefully closing the rear doors and climbing in behind the wheel.

As the ambulance pulled out the driveway, red lights again flashing, Jeff walked over to the just arrived sheriff.

"Glad to see you, Paul." He spoke as the two shook hands. "I guess José's filled you in with what we think happened. If you don't need me, I'll take off for the hospital." He paused to look around again, "Looks like a damn war zone – all this blood and wine!"

"Get going, Jeff. They'll need you down there. I'll call Julia."

"Julia? That friend of Pierre's I met at that Branding Iron affair?"

"Yep, one and the same. I'm sure she'll fill you in." laughed the sheriff. "As for this mess," he gestured around the big room, "I've already called for our techs to come out, we'll see what we can find." Shaking his head at the chaos before him, he continued. "Probably not much with all this wine everywhere, but we'll check for prints up on the racks." Turning, he looked back at Jeff. "Tomorrow, you and I need to meet—better bring Sam. After what's happened, I'm worried she's in real danger." Stopping to look around again, he gave a short laugh "Nice vacation you're havin', Dr. Thomas!"

———

Aside from the constant hum of the respirator, Pierre's room in the ICU was quiet. Wires attached to his chest and extremities led to monitors above the bed displaying his EKG and other vital signs. His fractured femur had been plated and screwed. There was no evidence of infection and the orthopedists felt that with no complications, he would be back walking in 6 - 8 weeks. The lung was well expanded and the ribs were splinted. Hopefully, the respirator could be discontinued in the next day or two…none too soon as far as poor Pierre was concerned. Being unable to speak, he was reduced to writing notes, a slow and laborious process. Like all alert patients on respirators, frustration ran high.

The neurologist had checked his head CT scans; there seemed no evidence of brain injury. It was his failing heart that caused all the worry. The trauma, blood loss and the long and difficult surgery, had severely impacted an already weakened heart.

———

"It's strange," Sam was speaking to Jeff as the two of them sat in the waiting room while Julia was visiting with Pierre.

"I've known 'Aunt Julia' forever. She was almost a second mother when I was a kid. I never dreamed that those two were anything more than longtime, close friends. I'm so glad Dad and Julia found each other, that they could share their twilight years together."

Jeff nodded. "When I watch those two old people looking into each other's eyes and holding hands, it makes me realize, maybe for the first time, how much more there is to love than the passion of youth." Jeff reached over, gently holding Sam's hands. "Maybe love is just as much the companionship and the closeness of two caring people."

As they were quietly speaking, Julia came back to join them. "Pierre's drifted off to sleep. I thought I'd let him rest while I came out and visited with you two." The waiting room was empty now save for Sam, Jeff, and this bright, alert little woman. No frumpy old lady, she stood erect for her age.

Dressed in a comfortable but now wrinkled dress, she was obviously unchanged since being urgently called from her shop. Pulling over a chair, she smiled at the two sitting on the couch.

"It must have come as quite a surprise, Sam, finding that your father and I are more than just long-time dear friends. We've done a pretty good job of keeping our relationship quiet, not that we were ever ashamed; we just liked it that way. I think the only people who ever guessed were Paul, Maria and José, they knew." Julia paused, looking out the window at the dark Monterey Pines with misty tendrils of fog weaving through their branches in the early evening light. "Sam, your Mother was my best and dearest friend. I would never have made it through the loss of my husband without her love and support. She helped me set up my antiques business; we did so much together. I lost my dearest friend when Annetta died."

Drifting for a moment in her memories, Julia collected herself and continued. "I never had a child of my own and you were such a little girl when your mother died. I so loved being your 'Aunt Julia'. For a long time your Father and I were just close friends sharing in our loss of your mother. We used to meet Paul, Tom and the others of our little group for dinner each month and as time passed, Pierre and I discovered how much we shared together, how much we cared for each other, how much we truly liked one another." She smiled to herself. "We were comfortable together." She paused, looking at the young couple sitting together. "Do we love each other? Yes, I think we do, I know I do. Love doesn't demand as much when you're older, it just slowly grows to encompass your life. You truly become one person together, I know we did." A few tears ran slowly down her cheeks as she reached for a tissue from a nearby box. "I don't know how I will survive if I lose that wonderful old man."

Sam, enveloping the small woman in her arms, pulled Julia from her chair onto the couch beside her. "Neither do I," she whispered as they held each other close and silently wept.

26

IME PASSED QUICKLY as Indian summer stretched into fall and each week Pierre seemed to show some improvement. First the ventilator had been removed, followed soon by the beginning of gentle physical therapy. Discharge planners began talking about the next move. The leg was healing well, and his punctured lung and broken ribs were almost back to normal. All was going well except for the Frenchman's weakened, failing heart. Each day Sam and Julia sat with Pierre reliving old times, helping him eat and take a few hesitant steps

"You've got to walk!" would say the therapist.

"*Sacre bleu!*"" he muttered, "How can I walk if I can't breathe?"

The therapist just laughed and urged him on. Little by little, Pierre's strength began to return, but his breathing failed to improve. The tan, weather-beaten face of the old Frenchman was now a pale, translucent parchment, all color drained away. As he sat in a chair for longer periods, even hobbling to the bathroom, long oxygen tube snaking behind, there had seemed hope. Then the cardiologist would drop by, look at Julia and Sam and silently shake his head. They understood.

As the weeks slowly passed, it was clear the old Frenchman's strength was failing once again. Pierre was a realist and brooked no polite, evasive answers from his doctors. He knew his heart had run its course. He had spent a number of hours with Tom DeBeers reviewing his will and the legal papers of the ranch and vineyard. He made clear to all that if he should die there was to be no funeral. His body was to be cremated and his ashes scattered in his vineyard where Annetta's had been spread so many years before. When and how was up to Sam and Julia. Pierre was clear about one thing. He did not want to die in the hospital. He wanted to be home at his beloved ranch, in his own bed, surrounded by his cherished family.

One evening while sipping his one and only allowed glass of wine, he gathered Sam, Julia and Jeff around his bedside. "What I want after I'm gone," declared Pierre, breathing in short gasps but with some of the old twinkle back in his eyes, "Is a party, '*Un célébration magnifique!*' " Pierre was very specific about who should be invited. There would be just twelve. First, there would be his family, Sam, Julia, José, Maria and Carmen. Hesitating for a moment, he took the young man's hand in his.

"Jeffrey, you know I have come to think of you as my son — will you become a member of my family?"

Unable to respond, Jeff gently squeezed the wasted hand and mutely nodded his assent.

The list would be completed with his oldest friends, the venerable Branding Iron Dinner Group. Attorney Tom DeBeers, Doctor George Demitross; his ever hopeful wine distributor, Bob Winter; and finally his long time hunting companion, Sheriff Paul Rodriquez.

Deep in thought, he gazed out his hospital window at the fast fading sunset. After a few moments, he looked back and emphatically declared: "It shall be at the winery and on a night with a full moon."

Turning his head, he winked at Julia, "I shall have a word with God about the weather!"

After catching his breath again, he continued, "Now as for the food." He noisily smacked his lips in true Gallic fashion. "We shall have Maria's magnificent *Cassoulet de Languedoc*." He laughed, "Who would have thought our Maria would become a superb French chef?" After taking a break to adjust the oxygen tube, he looked at the two women sitting beside him.

"There must also be Maria's sour dough baguettes to wipe out the plates, and Sam," Pierre stopped again to breath, "I think we should have that simple tossed salad of yours." He paused in concentration. "Yes, perhaps with avocado and tomatoes … a balsamic vinaigrette would be best."

"Oh, you fussy old man," Sam laughed, "you're always sticking your nose into the kitchen. For this party, Maria, Julia and I are in charge. You just keep out."

Pierre paid not the slightest attention to his daughter's ad-monition and continued without a pause "As for the dessert," he said, again licking his lips, "it shall be my favorite, a lovely Crème Brulée." His mustache twitched as he visualized this quintessential French desert. "The custard must have a perfect crust!" Bushy eyebrows drawn together, a stern look on his face, he admonished the three. "Do not embarrass me. There must plenty of everything!"

After resting on his pillows for a few moments, he now turned his attention to Jeff, "You and Carmen are in charge of the wine. I want there to be lots of wine, my best wine, my private, personal wine. Jeff, you know where it's hidden and where to find the key." Pierre laughed with pleasure as he thought of his secret horde and wagged a finger at the two young people. "I'll be keeping an eye on you, so you must not hold back!"

At the ranch the men were busy from dawn to dusk preparing for the coming harvest. The grapes were now bursting with color, their deep purple skin glistening in the sunlight. Maria took care of Peter, fixed the meals and ran the house. Jeff would drive to the hospital each evening, the old truck seeming to remember each turn and dip in the now familiar road. Like doctors do, Jeff always sat on Pierre's bed to talk, much to the annoyance of the nursing staff.

"If this warm weather holds we'll be picking soon," he reported. "The sugar should be perfect in another week, it's very close." Going over Jeff's vineyard notes, the two men would talk about all the many details of the fast approaching crush. Face animated, Pierre's eyes danced as he recalled the hard work and excitement the harvest brought each year.

"The men are still patrolling at night but so far it's been quiet," said Jeff. "We have your alarm system installed and it works like a charm. We'll know instantly if there's a break-in".

Jeff avoided any mention of Asia-American. Their lackey had been around a couple of times, always asking solicitously about Pierre. He never arrived without his threatening Asian thugs who would wander around just looking. To a suspicious José, it seemed they were getting the lay of the land. There had been no further report from the sheriff's office on the shooter's identity, nor had they heard from George, but his unseen presence was always present, always ready to strike.

When at last it came time to leave the hospital, Pierre adamantly refused the doctors' advice to move to a skilled nursing facility. "*Non!* If I'm going to die, I want it to be in my own bed and with my own family." he had vehemently replied. Julia had laughed and promptly declared, "If that's the case, you difficult old man, I'll just move up to the ranch and see that you behave."

A few days later the doctors had agreed it was time to move Pierre and Julia to the ranch. With the guest room to be occupied by Julia, Sam and Pete returned to their cabin. Each night after dinner Jeff would carry Pete up to bed, then he and Sam would talk quietly under the stars in the still warm Indian summer evenings. One such night, with the scent of the ripening grapes in the air and the occasional whinny of horses as backdrop, Sam talked about her life with George and the pain and misery of their divorce.

"What about your Caroline, Jeff. Can you tell me about her?"

Jeff paused for a long moment, then the words began to come. "Sam, you look so much like Caroline. That was what stopped my heart when I sat watching you up at the lake that first week. I wanted to reach out and take you in my arms, but luckily reality returned before I made a fool of myself. That was a very hard moment." He stopped, his eyes looking above the faintly visible lake into the star-filled night sky. "Sam, I loved Caroline very much. All I can remember of that terrible day was holding her torn and bloody hand. I knew somewhere in my mind that she was gone but didn't know for sure until the doctors told me just before my surgeries began ten days later in Germany. I hoped I'd die of my wounds—but somehow I survived." He stopped and looked at the woman sitting beside him. "That was three years ago. I thought I was over that terrible pain — that Caroline was laid to rest at last." He took Sam's hand. "Then you appeared."

Neither spoke for several minutes. Finally Sam gave his hand a gentle squeeze and stood. "Time to call it a day … but Jeff, thank you for telling me." Then without further words, she turned and walked quickly to her cabin. It was as though she was afraid to spend another moment in his presence.

A week later, on another such warm evening, exhausted by his long day at the vineyard, Jeff headed back to the trailer he now shared with Bruno. The little aluminum box on wheels, even though shaded by the sheltering oak, was still an oven. Opening the windows and with the door swung wide, Jeff showered then sat outside letting the air and faint breeze evaporate the moisture on his wet body. Bruno sat at his feet.

Later, while lying half asleep sprawled out on top of the bed, he and Bruno were suddenly startled when the screen door opened noiselessly and Sam stepped into the trailer. "Bruno," she whispered, "Out!" Then turning to an astonished Jeff, she put a finger to her lips and began rapidly stripping off her clothes. Jeff was instantly aroused at the sight of this beautiful woman standing before him. Hesitating for a moment in the dim light, she looked Jeff in the eyes as though daring him to speak, then without a word climbed into his arms. The fierce intensity of her passion brought out his own desperate need. Pulling her into his body, the two were joined together in a fierce embrace of love. As fast as it began it was over. The two lay clinging to each other, gasping for breath, the sweet scent of intimacy floating in the air. Still without a word, Sam placed a gentle kiss on his parted lips, extricated herself from his arms and stood looking silently at the man below her. Then she turned away, slipped on her sandals and picked up her clothes. With one last look behind, she opened the screen door and disappeared into the night.

Letting Bruno back in, Jeff sat catching his breath. "Dear God! Was that a dream?" Reaching down to scratch the dog behind the ears, he continued talking to his four-legged friend. "Bruno, that is the most amazing, beautiful and unpredictable woman I have ever met."

The next morning, in the early, coolest hours before sunrise, the harvest had begun in earnest. José and his crew had already put in three hours picking, sorting the grapes, selecting only the best and tossing aside the rest. That chosen fruit was transported quickly to the cement apron before the *cave* where Jeff was directing the final sorting before the fruit was de-stemmed and gently pressed. From there, the sweet, fresh juice and skins ran in hoses to large oak tanks in the winery to begin its fermentation cycle.. When the sun crept over the ridge tops, Jeff and José headed back to the busy kitchen for a quick breakfast. Sam and Peter had already arrived when Jeff walked into the kitchen. The warmth of the room, the smell of hot coffee and fresh baked bread awakened his now ravenous appetite. Jeff got his usual big hug from Maria, Peter climbed into his lap, and Sam handed him a cup of coffee with a pleasant, "Sleep well, Dr. Thomas?" Her inscrutable smile made his heart leap. Maria, observing the two from her place at the stove, sensed that something was brewing between the two. Whatever it was, she liked it.

After their quick breakfast, José headed back to the grapes and Jeff went to help the frail old Frenchman sit up, adjusted his pillows and replaced the oxygen tank. The room was dark, the shades still pulled. Permeating the room was that indefinable but unforgettable musty scent of long illness and impending death. Pulling up a chair, he sat briefly next to the bed, the only sound the rasping of the sick man's breathing and the hiss of the oxygen. Julia had already called George Demitross. Jeff wanted to stay, but Pierre, in a weak and gasping breath, had said, "*Non, Non*, the grapes come first." Then slowly catching his breath again, he whispered with a faint smile, "Don't worry, I'll still be here when you get back."

When the noon bell rang, everyone stopped for a short break and Jeff ran to the house. Dr. Demitross was just leaving as Jeff arrived, still dripping from dunking his head under the tap on his way past the barn. "Hi Jeff," the doctor called, looking the tan muscular young man up and down. "Looks like the life of a winemaker suits you." As they walked to his car, he paused. "Jeff, I don't think our dear friend can last much longer, his poor old heart is about gone. I told Julia and Sam ... I'm sure they already knew."

When the doctor had gone, Jeff hurried in to find Pierre sitting up almost vertically as he gasped for air, holding tight to Julia's hand. Sam sat quietly beside her father while Maria, holding Peter's hand, stood near. Pierre looked up when Jeff walked in and motioned him close. "How are the grapes?" he whispered, each breath a struggle.

"Wonderful!" exclaimed Jeff with a forced smile as he bent low over the bed. "José say's it's going to be the best harvest in years. The Cabernet will be fermenting by tonight We'll pick the Cab Franc and Merlot tomorrow."

A faint smile washed over the old Frenchman's face. "I knew you could do it!" he said between tortured breaths. "I thank God ... *merci*, Jeffrey." Panting with effort, he rested for a few moments then continued, voice now only a whisper. "Your wine … it will soon be better … than mine." Pausing again for several minutes and with what seemed a final effort he started to speak once more. "I pray that you and Sam …" but his voice failed, all sound obscured by his ever more labored breathing.

Tears running down her cheeks, Julia leaned over and with a soft kiss, whispered, "Rest, my dear, we're all right here." Pierre, holding tight to Julia with one hand, reached out to Sam, his grip for that last moment surprisingly strong. Then with a long, final sigh, Pierre's head sank slowly to his chest and his eyes closed for the last time.

27

JUST TWO WEEKS after Pierre's death, Jeff and Carmen had wandered in wonderment through Pierre's hidden treasures locked away in the back of the *cave*. Pierre's celebration was only days away. As they opened case after case, Carmen exclaimed, "Oh God, Jeff, this is unbelievable. There are wines here I almost never see, much less taste. People would kill for this collection."

For their first offering, they selected an *Oliver Leflaive Montachet Grand Cru*. Carmen knew this luscious wine from the Côte de Beaune in Burgundy was one of the most sought after (and most expensive) chardonnays in the world. It would be the perfect white. Carefully searching through the cases of reds they suddenly came across one smaller wooden box. Jeff carefully pried open the top and there before them lay four bottles of *1990 Domaine de la Romanée-Conti* from the Cote de Nuits. Carmen could hardly contain herself. "The last time I saw these priced, it was $5,000 a bottle! Jeff, since we can pick whatever we want, this would be the perfect wine for my mother's wonderful Cassoulet.... and it can't wait another year. If we're lucky, and with this amazing storage, it should be at its peak." She stood staring at the four bottles carefully resting in their wooden cradle and cushioned with straw. "1990 ...this must have been one of the last wines Pierre brought home." Looking at all the cases of world-class wines, she could only shake her head in wonder.

Jeff stood watching as she carefully examined one of the bottles. "Carmen, I've never heard of a bottle going for that price. I think this would be exactly what he'd want us to drink ... I bet he planned to have us find it just for this celebration."

As the two marveled at the treasure of wine surrounding them, they chose their last wines for the evening. To accompany the Crème Brulée, they would serve a *1989 Château d'Yquem*, the acknowledged crown jewel of Sauternes. In keeping with the Frenchman's desire, they made certain there would be an ample supply of each to satisfy all twelve thirsty friends.

"Carmen, do you have any idea what this stuff would cost today - if we could find it?" Jeff asked swinging his arm around the small room.

Her only answer was a shrug of the shoulders. "More than you or I could ever hope to afford."

Remembering Pierre's admonition and mentally reviewing the menu, they added three bottles each of an *'89 Petrus* and a *'90 Chateau Margaux*. They didn't bother to figure the thousands of dollars those wines might bring at auction.

It was a beautiful, fall evening when the appointed day arrived. Sam put Peter to bed close by in his grandfather's house, a special treat on this special night. There on the freshly mown lawn in front of the winery, the Frenchman's family and closest friends came together to remember and celebrate the remarkable life of Pierre Vaillard. The old man's request of God had been answered affirmatively with an unusually balmy, late fall Carmel Valley night; no wind and a lovely full moon. Rising over the ridge tops in the East, that luminescent globe cast a spell that encompassed each member of the group as they raised a glass in toast to their dear departed friend. No one doubted Pierre's presence. His spirit was among them, touching each in turn.

Earlier that evening, the kitchen crew had gathered around the imposing black stove. The moment of truth had arrived. Jeff, with an anxious Maria hovering alongside, used all his considerable strength to lift the very large, very heavy cast iron pot from the oven, placing it on the stovetop. With great care, Maria slid the lid partially off the top and leaning over the steaming vessel, inhaled the luscious aroma that had now spread through the room. Sighing with satisfaction, she stood and loudly proclaimed, "*Si, perfección!* Pierre's Cassoulet is ready! "The heavy container, now swathed with old blankets to maintain the heat, was moved with great care from the stove to the back of Jeff's battered pick-up, all the while Maria providing a steady stream of advise. "Careful … …don't tip that pot …watch out …Holy Mother of God, you're spilling … not there, over here …"

At last the truck was safely loaded to Maria's satisfaction. The salad, baguettes, and the Crème Brulée were packed around the well insulated Cassoulet and they were ready. The wine had already been delivered. With Maria, Carmen and Sam jammed in beside him, Jeff carefully let out the clutch and without a jerk or jolt they were off. Fully understanding its delicate mission, the Duchess proceeded cautiously and sedately up the hill to the winery just a hundred yards away.

———∞———

Pierre's celebration was a magnificent occasion by any standard. The moon, high in the clear night sky, illuminated the two long gingham covered tables now littered with the residue of a sumptuous meal. Empty dishes, rumpled napkins, countless glasses and innumerable empty bottles gave testimony to the evening's success. Around the table sat twelve happy, satiated and contented friends smiling at one another. Sheriff Rodriquez, wine glass in hand, ponderously hoisted himself to his feet for a final toast. "Pierre," he said, raising his eyes and glass to the heavens, "Thank you, old friend, it's been one hell of a party! Your wine was superb, the food delicious, and ...."

In mid-sentence, the sheriff's voice was chopped off by a massive explosion. Less than fifty yards away, the big red barn seemed to rise from its foundation and in one horrifying moment the roof and walls collapse inward amid a great cloud of dust and smoke.

Then, as suddenly, the whole area was illuminated by a burst of flames from Pierre's house just down the hill. With one terrified look, Sam screamed *"Peter!"* and started running towards the blazing building. "Oh dear God, *Peter.*"

Jeff, racing to the truck, grabbed a handful of old blankets and sprinted to the fountain in front of the house, plunging them into the water. Standing for a second holding a dripping blanket in his arms, he searched the flaming wall of fire for the best entry. Startled, he saw a fast running figure emerge from the darkness. Illuminated by the flickering flames now roaring up the sides of the house was a man dressed all in black running straight for Jeff.

"George, what the hell …."

"Is Peter in the house?" ccreamed the frantic man grabbing the dripping blanket from Jeff's surprised hands. "Oh God, where's my little boy?" Without waiting for an answer or losing a stride, he pulled the wet blanket over his head and shoulders, running straight into the burning inferno. Jeff, snatching another blanket from the fountain, was right behind him.

Inside, Jeff stopped to get his bearings in the acrid, choking smoke. George was lost in the darkness now illuminated only by the leaping flames coming from all directions. Dropping to his knees, he began crawling towards the barely visible hall leading to the bedrooms. Fighting for his breath, he moved fast through the burning living room and hall. Visibility was minimal and the heat unbearable. Shouting "Peter" over and over, all he could hear in reply was the noise of the fire and sounds of the disintegrating building. Once or twice he thought he could hear George calling "Peter" but there was no reply.

Jeff's brain, deprived of oxygen, was slipping in and out of consciousness. The heat and flames, the swirling smoke, the crescendo of noise, all added to his confusion. He tried to concentrate but was drifting in and out of a surreal world of past and present. At what he dimly recognized as Pierre's bedroom, Jeff was stopped as a section of the ceiling fell in his path. Backing away, disoriented, he thought he heard a muffled voice when suddenly from the flames a beautiful young woman's face materialized before him.

"Caroline!" he cried, but the visage only softly smiled and began to fade.

"Please Caroline, don't leave me," he beseeched. "Come back to me, Caroline."

"No Jeff," She slowly shook her head, her smiling countenance again bright and clear. "No, my love, we had our life together, now you are free once more. Jeff, it's Sam's time now."

Desperate, he reached out but the faint vision only smiled, shook her head and gently mouthed a kiss.

"Please, Caroline!" he called hopelessly but she was gone, vanished forever into the dancing flames and billowing smoke.

Slumping to the floor, Jeff felt tears form but vaporize before they could dampen his cheeks. As his mind drifted in and out of reality he became dimly aware of a new form, a new voice emerging from the smoke and flames. George, hardly recognizable with fire-blackened skin and burning clothes was calling him and clutching a blanket wrapped tightly around a small form.

"Take him," croaked George through the flames, thrusting the smoldering blanket over the burning beams. "Save my little boy …." but his voice was smothered as another section of the ceiling came crashing down on his now blazing body. With a dying effort, the man called out faintly again. "*Nacimiento* … the water's source…" The last Jeff heard was a faint but still urgent cry, "The treasu …." George tried to speak, his eyes staring at Jeff, but his voice had failed. Then it was over as fire engulfed the scorched, now lifeless body.

Clutching the blanket tight to his chest, head close to he floor, Jeff crawled back down the flaming hall. Through the noise of the now collapsing walls he could make out sirens and tried to navigate through the falling beams towards the sound. At last, through the smoke and debris, he saw the faint outline of a door. With a final surge of strength, he stood and forced his way forward. Then, with the blanket-encased child still clutched to his breast, he staggered out into the glare of headlights illuminating the chaotic scene.

Gasping for air, Jeff turned back momentarily hoping against hope to see George emerge from the holocaust. Shielding his scorched face from the heat, he watched as the roof collapsed into the conflagration with a roar of sparks, flames, and billowing smoke.

"The poor bastard's funeral pyre" Jeff muttered through cracked and bleeding lips. The sheriff, arms now supporting the swaying, smoldering man, also stared mesmerized into the blazing flames.

As Jeff slumped down, coughing and trying to breath, others rushed forward and many hands gently pulled the blanket encased child out of his arms. At the same time, Rodriquez, supporting Jeff's sagging body, dragged him away even as the flames roared higher consuming forever Pierre's once lovely home. Stretched out on the grass, he barely felt the cold foam being sprayed on his smoldering body by the fire crew. He could smell the stench of burning flesh, which he dimly realized was his own. The last voice he heard before losing consciousness was Sam's cry of joy. "Oh, thank God, Peter is alive!"

28

TWO FLIGHT NURSES in jumpsuits stared at their patient from behind masked faces while glove encased hands cut away the partially burned off, scorched and tattered clothing.

"Not as bad as it looked back there at that ranch," commented one as she peeled away charred cloth from the deep burns on the patient's arms. Looking down at the man strapped to a stretcher before them, she continued. "They said he was a doctor – wonder what a doctor was doing in that inferno?"

"Who are this Caroline and Sam he keeps mumbling about?" said the other. "Hope nobody else was trapped inside that charred mess!"

The steady thumping of the helicopter's rotors kept conversation to a minimum. Jeff's hair, eyebrows and eyelashes were gone, the skin on his scalp, face and lips blistered and cracked. The worst were his hands and arms – black and charred, most areas denuded of skin and many with burns deep into his flesh. They'd given him a liberal jolt of morphine before lift off and didn't expect to hear much more from their patient before arrival.

As the helicopter banged its way through the night skies headed for the San Jose Regional Burn Center, Jeff slowly came back to a dim consciousness. The crashing, tearing, sounds of the disintegrating building, the searing heat, the orange daggers of flame and the gagging, choking smoke seemed etched in his mind. His thoughts wandered in his morphine and pain induced confusion. In his semi-conscious state, he came to the realization this was a different helicopter and different time. The memory of another flight that seemed so long ago, of a broken, bloody body strapped in an evacuation basket flying low over Helmand Province, Afghanistan came flooding back. The same cluster of IV's, the same bags of plasma, the same oxygen mask, even the same female paramedics staring down — just different uniforms, a different aircraft and a far different world.

"OK, easy does it. Let's slide him onto the gurney real slow and careful."

"Watch those IV lines! We had enough trouble gettin' 'em in!" yelled one of the flight crew as they eased the stretcher out of the wide helicopter doors and onto the waiting gurney. Jolted wide awake, Jeff could feel the wind and hear the slow thump of the still rotating blades above him — then they were in the building and suddenly it was quiet, the noise and wind gone and he could hear voices around the gurney. Stopping for a moment, a nurse checked the monitor, rearranged some of the lines and draped a fresh sterile sheet over her patient's burned body.

"Welcome to San Jose Regional, buddy! We'll have you up to the unit in a couple of minutes." called one of the transport team pushing the gurney into an elevator. In moments they arrived, the wide elevator doors opened and he was suddenly under bright lights.

"You don't look so hot, friend." A doctor in green scrubs smiled down, assessing his new patient. "Let me check your record for a second then we'll strip off what's left of your clothes and have a look."

"Son of a bitch! It's Jeff Thomas!" exclaimed the doctor looking up from the chart and staring at the figure on the gurney. "Jesus, you look like shit, man. What the hell happened to you this time?"

Jeff tried to smile. "Hank Graften? "he croaked, "You bail out of the Navy too?" he questioned through cracked and bloody lips. "You a burn man now?"

"Yeah, I got into burns at Bagram after you got sent home for repairs. Lot of practice over there—you should know!"

It seemed the damage to his face was mostly 1st degree burns. No corneal damage. Of course he looked like a skinned, scorched rabbit, but hair and lashes would regrow and face and scalp would heal. Both arms and hands were much worse with 2nd and 3rd degree burns from fingers to elbows. Grafts were used to repair the biggest, deepest wounds. Over those early days he had soaked up morphine, the pain unremitting until slowly over time the paroxysms of agony had eased. Hank Grafton, his old friend from Afghanistan, and the team of burn specialists had debrided the deepest wounds under anesthesia. With his grafts taking well and healthy granulation tissue and new skin replacing the sloughing remains of burned tissue, his progress was good. Happily the muscles and tendons in his hands and arms were not too badly damaged. In the beginning, the biggest worry had been infection. By virtue of good luck and superb care, he'd passed that danger period without problems. During this same time his smoke and heat damaged lungs were healing and day-by-day, his breathing was returning to normal.

As time permitted, Jeff and the doctor had enjoyed talking about their time together in Helmand Province before Hank had transferred to the hospital at Bagram. He had heard all about the raid and Caroline's death from friends at the Trauma Unit. Hank was part of the medical team that took care of Jeff during his short stay near Kabul where they had met and become friends with Captain Ali who visited daily. Those days after the I.E.D. explosion, Jeff had seemed unable to comprehend what had happened and continued to talk of Caroline as though she would be joining him soon. At the psychiatrist's urging, his friends had talked very little about her and nothing about her death. Although Jeff was soon sent on to Germany, Hank had remained friends with

Ali until his own rotation back to the States. Now here in San Jose, the two doctors often reminisced about old times at the trauma unit, but very little was said about Caroline. Hank had wondered how Sam, who came so frequently, fit in. It was obvious she cared for him a great deal. Knowing the past, he had watched Jeff's reactions on these frequent visits. The shadow of Afghanistan seemed always present in his eyes.

At the end of six weeks, it was time to think about sending this patient home. The only thing now holding up his discharge was the patient's mental state. He had become more withdrawn and depressed than matched his injuries A psychiatrist had been consulted and anti-depressants advised. Hank Grafton didn't agree. He had seen a great deal of Post Traumatic Stress Disorder and knew Jeff's medical history. He also knew there was much more to this withdrawn man's story than appeared in his medical record. As the doctor watched and talked to his friend he realized that in addition to the symptoms of PTSD, there was unspoken unfinished business locked in the hidden recesses of Jeff's mind. Hank Graften suspected there must be a connection to the terrible events in Afghanistan and these recent tragedies in Carmel Valley.

Starting as soon as allowed, Jeff had had regular visits from José, joined always by Sam and Maria. To protect against infection, the great fear of all burn units, friends and family could only enter fully attired in cap, mask, gloves and gown. Jeff's first question to Sam had been about Peter. He was overjoyed to hear that the little boy had survived with only smoke inhalation and no significant burns. He learned that Sam and Pete were staying with Julia in the Village to be closer to the pulmonary specialists and the boy's pediatrician. Most of the talk was about the ranch and vineyard. Studiously avoided was any discussion of the fire or its aftermath.

Dr. Grafton had watched these encounters with interest. He had talked to the young woman who came with each visit, had watched and understood her anxious, apprehensive face. He'd observed Jeff search her eyes as though seeking some answer, but to what?

On several occasions, the doctor had spent extra time in the waiting room with Sam in hopes of reassuring her and learning more. It was clear this attractive, apprehensive woman cared a great deal for Jeff. Like his doctors, she had no answers for his strange, withdrawn state.

Sam had tried to find a way to give Jeff a kiss of thanks through her mask without much success. She couldn't even hold his hand with all the fluff bandages. "Jeffrey, you saved my child's life, how can I ever thank you?"

"No Sam, thank George." Jeff wheezed in reply. "He found him. I just carried him out. Thank God Pete's alive—that's all that really matters."

"You should have seen yourself when you staggered out of that bonfire." José chuckled on one occasion when the women stepped out to talk to the doctor. "You looked like a roman candle belching flame and smoke."

Jeff tried to smile. "Sounds pretty dramatic ... a roman candle ... I must've looked like an apparition straight from hell."

As the two friends talked, Jeff vividly recalled the moment when a burning, dying, Jorge had passed the smoking, blanket enclosed child through the flames. The scene was still vivid in his mind but he had trouble comprehending what George had said. "Save my boy" had been clear. It was the rest that he couldn't understand. Had it been something like "Nacimiento" and then, "The water? There was another word, but I can't remember the rest."

It all made no sense to José. "The old Spanish Rancho's name had something to do with 'Nacimiento'. But those other words – maybe the poor *hibrido* was just desperate for water?"

"No, I don't think that was it. He was trying to tell me something, but what I don't know."

The subject was quickly dropped and soon forgotten as Maria and Sam walked back in his room. "Jeff," Sam had said. "They only let us stay fifteen minutes and you've got to decide your next move. We all want you back at the ranch. I'm staying with Julia so you can move into my cabin for a few weeks. It's close to Maria's place where we're now eating. She can fix your meals and help you eat until those bandages come off." As Sam spoke, José had turned serious. "Amigo, even if you can't get out in the vineyard, you'll soon be able to visit the winery. I can handle the grapes, it's the wine I worry about,

Pierre always took care of that stuff." José stopped, big hands clutched tight in his concern. "Jeff, I gotta have your help!"

And so it was decided. Sam and Peter would continue living in the village with Julia for a few more weeks and Jeff would move into her cabin until he was able to be on his own in the trailer. There wasn't much choice—he had no other place to go.

On the next Saturday the Burn Center released Jeff with a bag of medicine, multiple tubes of Silvadene, the special burn ointment, and a large box of dressings. José and Sam had driven over in Pierre's old Buick where there was plenty of room for Jeff to sit with his still bandaged extremities. Unable to wear any clothes, everyone thought him quite fetching as he climbed gingerly into the front seat with his hospital gown flapping in the breeze.

On the long drive back to the ranch, Sam filled Jeff in on the FBI's discoveries at George's apartment and at the Asia-American office. There was no question about the heroin trade. With the information found, the Feds hoped to shut off one important link running from Afghanistan, through Mexico and up into the States. In addition to that, they had found the stolen Deed and the old Land Grant papers from the Monterey County Hall of Records. With access to George's safety deposit box, they found what appeared to be a valid holographic will written and dated by Pierre on the day of Sam's marriage to George. In a couple of terse sentences, Pierre had bequeathed the ranch and the winery to George and Sam on his death. None could guess what threats had been used to force Pierre to create that small critical document that may well have proven his own death warrant. They also found Segovia's personal will dated much more recently giving his entire estate to Peter.

Jeff had listened to this recital with increasing interest. "My God, then he did own the ranch along with you after Pierre died. If that will holds up, you now have title to the whole place!"

"No, it's not as simple as that. Tom tells us my father cancelled that codicil immediately after the divorce. Dad wrote an entirely new Will while he was in the hospital. None of us know the contents of that latest one. My Dad must have known there were going to be problems with George because he specifically stated it could not be opened until three months after his death."

"Well, are you or aren't you the legal owner?"

"It's all in limbo 'till we can read the will and that's still locked up."

Arriving at Highway One and heading for Monterey, they talked a little about George. How he was probably responsible for Pierre's death and without question caused the destruction of the barn and the main house. They also spoke of how, in spite of his terrible actions, he had sacrificed his life to save his son.

"How can I hate a man who does something like that?" Sam looked out the window at the blue-green ocean, white caps dancing in the wind before turning back. "I'm so glad

Peter can remember his father like that, how much he really loved his son. What a waste that man made of his life."

"Hey, don't forget this guy in the front seat," called José from behind the wheel. "Look at him, *el pobre!* Maybe he deserves a little credit too!"

Sam blushed. "Of course he does! Oh, Jeff, We all know Peter would never be alive without you." She stopped, not quite sure how to go on, instead she just leaned forward and gave Jeff a small kiss on the dark stubble now growing on his bare skull.

Driving up Carmel Valley, they stopped at Julia's little house in the Village. As they pulled up, Peter and his now "Nana Julia" came running out to greet Jeff. "Boy, you're a mess, Jeff!" said Peter craning his neck in the front window. "Dr. Jeff to you, mister," said Jeff with a smile. "How ya doin' little buddy?" He reached out with a bandaged hand and rumpled the small boy's hair.

Julia pulled Peter away and gave Jeff a big kiss on the lips. "Nice to have you home, Jeffrey. We've all been missing you more than you'll ever know." Peering in the window, she looked over at the driver and gave a command. "All right José, we've had our visit. You get this boy back to the ranch and to bed. He needs a rest before dinner. Maria's been cooking all day so I hope you're hungry!" She gave Jeff a careful pat on the shoulder, and then thinking better of it, leaned in and gave him a peck on the cheek. "We'll all see you for supper, so get going."

"Yes, Mother!" Jeff called out the window as the big Buick pulled away.

Forty-five minutes later they turned off Carmel Valley Road and through the old familiar gate. As they drove over the hill he was struck by the change. No big red barn, and nothing at all where Pierre's house had once stood so peacefully under the great oak. All was level, all scraped clean. Only José and Maria's little house, Sam's cottage, a few of the outbuildings and Jeff's trailer remained. In the background, the lake alone was unchanged, placid water disturbed only by a slight riffle from the afternoon breeze.

José stopped for a minute at the top of the knoll as they looked at the strangely altered scene. "What a tragedy." spoke Jeff. "The ranch will never be the same without Pierre."

"Perhaps and perhaps not, *amigo*. This ranch has been around for almost three hundred years. You and I may come and go, but this Rancho will be here forever."

As they watched, a great white streak of fur came racing up the hill, tail wagging furiously, tongue at the ready. Feet up on the windowsill, Bruno greeted Jeff with a slobbering kiss he'd long remember. In the distance smoke was drifting up from José and Maria's chimney and as he watched, Maria stepped out the kitchen door waving. Blinking back tears, Jeff knew he was home at last.

—⟨⟩—

As each week passed, Jeff showed continued improvement. New skin grew stronger and the grafts were blending with healthy tissues. Bandages were removed one by one. Maria would bring him his meals and José would come by each evening to talk about the vineyard. It wasn't long before it was time to move and in spite of Maria's loud disapproval, Jeff had returned to the trailer. Frequently Sam and Peter would come to visit and occasionally Julia would drop by to spend a few hours. They were all pleased with his physical change, but the visits had been strained and at times Sam felt almost a stranger. Jeff would go outside by himself to tinker with his truck or to take short walks, always under the watchful eye of Maria. Usually alone except for Bruno, his wanderings seemed purposeless. Sometimes he went down to the raw, bare patch of ground that had once been the site of Pierre's lovely old home. Here he would stand motionless for long minutes, his mind seeming far away. Other times he would walk up to the lake and sit on Peter's rock, gazing into the distance. Maria, from her vantage point, observed this strange behavior day after day with growing concern. More than once she had spoken to José and Julia. She tried not to worry Sam or Peter. The little boy couldn't understand what had happened to this man who had become almost a father. Sam spoke of it seldom, but her pain was obvious for all to see.

"Jeff is getting better every day but something is wrong with that boy." Maria worried aloud. "He's not been the same since the fire."

"He seems in another world half the time." agreed Julia.

José who sometimes joined Jeff on his walks concurred. "When I take him to the Doctor next week I'll have a chance to talk to the boy alone. Maybe he'll open his heart and tell me, I will try."

As scheduled, José drove Jeff back to the Burn Center for his follow-up visit. Dr. Grafton was duly impressed by the obvious improvement and medically the visit was a great success. It was decided that Jeff could now experiment with limited work wearing protective clothing, hat and gloves. The doctor was nonetheless troubled by the still distant tone of his friend's voice. While Jeff was dressing after the examination, Dr. Grafton took José aside and they talked of their mutual friend. "Mr. Sanchez, I don't know if Jeff has ever talked much about his heartbreaking experience just before leaving Afghanistan ... about his horrible wounds and the death of his fiancée. I suspect he hasn't spoken much about either to anyone. I think somehow this recent fire and the trauma of his burns has rekindled that terrible time in his mind. Like all of you, I worry a great deal about our friend." Spotting Jeff coming back down the hall, Dr. Grafton finished hastily, speaking under his breath and handing José a card. "Watch him closely. Call me anytime if you have questions."

The three-hour drive back to the ranch had been strained. José had tried to talk about the vineyard, even brought up Jeff's earlier question about George's strange dying statements. Jeff's replies had been brief, his mind elsewhere, he was not even listening. Then as they passed through Carmel and turned up the valley, something suddenly took place; it was as though he had made an important decision, as though a cloud had been lifted from his mind. He became much more talkative; he inquired about the state of the vines, about Sam and Peter. José, when the road allowed, turned in astonishment to look at his friend. For the first time since the fire, Jeff seemed at peace.

That night at dinner Maria was also aware of the change her husband had mentioned that afternoon. Jeff played with Bruno like old times, scratching the big dog's ears and patting his head as much as his stiff hands allowed. Best of all for Maria, he had an appetite for the first time in weeks. After supper they talked comfortably together for an hour or so until at nine o'clock, Jeff had looked at his watch and declared it time for bed. He gave Maria a big hug and a tender kiss. He shook hands with José and thanked him again for all his help since his return. After he had walked out the door with Bruno, the two turned to each other in wonder. Something had happened, but what?

Next morning, well before dawn, José and Maria were awakened by a loud and insistent scratching at their front door. There in the dark stood a whining Bruno looking anxiously back at the trailer; the usual light at the door was out, the trailer was dark. Dr. Jeffrey Thomas and his old truck were gone.

Quickly pulling on his pants and boots, José ran to the trailer. Switching on the lights, he hurriedly took in the scene. The small box of medicines and the few remaining tubes of Silvadene were missing from the tiny bathroom shelf. The small hanging closet was empty; Jeff's few clothes and his duffle had disappeared. On the table a single piece of notepaper was taped to the spotless surface. The message was brief, just three short lines printed in block letters.

"FOREGIVE ME, DEAR FRIENDS.
THIS IS A JOURNEY I HAVE TO MAKE.
TELL SAM AND PETE I'M SORRY."

Not bothering to close the door, José ran to the one remaining out-building still standing after the fire. Here by the horse corral, he rapidly swung his flashlight over the saddle racks. Seeing what he was searching for he let out a sigh of relief. Hurrying back to the trailer, he lifted the mattress and peered into the small storage space hidden beneath. Satisfied by what he found, he replaced the mattress and stood with a slight smile.

Walking quickly back to the house, Bruno glued to his heels, José went directly to the bedroom. The light was on and Maria was sitting bolt upright, her face a mask of anxiety. "Where has he gone?"

"I don't know. He doesn't say." José handed the frightened woman Jeff's note. "But I know one thing is certain – he will be back. A man does not leave his saddle and rifle unless he plans to return."

29

EARLY THE NEXT morning, a shattered Sam called Hank Grafton. The Doctor, dressed in hospital scrubs ready for morning rounds, listened quietly. He shared her concern; Jeff was not ready to go out on his own. Grafton did his best to reassure Sam that all would be well; he promised to do what he could to track down their mutual friend. Putting down the receiver, Hank Grafton let out an explosive expletive. "Son of a bitch! That crazy bastard, I bet he's done it!" Quickly checking his watch he saw it was almost 9:00 AM. Remembering that it was exactly 24 hours later on the other side of he world, he reached for his phone.

After a series of failed calls, long waits and much twisting of arms, Grafton got through to his goal, the Afghan National Army Intelligence. "Thank God I learned some Pashto." He muttered to himself as he was passed from phone to phone in the A.N.A. headquarters. It was almost an hour before he found his man: Captain, now Colonel, Ali Mohamoud. It took another 30 minutes to explain Jeff's history since returning to California. Hank explained the depression and withdrawal that they had all noticed since the fire. Ali had not been surprised; he'd had letters from Jeff that told the same story.

"Ali, I think he's on his way back to Afghanistan. The poor bastard's got too much unfinished business he has to deal with. I'll bet he'll fly to Kabul, then catch an Afghan Air flight south to Lashkar-Gah."

Except for occasional sharp questions, Ali had listened in silence. "You may well be right." Ali finally said in his strange, clipped, half Cockney, half Etonian, accent. "I think that is what he must do to get on with his life. If he is going to Helmand Province he will go to my cousin Ahmed Kahn and his wife Saire. They became almost family to Caroline and Jeff."

There was a long pause interrupted only by static. "Hank Grafton, are you still there?"

"Yes, Ali, I'm still here."

"If I can get away, I shall catch the morning Air Force flight to Lashkar-Gah and requisition a helicopter on to Quah-ye-Gaz. I'll be there by evening... maybe even beat Jeffrey if we have guessed correctly on his destination."

"How in hell can you manage all that in less than 24 hours?"

"Rank does have its privileges. I find that on-demand transportation is one of the happy benefits of being a colonel." There was a loud laugh on the other end of the line. The same happy laugh Hank remembered so well from his days at Bagram and Kabul. "If I find him, perhaps I can help

him. I will …" Ali's voice began to fade. "… my cousin …
I can … a Humvee… "

"Your transmission's breaking up," yelled the doctor into
the phone. "Call me on my cell phone when you learn something, you have my number. Good luck!"

Hank Grafton sat back at his desk. If anyone could find
Jeff, it would be Ali.

⸺∞⸺

It was a blustery late afternoon in March when family and
friends gathered again at the winery. The same company
had come together last December to celebrate and honor the
life of their old friend Pierre Vaillard, a day none would ever
forget. Today, a much more somber group had been sum-
moned by Pierre's executor, attorney and friend Tom DeBeers
to learn of the old Frenchman's final wishes. All were present
except Jeff whose absence the past month was made obvious
by an empty chair placed next to José and Maria.

Tom DeBeers was clearly enjoying his role as executor.
Attired formally in a dark business suit, he had dressed befit-
ting the seriousness of the moment. He alone was privy to
the contents of Pierre's new holographic will written in those
last days of his hospital stay. He also was the only one present
who had access to the Pierre's Safety Deposit Box and broker-
age account. The crime leading to the old Frenchman's death,
the subsequent torching of the property, and the internation-
al implications discovered in investigating Asia-American

Development Company had required the sequestering of all documents and records pertaining to Pierre Vailard's estate for months. Finally the FBI, the Bureau of Alcohol, Tobacco and Firearms, the Monterey County Coroner and the District Attorney's office had completed their investigations and released the documents.

At the attorney's direction, José had set up a table in the small building and collected all the remaining chairs left after the fire. Although an electric space heater was doing its best, it was still cool and all were bundled in jackets and sweaters. At last Tom stood, put on his reading glasses and pulled a gavel from his briefcase. After a few loud raps on the table, he began to speak. "Dearly beloved," he intoned in a doleful voice, "we are gathered here together …"

The attorney was promptly drowned out by catcalls and shouts "Get on with it, Tom. It's cold in here!"

"All right, everybody settle down. What I'm going to say this afternoon may come as a surprise. Our friend Pierre led a much more complicated life than we all knew. Everyone knew he was a skilled and proficient rancher. That he made great wine, we also knew. What we didn't know was that Pierre was also a very astute investor. That, it appears, may have been both good and bad. First the good news."

Everyone was silent for a moment until Sam, her face drawn and pale, spoke up. "What do you mean? What bad news?"

"We all were aware, of course," the attorney continued, paying no attention whatsoever to Sam's interruption. "that

Pierre bought the ranch with Intel stock he'd acquired when he worked as one of the company's first employees long before it went public, he told us that many times. What he didn't tell us was that he used only about half of the stock he had been given to purchase this ranch. He apparently was fascinated with the new technologies growing all around Intel in the early days of Silicon Valley. He began to buy stock, very early stock, in companies like Apple, Microsoft, HP, Varian and Rolm. The last stock he purchased was Google when it first went public. Like Warren Buffett, he rarely sold a share in any of this amazing portfolio. Those shares just grew in value and multiplied in number with the passage of time." Tom stopped and looked around the room. "I should tell you that the conservative value of that stock is now twenty, perhaps even twenty-five million dollars."

A hush fell momentarily over the group, then everybody began talking at once. "Quiet!" called Tom, peering over his glasses and rapping his gavel. "Now let's get to his Last Will and Testament. It is quite remarkable." Reaching into his briefcase he pulled out a folder. Carefully opening the clasp, he extracted a number of handwritten pages.

"Let me tell you that our Frenchman was one clever and devious fellow!" He shuffled the papers and began to read. "In his will, he has requested that all his stock be sold and the proceeds divided into 20 equal shares."

No one said a word but several sharp intakes of breath punctuated the silence. After pausing a moment, perhaps for dramatic effect, Tom proceeded.

"First, to my dear daughter Samantha, the joy of my life, I give the entirety of my ranch, approximately 640 acres plus one-half the water rights to our spring. There are two exclusions. The first exclusion shall be the 20 acres of vineyards plus easements for access and one-half the water rights to the spring. The second exclusion is the winery and the *cave* and all its contents. I also give to my daughter four shares of the proceeds of my stock portfolio." Tom paused and smiled at Samantha.

"Second, to my dear friends José and Maria Sanchez who have lived and worked with me since I acquired this ranch, I leave the 20 acres of vineyards, one half the water rights, and an easement for access to both. I also leave them the house they have lived in all these years and three shares of my stock portfolio."

Maria, now openly sobbing, held tight to José's arm with one hand while clutching a handkerchief tight to her breast.

Carefully adjusting his wire-rimmed glasses, Tom looked back at the papers held in his hands, cleared his throat and continued. "And third, to Julia Barnes, my Annetta's closest friend and the dear companion of my later years, I leave my everlasting thanks and two shares of the proceeds of my stock portfolio. I have also arranged for the full payment of any mortgage on her house and business facility. As of this date, these titles will be in her name and free and clear of any and all encumbrance."

Julia appeared stunned, her face frozen. Bruno, seeming to sense her sadness and surprise, rose to his feet and gently placed his head in Julia's lap.

"Fourth," continued the attorney without pausing, "To Jeffery Thomas, M.D.," Sam caught her breath and gripped Julia's hand. "Whom I have come to consider the son I never had, I give the Winery, the *cave* and all their contents, equipment and stored wine. I also give Dr. Thomas two shares of the proceeds from my stock portfolio." DeBeers stopped to chuckle as he looked at the next sentence. "In addition, I give Dr. Thomas all rights, privileges and obligations for the ownership of my dog Bruno. Should for any reason Dr. Thomas be unable to accept any or all of these bequests, they shall revert to my daughter, Samantha."

Tom stopped and looked for a long moment at the empty seat and then around the room. "Where is that boy!" He exclaimed in an exasperated voice. To make this surreal moment complete, Bruno rose from his place by Julia and lay down in front of the empty chair.

"To Carmen Sanchez, the daughter of José and Maria Sanchez, who grew up on our ranch and has loved wine since childhood, I leave two shares of the proceeds from my stock portfolio."

Tom paused to clear his throat, then removing his glasses, he looked over at Sam, José and Maria, his face now creased with a broad smile. "I told you that old man was devious. He's tied you all together in one big knot."

"And now comes the best part," said Tom looking around the room with a big smile. "To the Branding Iron Eating and Drinking Group I leave: a) Free Vaillard Wine for life. b) Dinner each month in perpetuity at the Branding Iron Saloon and Café or any such other site as they may choose."

After a momentary silence, the members of the group erupted with a cheer for Pierre!

"Quiet! There's more." The attorney shouted with mock severity, pounding with his gavel. "There is a stipulation to that last bequest. Let me read: 'These gifts to the Drinking and Dining Group shall continue so long as they, joined by my extended family previously named, do jointly provide an Annual Celebration Of The Grapes and give at least one toast to their late lamented host'."

"Sounds just like Pierre," laughed the Sheriff, clapping his hands. "That man did like a party!"

"Carmen and I will select the wines" piped up Bob Winters. "Maybe, if we ever find Jeff, he'll let us use some of that special collection Pierre locked away."

"He better show up!" Sam answered with feigned indignation. "I bet that's exactly what my Dad intended."

Tom pounded loudly again with his gavel. "Settle down. I'm not finished! There is a final codicil to his will that is very important." He stopped, his face now serious as he searched his papers for one final page. Once found, he raised his head and again began to read.

"I hereby direct my attorney Thomas DeBeers (that's me), "and my daughter, Samantha Vaillard, (that's her, pointing to Sam), to establish an Educational Trust to be named the Pierre Vaillard Educational Trust for the Children of the Vines. This Trust shall be funded by the sale of the remaining shares of my stock portfolio. These monies shall be invested at the direction of the trustees and the interest accrued shall be used for the educational support of the children of the vineyard workers of Carmel Valley, Cachagua, Arroyo Seco and Santa Lucia Highlands appellations of Monterey County, California. Following its establishment, this trust shall thereafter be administered by the before mentioned Board, the Trustees consisting of Samantha Vaillard, José and Maria Sanchez, Jeffrey Thomas, M.D. and Julia Barnes."

Tom banged his gavel one last time as he gathered up his papers and stuffed them in his briefcase. Looking up at last, he gave a startled look towards the back of the winery as the door silently opened and closed. Quickly collecting himself, he returned his gaze to the still stunned assemblage. "Now for the bad news… and this is a shocker."

Before continuing, the attorney warily pulled an envelope from his briefcase, holding it up to clearly show a foreign stamp. Deep in thought, he turned it over in his hands, then with a long sigh, placed it carefully on the table. Looking up at the now concerned faces, he began to speak. "It seems that for several years, unknown to anyone including myself, Pierre has been quietly purchasing a well-regarded vineyard in the heart of Bordeaux … near Saint-Émilion, to be exact. There are almost 30 hectares, that's almost 75 acres, of Premier Grand Cru vines."

Peering over the rim of his glasses, he studied the stunned reaction to this startling information. "I only learned of this purchase last week when the French attorneys representing the Chateau owners contacted me about the next and final balloon payment due in exactly two months." He paused to pick up the envelope again. "Pierre never mentioned this transaction, not once. Perhaps he hoped to complete the purchase before telling us; perhaps he was worried about the very large sum of money involved. Perhaps he had some other plan in mind. Whatever his thinking, it makes no difference now."

A shocked Sam was the first to speak. "How much money are you talking about, Tom? A Chateau in that part of France should belong to the Rothschild's, not the Vaillard's."

"The representatives of the vineyard have presented me with this final bill totaling ..." The attorney sneezed loudly, blew his nose vigorously, then tucking his handkerchief back in his breast pocket, he tapped the envelope with his pen and looked up. "... 22 million dollars."

Sam jumped to her feet. "Twenty-two million dollars?"

"22 million dollars."

"How can we pay 22 million and still run the ranch? My God, we don't know if Dad's stock is worth 22 million. Tom, my father would never do something so crazy."

"He did, Sam." Came a quiet voice from the back of the room. "He told me."

"Jeff!" cried Maria.

30

THE SMALL GROUP leaving the winery that evening talked quietly, their voices restrained. It was as though all had become mute in the face of the evening's revelations and the return of the prodigal son. Jeff's appearance was interesting at best. His head was now covered with a ½ inch frizzled thatch of dark brown fuzz, flecked with grey. His eyebrows and eyelashes had partially regrown. His face was a variegated patchwork of red and pink skin. Unchanged were his eyes, as dark and intense as ever. People greeted Jeff, careful not to shake his still scarred hands. No questions were asked. After seeing off the others, José, Maria and Carmen led the way to their home. Tom DeBeers took Sam's hand as they walked down the rough path in the growing darkness. Following behind were Jeff, Julia and a joyful Bruno.

After they were all seated in José and Maria's small living room, Sam was the first to speak. "Jeff, we're all so glad ...." She faintly blushed. "Peter will be in heaven. Last week Doctor Grafton called. He told us why he thought you had to leave and where you had gone. I think we all understand." Sam hesitated, tears welling up in her eyes. "I know I do."

As the rest watched in silence, Jeff picked up his chair and moved close to Sam and took her hands in his. Finally, Tom DeBeers cleared his throat and broke the silence. "Jeffrey, we're all glad to have you back. This ranch needs you now more than ever."

"Si, Amigo!" cried out José, who could contain himself no longer. "You scared the sh ..." Maria clapped her hand over the big man's mouth before he could finish the word. "Stop that!" She angrily whispered. "What a way to greet our Jeff." Turning, the smiling Mexican woman walked over and planted a big kiss on Jeff's cheek. "Now, that's how we welcome home our family on this ranch!"

That large, wet, heart-felt kiss broke the ice and everyone started talking. Finally DeBeers held up his hand for quiet. "O.K. everybody. Jeff, you came in late, I think you only heard that last little bit about the Bordeaux vineyard. This whole French business is a bolt out of the blue to all of us — but did I hear you correctly? Did Pierre tell you about the Chateau?"

"Yes he did ... and swore me to silence." Jeff released Sam's hands and looked over at Tom. "He told me about the Chateau just a week before his accident. I know it sounds crazy, it sure sounded crazy to me at the time but never forget, that old man was crazy like a fox. First, you all know that our Pierre never forgot his roots. Second, he thought he had plenty of time to enjoy a few years travelling back and forth - if he cut back here. He'd said often enough he wanted to enjoy life at a slower pace. Now, here's what he told me. Exactly what he told me."

—◦◦◦—

It was late before the meeting broke up. Somewhere in the evening Maria had served sandwiches and coffee, but no effort at dinner was attempted. It seemed forever before Jeff was able to return to the trailer. It took just moments for the exhausted man to peel off his travel-worn clothes and fall into bed. His many flights and transfers from Helmand Province to Kabul, then on to Delhi, Hong Kong and finally to San Francisco had taken almost 60 hours. It took another 3 hours in a rental car to reach Carmel Valley. He was dead on his feet by the time he collapsed on the bed. Even Bruno seemed to understand and for once curled up on the floor. Jeff didn't stir an hour later when Sam quietly slipped in, looked in silence at the still form for a few long moments, then carefully pulled a blanket over his unconscious body. Leaving the door ajar for Bruno, she departed as silently as she had arrived.

Jeff was awakened at last by the sound of the noon call ringing loudly not far away. That old Spanish bell had been the sole survivor of the fire at Pierre's home and now stood watch near Maria's kitchen door. Jeff opened his eyes, stretching out arms and legs with a long sigh of pleasure. Lieing back, arms behind his head, he smiled. He had slept for 16 hours. He was home.

After a quick, frigid shower, he shaved and pulled on a clean shirt and jeans. He had eaten nothing but airline snacks and one sandwich in almost three days. He was ravenous and he knew with a satisfied smile just how and where to solve that problem! When he reached the kitchen door, Jeff was almost knocked off his feet by a combination of large dog and small boy. Peter attached himself like a limpet and with the big dog in tow, the threesome made their way to the table. Sam, helping at the stove, watched bemused as Maria clucked happily like an old mother hen. "Coffee! I need coffee!!" Jeff cried hopefully over the heads of his captors.

At lunch they were again joined by Tom DeBeers, Julia and Carmen. It was a magnificent lunch. (Any food qualified as magnificent after airline fare from half way around the world.) Later, the adults relaxed over coffee as the remains of lunch were cleared away. Sam sat quietly, aimlessly stirring the sugar in the old china bowl as the others worked around her. "You say the price paid for that Chateau was a terrific bargain." She now looked directly at Jeff. "What I don't understand is how my father thought we could take care of our obligations here at the ranch? You may not realize it, but all the ranch records went up in that holocaust. I do know from my conversations with Dad in the Hospital that there were a lot of bills to be paid. He told us about some. Jeff, we don't even know what our tax bill will be next year. Everything is gone." She looked at the attorney. "Correct me if I'm wrong, Tom, but aside from less than two thousand dollars in the bank, if we pay that bill from France, this ranch is basically bankrupt."

Jeff shook his head in astonishment. "He planned to sell off two-thirds of the Bordeaux vineyard – keep just a small vineyard, only a few hectare, around the Chateaux for himself and his family. He was sure that would bring in a great deal of money, much more than his original cost. His plan was to do that as soon as the purchase was complete. He just had his life cut short a few years too soon. Did I mention last night that back before the fire, I checked the land prices around Saint-Émilion. Decent vineyards had more than doubled since Pierre's price was set almost 10 years ago … and don't forget, this is a *Premier Grand Cru* vineyard, it's pure gold."

"But right now that doesn't pay bills." Interjected Sam.

"We all know this ranch was never expected to make money," broke in DeBeers. "Since the fire, the accountant and I have been going over what records we could resurrect. So far as we can see, the ranch and the winemaking operation have never come close to breaking even. Pierre always covered his deficit by selling some of his stock. Now that's all going to France."

"You're right," responded Jeff. "But remember what I said last night. Pierre knew this would happen. His plan was perfectly good as far as it went. His basic idea was to quickly sell that excess French land. He was also going to sell a significant part of the ranch here in Carmel Valley. He planned to keep the vineyards, the spring, the lakes and the land around the house plus ample protecting acreage. That leaves almost 400 acres, maybe more, available for sale."

"But that takes time", said the attorney. "Cattle prices are down and ranch land is a glut on the market. What about the wine?"

Jeff was now nervously pacing the floor. "He planned to enlarge the vineyards, quadruple our case output and sell the wine under a new label at an affordable price. He told me he had talked at length to Tom Winters, they were sure it could be very profitable."

"Amigo, we are too small! We would have to lease winery space and equipment. Also it is very expensive to plant new vineyards. You know yourself this all takes time and many dollars. Right now we must pay our workers and we must re-build the barn. Maybe even the house. That all costs money — money that we do not have." José flung up his hands to express his concern.

"I know you're right, José. If he had just had more time…."

Carmen had remained quiet during this recital of woe. Finally she spoke out, interrupting the unhappy discussion. ""If we need quick cash, and I mean in the next 3 or 4 months, I think I know a way to solve some of our problems." Carmen looked at Jeff. "You and I are the only ones who have seen Pierre's personal stockpile of wine. After we had chosen those bottles for his celebration, I did some calculating. I am sure his collection of rare, almost unobtainable, wine he has locked away is worth at least $500,000, perhaps much more. Christie's would love to auction that treasure. We could also sell it almost immediately, one lot at a time, to some of the rare wine dealers in New York."

Maria audibly sucked in her breath. "$500,000! That could carry us through the year."

"I had no idea my father had such a horde!" Sam whispered. "He would just bring out a few bottles at Christmas and tell us he'd brought them from France on one of his trips. You've seen it, Jeff, is that really true?

"Carmen knows the prices a lot better than I, but she's right, that wine is available right now and I'm sure it is worth a great deal of money – if you want to sell."

"Young man, that's pure manna from heaven." The attorney spoke, rising to his feet. "That would cover the ranch costs for the next six months, maybe longer. It would allow you all to complete the purchase of the Chateau and still pay most of your bills. Bless my soul, you might even be able to pay mine!" He stopped suddenly and looked straight at Jeff. "Jeffrey, you didn't hear the reading of Pierre's will. Among other things, that wine is now yours. It was given directly to you."

"To me? " Jeff stopped in his tracks. "Do you mean I'm mentioned in Pierre's will?"

"Not just mentioned, my boy. You are one of the six primary beneficiaries of the Pierre Vaillard Estate."

Jeff, who had been standing, dropped onto a chair. "My God, I didn't know."

"But don't count your chickens before they hatch," The attorney wagged his finger. "Until this Bordeaux situation is cleared up there is nothing for anyone. What do you think about Carmen's suggestion? It's your decision to make."

Jeff was still at a loss for words. Looking helplessly into the faces around him, he finally spoke softly. "That wine is not mine; it belongs to all of you much more than it could ever belong to me." He paused to look around the room. "It's what you think; you will have to make the decision."

31

LATE SPRING RAIN had turned the hills and valleys a glorious, iridescent green. Splashes of lupine, buttercups and a host of other wildflowers announced the awakening of the land. Above, the sky displayed a brilliant azure blue and towering clouds rose high over the distant peaks. In the vineyards, the resurgence of life was everywhere. Small new branches were fast emerging from the gnarled old trunks and emerald tinted leaves festooned the new growth. Last year's harvest, so drenched in sorrow, was now a distant past. The sweet essence of grapes lay quietly in oaken barrels, carefully stacked in the dark recesses of the *cave*. As it was for Pierre, the wine was at last at rest.

As Sam and Jeff rode their horses over a high crest they could see the vineyards stretched out below. Sweating from their morning ride, they stopped to look out over Pierre's beloved ranch. Gazing out over row on row of vines below, Jeff, rested both hands on the horn of his saddle.

"This vineyard is where your father always hoped to end his days. Now he can rest forever among his beloved vines." Sam nodded silently.

The two of them had spent the morning riding to all four corners of the vineyard scattering Pierre's ashes among the vines. They had ridden hard and the horses were as tired as their riders. "Funny," he spoke quietly, "I should be feeling sad – but I'm not. What a wonderful man and what a remarkable life." Moving their horses under the shade of a nearby Oak, the two dismounted and sat quietly on a large, lichen encrusted, boulder looking out over the vista spread before them. "Sam, I don't know how, but there must be a way we can save this ranch … there has to be a way."

"There's Dad's private collection. That will provide some quick cash for the next few months." She looked out over the vines. "Thank God, the I.R.S. will value that wine on its price at the time of Dad's death. The capital gains would have been huge. Tom and the accountant say we'd be bankrupt in less than a year if it weren't for that." She paused again. "I still can't understand why he got into that crazy business in France, maybe it was just old age."

Warmed by the late morning sun, Jeff's mind drifted away and he began thinking aloud. "Much as I love this vineyard and making wine, I'm going to have to go back to work. My savings will run dry before too many months and medicine is still in my blood," Jeff seemed to be speaking to the clouds as he gazed out to the distant horizon. "Not the impersonal turmoil of the emergency room. I learned the hard way these past couple of years how much I want to be part of my patients' lives ... it's the people I love." He turned to Sam. "George Dimetroff wants to cut back, take more time off. He asked me to join him part time. I could work with him and still make the wine." As he looked out over the vineyard he suddenly began to laugh. "Hell, I bet we could make a fortune bottling the spring water – call it Pierre's Pure Artesian Water, or maybe Nacimiento Spring Water ... " Jeff stopped suddenly and sat bolt upright. "Nacimiento ... The Spring. Dear God, Sam, The Water! That's what George was trying to tell me!"

Jeff was on his feet in an instant and calling Sam to follow, jumped on his horse and galloped straight down to the spring. Arriving in minutes, he jumped off and stripped to his shorts. When the other horse and rider arrived he was already standing by the pool. "Sam, quick find José and get him up here. While you're there, look in the trailer for my skin diving mask – I think there might even be two. Hurry!"

"What's going on?" But it was too late — he had already disappeared into the deep blue water of Pierre's magic pool.

―∞∞―

José arrived in minutes on his ATV and the two men had been diving for almost an hour when Maria hurried up the path with Peter in tow. "Holy Mother of God! What are they doing ... have those men gone crazy?"

"I don't know. Jeff yelled for me to find José and he hasn't said another word except to tell José something I couldn't hear. Now they just come up for air every couple of minutes." As she spoke, José broke the surface on the opposite shore as Jeff popped up beside him. Both men pulled their masks on their foreheads and were yelling at each other.

"I think I found it! It's there behind the reeds under the rock,"

"Si. I saw it also."

"We'll need a crowbar, maybe some rope." Paying no attention to the two anxious observers standing across the pool, the two men climbed up and flopped on the grass laboring to catch their breath.

"Amigo, there is a towline and winch on the ATV. The crowbars are still in back." He got up, testing the ground with his heel. "I should be able to park right here. We can drag it out from under that rock."

"We'll have to break up some of the rock, but I think you're right, that just might work. The steel should hold up; God knows how it's stayed so strong and solid. "Jeff dipped his hand below surface and ran water through his fingers. "I wonder what's in this amazing stuff that could preserve a chest for two centuries?"

As José dove in to swim over for the ATV, the women were hurrying around the end of the pool, crossing the plank that served as a bridge and fast approaching.

"Jeff Thomas!" called Sam. "What in God's name are you two doing?" Maria, panting up beside the younger woman, stopped dead in her tracks, staring wide-eyed at the long jagged scars running irregularly up and down Jeff's back and thighs. "Oh Sam," she taking the younger woman's hand. "I never knew it was so bad." She whispered. "No wonder the poor boy …" her voice trailed off as she clutched Peter's hand tight.

"Sam, It's just possible …" Jeff was staring at the spring. "It's just possible," He repeated looking up, "That George had the answer to our prayers."

"George?"

"Yes, George." Jeff turned to face the women. "Do you remember Pierre telling the story of the famous high jacking of Spanish gold en route to the Monterey Presidio two hundred years ago? He said the *bandidos* were captured in these very canyons and promptly strung up – but the gold was never found. Your Dad told me ranchers still find holes up and down the valley where treasure seekers used to dig. He said it was all forgotten when the Gold Rush of 1849 changed everything in California. Well maybe, just maybe, that story was true." He waded into the water pointing. "There is something buried down there under a lip of rock and covered by moss and reeds. It looks like a Spanish strong box. Both of us saw it. I'm sure that must be what George was trying to tell me when he died. What ever it is, it's very old and yet it still looks almost new."

"Dear God! I always thought that old legend was just a folk story. Dad always laughed about it when Carmen and I were growing up."

As the three talked, José navigated the ATV around behind the rock and down the grassy slope. Reversing the ungainly machine, he carefully backed up towards the water's edge. Once parked and the handbrake pulled tight, he hauled out two crowbars and handed one to Jeff.

"*Hombre*," he laughed glancing first at Jeff's back and then at his wife. "You better get back in the water. You're scarin' hell outta my poor Maria."

They found the lip of the overhanging rock seemed to have grown around the chest over the years. Working at a depth of about ten feet, they could only stay down a minute per dive. Breaking up that shelf of volcanic *briccia*, one lung full of air at a time, took almost two hours. On about his 20th dive, José popped to the surface and gave a yell. "It's free!" When his breathing finally began to ease, he looked at Jeff and grinned. "Get the cable ... " he gasped as he sucked in great gulps of air. "I think ... we can ... pull it out." Working like men possessed, the two unwound the long wire cable, checked the hook at the end and Jeff prepared to dive.

It took three tries to secure the cable to the chest. At last he pulled himself up on the grass, lungs fighting for air. As soon as he was able, the two men stood by the ATV and talked. Jeff would dive with another thin rope. As soon as he was positioned he would give the thin line a yank and José would start the winch slowly reeling in the cable. Two yanks meant, "stop!". Soon, inch-by-inch, the chest broke free from of its long hidden rocky niche and came to rest on the sandy bottom. It wasn't long before the final leg of the journey brought the ancient strong box to the surface and up on the shore.

While the men were busy underwater, Sam had run back to collect her cellphone. Worthless at the ranch for its primary purpose with no reception this far from civilization, this modern successor to a digital camera was ideal to record each step of the recovery. Using a tape measure from the ATV, the dimensions of the chest were carefully recorded. The heavy steel box was 2 1/2 feet long, 2 feet wide and 1 1/2 foot tall. Although still covered with moss and weeds, the metal looked surprisingly sound. Jeff carefully scraped the debris off the top and there, still faintly visible after more than 200 years, was the Spanish royal coat of arms. Dripping wet, the chest was lifted with care onto the bed of the ATV. Jeff thought it must weigh 100 pounds or more. Next stop would be Maria's kitchen with its linoleum floor and good light.

It was almost five o'clock when the procession reached the Sanchez home. With a final effort and with Maria directing traffic, the two men lifted the heavy steel box and carefully carried it still dripping into the kitchen where it was deposited safely on a bed of old newspapers.

"This lock is rusted tight ... looks pretty solid. We're going to have to saw it off. These old hinges," he said using a screwdriver to test their strength, "Are almost rusted through – no problem there." Peter, who could hardly contain his curiosity, held a light for Jeff. "Yep," said Jeff, "They just fall apart. Amazing, the rest of the steel looks almost new. José, where's a hack saw?"

"Right here, *amigo*. Let me get in close." Kneeling down the big Mexican began to saw. The shank of the ancient lock was surprisingly tough even after all those years in the water. Finally, after about ten minutes of effort, the shackle fell apart and the chest stood ready to open. Jeff, taking the light from Pete, held it aloft as José slowly pried lose the top and carefully lifted the lid.

The room was silent as José stepped back revealing the contents for all to see. There before them lay shreds of rotted sacking and what must have once been straw. Clearly visible beneath were coins, masses of large, still brilliant, gold coins. Peter was the first to speak "It's a treasure chest!" he cried. And a treasure chest it was.

Jeff sat back and stared. "I read in the paper the other day that gold was pushing $1,500 an ounce. If we've got 80 pounds of gold," he was doing some quick calculations in his head. "That would be about two million dollars! God knows what collectors might pay!'""

Maria dipped her hand into the chest and dribbled some of the beautiful coins through her fingers and let out a long sigh. "*Ay dios*! How could it be … all these years right here at our spring."

Sam was holding Peter's hand tight. "Jeff," she whispered. "Is it really ours?"

"It's all yours, Sam. Maybe the law will say it belongs to the estate, but however they decide, I think it will save the ranch."

32

For the next week, life at the ranch was tumultuous to say the least. It had begun when the fully dried strong box had been transported by armored car to the Monterey County Assessors' office in Salinas. Present were Sam, Julia and Jeff, the Vaillard family attorney, an Assessor's deputy, two deputy sheriffs and a well-known San Francisco rare coin dealer. There in their presence the contents were carefully inspected. First, the coins were weighed on the Assessor's official scale, then the coins were   counted in stacks of 100. The results stunned them all. The net weight of the gold was 76.4 pounds; the "doubloons", as the expert called them, seemed uncirculated. All had been minted in 1764 in Mexico City; they numbered a remarkable 3,217. By weight, the value would be more than a million and a half dollars. Valued by their uncirculated condition and rarity to collectors, the horde could be worth well in excess of 20 million dollars.

It took almost three hours to weigh, count, photograph and then repack the treasure before it could be transported back to the Wells Fargo vault. There it would be stored until its future sale and disposition.

It was a very quiet ride back to the ranch from the Assessor's office. As always, Highway 68 was jammed with commuters returning to Salinas in the late afternoon. Tom DeBeers was driving his large SUV with José beside him in the front seat, Sam, Maria and Carmen rode in the second and Jeff and Julia in back. Once out of town, Tom was the first to break their silence.

"Well now, wasn't that an interesting afternoon! I think, Sam, your financial worries are over. As soon as you decide how you'll dispose of that amazing collection, I can pay off the Bordeaux people." Leaving the highway at the Laureles Grade turnoff, the big vehicle wound its way up the hill heading for Carmel Valley. Tom paused momentarily at the summit. "Now," he spoke with finality, "We can all take a big sigh of relief and settle Pierre's estate."

"I still can't believe any of this," said Sam, sitting behind the driver. "It's like some fantastic fairy tale. Who would even dream of a buried treasure in this day and age."

"I think," said José, "We should nail up one of those shiny gold pieces over the barn door when we rebuild it."

"Never!" Laughed Maria. "It should be glued to the kitchen stove! Don't let me ever see you pound a nail through a single one of those golden coins."

"I think we should have a party," called Jeff from the back as they started down into the valley. "We need to drink a toast to George. He sure as hell saved the ranch."

"No Jeff," Sam turned as she spoke, "You saved the ranch. You remembered and you found it."

———

One morning after they had all returned to the ranch, José and Jeff were walking through the vineyard. It was early on a crystal clear, unseasonably warm, late spring day. The vines were leafing out and it was time to think about the grapes and the fall harvest.

"Man, we really need those summer fogs. The vines are gettin' too hot, way too early." José gazed up at the cloudless sky and shook his head.

Leaning against a post, the big Mexican pulled off his hat and dug a faded red bandana from his hip pocket, wiping his sweat-covered face. "Well, *Amigo*, what're you gonna do now? I remember you told Pierre you'd come an' help for a few weeks — that was more'n a year ago."

Jeff laughed aloud. Looking down the long rows of vines his smile faded and his face grew serious. "Back in those evenings at the hospital I made a promise to Pierre. He knew he was dying, that Sam would need help getting through that first year. The vineyard was safe in your hands, but he worried about the wine. I told him I'd stay for the next six months. Smart old bastard, he knew how this place gets under your skin." Jeff was quiet for a few moments then looked at José with a faint smile. "It's not just the ranch, José, it's you and Maria … and Sam and Pete…." His voice trailed off as he looked at his friend and shook his head. "I don't know, somehow the decision's not up to me."

Walking down the slope they met Sam coming up the path alone. Making a rather lame excuse to a smiling José, Jeff joined her and the two walked slowly down the hill talking about Pierre's ranch and its future. It wasn't long before the enormous outcrop of rock with its gushing spring came into view. Jeff led Sam over to a grassy spot under the canopy of an ancient oak. The bright sounds of fast flowing water cascading into the azure blue pool had a hypnotic effect.

After a few quiet minutes, he turned and smiled. "Pierre made one last request when we were alone that night before he died. After we finished scattering his ashes, l was to tell you his last wish, and these are his exact words: 'only after you both have taken a swim in my magic pool'"

"But I didn't bring a towel … " Jeff didn't wait for her to finish. "Since when did you need a towel!" He retorted, already on his feet and pulling off his boots and clothes.

"Last one in's … "yelled Jeff as he dove deep into the clear, cold pool.

Sam, unable to resist the challenge, stripped off her clothes, let a loud squeal as her body hit the chill water. Leaping on Jeff's head, she dunked him below the surface. Yelling and splashing, they played until exhausted, then swam slowly in the healing water letting the sad events of the recent past be exorcised forever in that magic, healing pool.

At last, hearts and minds restored, they swam to the water's edge and walked hand in hand to the sheltered, grassy slope. Settled on the soft green carpet, Jeff let his eyes roam over the woman stretched out beside him. Wet hair fanned out, eyes closed; her still damp body lay open before him. As her soft breasts rose and fell with each quiet breath, she seemed totally at peace. Leaning over, he kissed her closed eyes and brushed her open lips. Looking at her silent form, Jeff could hardly believe how beautiful this woman was, how much he loved her, how much he wanted her now and forever. Seeing her eyes watching him, a faint smile on her lips, he reached over and took her tenderly in his arms.

"Sam ..."

"Yes!"

"Yes, what?"

"Yes, I'll marry you."

"But I haven't asked you yet!"

"Oh, sorry." Hand over her mouth to conceal her smile, she tried to look contrite. There was a long pause while he collected himself to try again.

"Sam, will you marry me?"

"Yes! Yes! Yes!" She laughed aloud planting a big kiss on his startled lips. "I thought you'd never ask. You silly man, I was about ready to propose to you if you didn't say the words today." Laughing, they fell into each other's arms.

"Jeff. I've been waiting for this moment for months. I've loved you ever since those first few weeks, you must have known. Now we're both free, we both love each other ... Oh, Jeff, we both need each other." She rested her head against his chest.

Holding her in his arms Jeff began to speak again. "Sam. I haven't talked to you about why I left two months ago."

"Dr. Grafton told us where you went. Jeff, that was about your life."

"No, this is about *our* life." He leaned back and took a long breath. "Sam, something happened while I was in that inferno before I found Peter. I saw Caroline. I know it sounds crazy, but in my oxygen starved mind she was there before me, so alive, so real. She spoke to me and smiled … she said I was now free … she said I now belonged to you." He paused, staring into the eyes of the woman beside him. "Then she blew me a kiss and faded back into the flames forever." Sam said nothing, hands clenched, not knowing what might be coming.

"I knew I had to go back. I'd never had a chance to say goodbye to the Afghan family that Caroline had come to cherish. I had to close that chapter of my life."

Silent for a few moments, Jeff turned and raised himself on one elbow. He spoke quickly as though hoping for understanding. "I flew to Kabul, then on to Helmand Province and hitched a ride up to the town where it all began. I stayed two weeks with Ahmed Khan and his wonderful wife, Saire. Talking with that remarkable couple, experiencing again their faith and love, I felt a weight lift from my heart. Later, with a couple of Marines riding shotgun, I joined a convoy and drove back over my personal road to hell. We found what remained of the Humvee, now stripped clean and what was left still lying crumpled by the side of the road. I will never understand how I survived that explosion. Saire, in her quiet way, told me it was Allah's will. That she had always known I'd been saved for someone else."

For a few minutes all was quiet other than the insistent voices of tiny frogs calling each other across the pool and the raucous noise of a blue jay not far away; the only movement, a family of quail dashing across the grass. Oblivious of their surroundings, the man and woman lay silently together.

After a bit, Sam looked up and spoke again. "So, Dr. Thomas, we've had our swim. Why haven't you told me about Pierre's last wish? I'll bet I can guess!"

"And you'd probably be right. Pierre told me that saving this ranch and our joining together were his two greatest hopes. I think we've given that wonderful man his fondest wish."

Holding each other, warmed by the late morning sun, they began to talk of a future together, of rebuilding the house, of Jeff adopting Peter, of the Chateau in France. Jeff spoke of his love for medicine and the pleasure he would have making Pierre's wine.

Time had no meaning as they poured out their hopes and dreams. They were brought back to reality only by the distant peal of the noontime bell. Jeff let out a long sigh pulling Sam close. "Damn!" he groaned, "I promised Maria I'd be down for lunch. I could lie here with you forever."

After a long pause, he laughed aloud. "I think we should tell her as soon as we get back. That woman has been hoping for this day even more than Pierre!"

"I don't think you have to worry, Jeff." Sam smiled, as she stood and collected her clothes, "Never doubt that old Mexican woman's intuition. I think our Maria has known for a long, long time."

Dressed, they walked hand in hand down the valley following the burbling, tumbling stream. The scrub oak on the hillsides had turned from dark green to the soft tones of late spring. Tufts of blue shown on the *Ceanothus* scattered over the hillsides. The Buckeye glistened with their multitude of white blossoms. Patches of bright poppies and scattered clusters of lush blue and yellow lupine were painted over the landscape as though dropped at random from an artist's palate. The joyful harmony of birdsongs and the sweet scent of wildflowers followed them each step. Outside the *cave*, standing as it had for countless years, the old White Oak had shed its dark winter cape for an emerald canopy of new growth. Along the stream, white-barked sycamores gracefully arched over the now fast flowing water. Spring was leaving the ranch and a summer's sun would rise to warm Pierre's valley and its still green, soon to be golden hills. For life on the ranch, it was a new beginning. It was the same for Sam and Jeff.

Coming around the last bend, the two could see the small dwelling standing alone not far from the lake. As they approached the garden gate, the kitchen door swung open and Maria appeared, arms stretched wide in welcome. Illuminating that round, bronze, happy face was a broad and joyous smile. Sam was right, Maria knew.

Made in the USA
San Bernardino, CA
29 September 2015